Praise for

"M.
—*New York Times* b

"Potentially explosive…R
[Dr. Morgan Snow] is an engaging guide to the world of
dysfunction that Rose painstakingly constructs."
—*Publishers Weekly*

"Dr. Morgan Snow is a refreshingly vulnerable character whose
spunky decision to go undercover in the demimonde is both
believable and hair-raising. *The Halo Effect* will have you
on the edge of your seat from page one."
—Katherine Neville, *New York Times* bestselling
author of *The Eight*

"I dare you to read the first five pages of *The Halo Effect*
and not be in its thrall: this is a compulsive, artful
page-turner of a novel. Suspenseful, sleek and sexy,
this is M. J. Rose at her best."
—Douglas Clegg, author of *The Hour Before Dark*

"Rose writes fearlessly about sex. This is a true erotic thriller.
The end will take your breath away."
—Lisa Tucker, author of *Shout Down the Moon*

"Rose has written a steamy and sexy novel that keeps the
adrenaline running until the very end. Sex, romance,
and murder are artfully combined to produce a
page-turning novel that shouldn't be missed."
—*New Mystery Reader*

"Interesting…thrilling…like a femme…Jonathan Kellerman."
—*Kirkus Reviews*

"Elegant, arresting and so suspenseful I was gripping the pages.
Rose's alchemy is to take the psychological mystery and spin it
into something literate and new, giving us complex, beautifully
complicated characters which are so real we hear them
breathing in our ear, prose that's both subtle and moving,
and a plot that can only be described as a knockout."
—Caroline Leavitt, author of *Girls in Trouble*

Also by M. J. ROSE

Fiction

THE HALO EFFECT
LIP SERVICE
IN FIDELITY
FLESH TONES
SHEET MUSIC

Nonfiction

HOW TO PUBLISH AND PROMOTE ONLINE
(with Angela Adair-Hoy)

BUZZ YOUR BOOK (with Douglas Clegg)

M. J. ROSE

THE DELILAH COMPLEX

ISBN 0-7783-2215-7

THE DELILAH COMPLEX

Copyright © 2006 by Melisse Shapiro.

www.MIRABooks.com

Printed in U.S.A.

To my wonderful agent and dear friend,
Loretta Barrett.

Delilah, n. The name of the woman who betrayed Samson to the Philistines, used allusively to mean a temptress or treacherous paramour.

"And she made him sleep upon her knees; and she called for a man, and she caused him to shave off the seven locks of his head;…and his strength went from him." (*Judges* 16:19)

complex, n. *psychol.* A group of emotionally charged ideas or mental factors, unconsciously associated by the individual with a particular subject, arising from repressed instincts, fears, or desires and often resulting in mental abnormality; freq. with defining word prefixed, as inferiority complex, dipus complex, etc.; hence *colloq.*, in vague use, a fixed mental tendency or obsession. Also *attrib.* and *comb.*

The use of the term was established by C. G. Jung in 1907 (*Ueber die Psychologie der Dementia Praecox*), but it originated with Neisser in 1906 (*Individualität und Psychose*).

'Tis not in the high stars alone,
Nor in the cups of budding flowers,
Nor in the redbreast's mellow tone,
Nor in the bow that smiles in showers,
But in the mud and scum of things
There always, always something sings.
—Ralph Waldo Emerson

One

Warm, engulfing, darkness surrounded him. Flesh moved over him. Naked legs held him, vise-like, rocking him, rocking him, lulling him back into haze. Shoulders, neck, torso, blocking all light. Hot breath on his neck. Soft hair in his face, soaking up his tears.

He was crying?

One wrenching and embarrassing sob escaped in answer.

No. Take me back to the threshold of coming.

Let me loose in you.

Please.

The pleasure was too much pain. He wasn't taking, he was being taken. Sensations were being suctioned out of him. No control over the pulsing now.

He didn't know what time it was or how long he had been sleeping. Or even if he still was sleeping. He only knew that he had never been used like this and never cried like this before. Never cried before at all. Now he was reduced to weeping because—

He didn't know.

Why was he crying?

He could taste someone else on his lips. Smell someone else in his nostrils. A sour smell. A sweat smell. Not sweet. Everything stunk of stale sex. He wanted more.

Please, come back.

Nothing for a few more minutes. Or another hour? Ribbons of sleep. Weaving in and out of unconsciousness. Fighting through the interwoven dream web. Or had he awoken at all?

Must be in bed. His bed? He didn't know. Focusing, he forced his fingers to feel for smooth sheets but only felt skin. His own. Moist and frigid. He tried to move his hands away from his chest, to his sides, but he couldn't.

What was happening?

Remember something, he told himself. *Try to catch something from last night.* No memory.

So he had to be sleeping. All he had to do was wake himself up. Open his eyes. From there he'd sit up, stretch, feel the damn sheets, put his feet down on the carpeted floor and get to a shower where he would wash away this fog.

But he couldn't be at home.

The body had not been his wife's.

Was it any lover he'd ever known?

He fought, ignoring the tears, to open his eyes. To push one more time through the last vestiges of the milky-blue fog. Part of his brain, the small section that was functional and was informing the emotion that led to the weeping, knew that something was desperately wrong. This was not just about fucking. Hot streams of tears were sliding down his cheeks and dripping off the sides of his face. His rib cage hurt from the crying.

He gulped air, hoping that would help clear his head, and became aware that the air was icy.

Weak, helpless, spent, he lay there.

Why was he crying?

Because...

Because...

The hands stroked his hair. Cupped his skull. He felt himself stiffen again. Tears and erections. What was wrong with him? Fingers played with his curls. Where each hair follicle met his scalp, his blood singed, sending shivers of pleasure down his neck, his spine, to his solar plexus.

Please. Take me back inside of you.

He moved to reach up and brush the wetness off his face, but his hand wouldn't lift. A metal bracelet, hard and icy, dug into the flesh of his wrist.

Silver cuffs flashed in the darkened room.

When had he been chained?

He tried to lift his head and shoulders and felt another pressure holding him in place. A band across his chest prevented him from rising. Falling back, his head hit the thin pillow. Not the overstuffed down pillows on his own bed, but a poor substitute that offered only a few inches of padding between his head and the inflexible cot.

Was this more of the dream? It didn't matter, as long as the fingers kept playing so exquisitely with his hair. He tried to move his legs so that he could thrust up, but the same pressure that radiated across his chest also held his ankles. The same sound of metal against metal rang in his ears.

On his back, naked, shivering, he gave up wanting to understand.

The fingers were torture now. The rhythm of the stroking was making him harder. He opened his mouth, wanting to lick the skin he could smell.

His tongue wouldn't move. He tried to speak but his

mouth was filled with a dry thickness that absorbed the sound. How could his tongue be so swollen?

He worked at it for a few seconds, then tasted the cloth gag.

Suddenly the fingers stopped.

He saw a glimmer of silver. Bright in the room's darkness. Heard the murmur that razor-sharp metal makes as it cuts, exacting and fast.

The only thing he was capable of bringing forth from his body was more tears.

Weak. Like a woman, he cried.

Because he, Philip Maur, who was fearless, was scared. Scared to death.

Two

The lights on the subway flickered off and then returned. In front of me someone gasped prematurely, as if expecting disaster.

"Boom! Boom! Boom!" A man shouted in the rear of the car.

We all turned but there was nothing to see. An irrational outburst from someone who had already disappeared into the crowd.

Since the terrorist attacks on the city in 2001, we looked out for the stranger among us who might spell danger. And since the killings I'd stumbled on to last summer, and the murderer who hid from me in plain sight, I no longer trusted my ability to identify a threat.

I used to suffer the hubris of thinking I could identify who was dangerous and who wasn't, blindly enjoying the fallacy that, as a trained psychotherapist, symptoms would present themselves to me as long as I remained aware. But now I know that's not true.

The genuine lunatic, the real psychotic, can fool me as well as you, so I have become ever more vigilant and ever less sure that I can protect those I love. Questions keep me awake at night: Will I be prepared when someone comes for me the next time? Or worse, if someone comes for my daughter, Dulcie?

Beside me, Dulcie sat oblivious to what I knew could catch us unawares. A pair of expensive headphones—a gift from her father—covered her ears, and her head bobbed to the soundtrack that was audible only to her. Silently, my lovely young daughter mouthed the lyrics to the score of "The Secret Garden," because in four months, on January 5, she would stand on a Broadway stage and take on the role of Mary Lennox in a new production of the classic. Every day now on our way to and from the rehearsal studio on Lafayette Street in lower Manhattan, she burned the nuances of the music into memory, working tirelessly on her part.

A thirteen-year-old girl should not have a job, not even if her talent has bloomed early and she has acting in her blood. But the price of stepping on my daughter's dream wasn't something I was willing to pay. And so, more intently than I surveyed the strangers on the train, more doggedly than I observed my patients, I watched my daughter. Carefully. Always monitoring. Maybe too closely sometimes. But if the anxiety or pressure of performing weighed on her too heavily, I wanted to be prepared to step in.

Since she had been chosen for the part back in June, Dulcie was thriving, doing better than she had at her private school where too many label-obsessed kids had goals no more complicated than getting the next Prada bag. The Bartlett School, even with its emphasis on the arts and its high number of scholarships, still had its share of kids with limitless gold credit cards and limos at the ready.

The train doors opened. A middle-aged businessman entered and sat in the seat on the other side of me, despite the empty seats across the aisle. I reached into my bag, pulled out a peppermint, unwrapped it and popped it in my mouth.

As I'm overly sensitive to smells, public places are sensory nightmares for me. I bit down. The intense flavor burned as the cool blue-green scent rose up and insulated me against any possible assault.

I felt his glance.

A dark-haired woman in narrow black slacks, a long-sleeved white shirt and a black leather blazer, sitting next to her lithe thirteen-year-old daughter, who was wearing jeans, a pink T-shirt, a jeans jacket and a wristful of purple and light green beads, listening to a CD, was not a threat.

When I turned a minute later and he looked at me, I didn't turn away. I don't do that.

No, that's not true. I look away from myself all too often, especially in the four months since my divorce. I ignore what is not in my life anymore and shy away from facing the one issue I spend my days helping other people deal with: sexuality. Dr. Morgan Snow, in denial. It isn't something I'm proud of. But it is how I cope.

Once more the lights went out and the train came to a dead stop. It didn't bother me, but I wasn't certain about Dulcie. I didn't have to search for my daughter's hand. I just reached out, instinctively knowing where it would be, even in the dark.

"You okay?" I asked her.

"Yeah. It's kind of creepy, though. How long do you think we're going to be stopped here?"

"Hopefully not long." I squeezed her hand.

She squeezed back and then pulled away to switch on her CD player again.

The lights flickered on but the train still didn't move.

Down the aisle, a man in a ripped jacket streaked with grime turned and ogled my daughter's legs. Dulcie didn't notice him, but I did and stared him down.

Why was his jacket dirty? What had broken his spirit? What had cracked his self-esteem?

Occupational hazard #1: Reading the body language of strangers. Like judging a book by its cover, it is tempting to make a diagnosis based on insufficient information.

A woman with downcast eyes opposite us kept flexing her fingers in a habitual way that suggested she was slightly compulsive. About what? It would take hours on my couch to find out, but I could guess at the darkness that bound her mind like barbed wire.

The lights went off again, suddenly, and we returned to stuffy blackness.

You will be on a dark street and he will jump out at you, his knife gleaming in the lamplight. Or you will be on the sidewalk below a fifty-floor office building and the noise will take you by surprise, as will the glass that rains down and slices your skin. There are so many possibilities of catastrophe that sometimes you do not know how you stay sane.

You manage because you have a child. You accomplish it because you still have hope, which, most therapists agree, is the hardest emotion to give up.

We started moving again and the lights came back on. Another five minutes passed and we were at the stop before ours.

"Hon." I touched Dulcie's hand.

Dulcie hit the stop button and turned, cornflower-blue eyes wide and waiting.

"Yeah?"

"Next stop."

"Really?"

She was always surprised the rides between our apartment on the Upper East Side and the rehearsal studio in SoHo were over so quickly. As she listened to her music, her sense of time deserted her.

Peering out the slimy windows into the blackness, Dulcie looked for a marker, not trusting how much time had passed.

"Mom?" Her face was still focused on the hollow tunnel. "Did you get nervous when the lights went out?"

"A little. I bet a lot of people did."

"Will I get that kind of nervous if I'm onstage and just forget the words? Will I get sick from it? What will being nervous do to me?"

"I don't know. But it's not a bad thing to feel anxiety. We can talk about how you can overcome the feeling and learn from it."

My job wasn't to protect this budding teenager from the darkness as much as it was to teach her how to find the switches so she could always turn on the lights.

But I would have preferred to protect her. To wrap her in my arms the same way I had when she was only months old, to keep her away from the open windows, from the cold and the poisons.

Three

The telephone was ringing as we walked into the apartment.

"Do you want me to get it?" Dulcie asked as she raced ahead of me.

"No, I've got it. You get ready for dinner."

While I picked up the receiver, Dulcie threw her backpack on the floor and immediately opened the refrigerator. Pulling out a bottle of carrot-apple juice, she drank almost half of it without stopping.

I watched my daughter's delicate throat as she swallowed, drank again and swallowed once more. It was eight o'clock in the evening and she was starving. Between working on the play, the tutoring that interrupted the rehearsals, and homework, she was burning energy. I didn't like her having to wait this late for dinner as it was.

"Dr. Morgan Snow, please."

"Yes, this is Dr. Snow."

The last thing I wanted to do was get stuck on the phone and delay it even longer.

"I'm sorry for bothering you at home, Dr. Snow. Dr. Butterfield gave me your number. My name is Gail Danzig. I'm a producer for the *Today* show. I was hoping you'd agree to do a segment on Friday morning."

While my name and involvement had made it into the news last June, when I'd been pulled into a hunt for a serial killer after one of my patients had disappeared, I'd refused to be interviewed. Dr. Nina Butterfield, my mentor, my closest friend and owner of the Butterfield Institute— the sex therapy clinic where I work—had supported my decision not to comment in the press. But lately she had been pushing me to become more visible in the psychoanalytical community. This obviously was one of those shoves. As with the paper she'd asked me to deliver on women's aggressive sexual tendencies at an upcoming conference, Nina wanted me to get out there. Success as a therapist was something that mattered to me. But notoriety? It had never been on my list.

"Dr. Butterfield didn't mention it to me."

"Oh, damn. She said she was going to call you—she felt this was something you would be interested in. First, let me tell you we're very sensitive to what you do, and don't want to exploit your profession at all."

From the refrigerator and the cabinets, I took what I needed for dinner and put it on the countertop. "I'm sure the *Today* show is a big draw and that there are a lot of therapists who would jump at the chance, but I really don't think that television is something I want to—"

Dulcie spun around from leafing through the mail and walked over to me, standing so close I could feel her breath on my neck as she whispered, "They want you on television? On the *Today* show?" Her eyes shone with admiration.

I nodded to her.

"Why?"

I shook my head—I couldn't listen to what the producer was saying and what Dulcie was saying at the same time. "Excuse me, Miss Danzig, could you hold on a second?"

I put my hand over the mouthpiece. "Dulcie, wait till I get off the phone, okay?"

Her words rushed out of her. "You have to do it, Mom. You have to. The *Today* show? How could you say no to that?"

My daughter's eyes didn't typically shine over anything having to do with my occupation. Quite the opposite. She thinks my being a sex therapist is embarrassing. Occasionally, she even calls me Dr. Sin, in the derisive way that only a thirteen-year-old can. All too often, she's introduced me to her friends or their parents as a heart doctor.

But here was something that involved me professionally that Dulcie wanted me to do. And I'm a sucker for making my daughter proud of me. I'm a softie for bending my own rules to see her smile.

"What is the subject of the segment, Miss Danzig?"

While the producer explained that the show was doing a week-long series on the sexual dissatisfaction of women in long-term relationships, I filled a pot of water and put it on the stovetop to boil.

"It's a trend we've spotted. Women seem more frustrated sexually than their male partners. Especially working women. For many of them, their interest in sex increases the more they work, while men have the opposite reaction."

I poured salt into the water. Supposedly salt makes the water boil faster and the pasta taste better. I saw that once on an episode of *Martha,* and anything I can do to make the food I cook taste better, I remember. I seem to be missing the cooking gene; I can even ruin prepared food.

"It's not a new trend as much as women's sexuality is a hot topic now, thanks to drug companies who are making huge public relations efforts to hype their female sexual-dysfunction drugs." I tried not to sound as if I was educating her, but I wasn't sure I'd succeeded.

"That's a good point. I'm making a note of it and will pass it on to our writers and researchers."

I cut through the plastic of a package of precooked chicken breasts and started to slice them into strips. I was probably using the wrong knife—they were shredding.

"So, is that what you want me to discuss?"

"No. We'd like you to be on the show the final day of the series to talk about when it's time to stop trying to cope with your sexual frustrations yourself and seek a sex therapist."

The water wasn't boiling yet.

"We'll need you here at 7:30 a.m. for hair and makeup. Your segment will probably air between eight-thirty and nine. Is that doable? Do you need a car to pick you up?"

Dulcie's face broke into a grin as I gave the producer my address. Meanwhile, the water in the pot still wasn't boiling. I checked for flames. I'd forgotten to turn on the burner. I sighed.

"Something wrong?" Miss Danzig asked.

Once I hung up, I continued making dinner: pasta with chicken and pesto sauce.

When the penne was almost cooked, I opened the last of the prepared food—the sauce. Scooping the emerald paste into another pan, I turned the heat on, added the chicken, and gave it a quick stir. Then I left it on low to find Dulcie and tell her it was time to eat.

She wasn't in her room. Or in her bathroom. And she wasn't rummaging around in the makeup box in my bathroom, which was one place I found her too often.

Our six-room apartment, on the fifth floor of a prewar building on the corner of Eightieth East and Madison Avenue, was not that big. Since she wasn't in either of the two bedrooms or bathrooms, and obviously not in the kitchen, she had to be in the den.

I'd taken the formal living room and dining room—spaces we'd never used—and had the walls ripped down, creating a large, cozy, book-lined space with comfortable couches and an entertainment area in one corner and my ersatz sculpture studio in the other.

Dulcie was standing in the dark, looking out of the windows that faced the street. Her shoulders were slumped and her forehead was pasted against a windowpane. She was too preoccupied to sense my presence.

Too often I can feel my daughter's pain. Both physical and mental. I can't read her mind—I am not psychic—but we're in sync in this way. So without knowing why, I knew she was sad, because I was suddenly sad.

When it comes to my daughter, I'm not a good therapist: I'm just another parent. All I could think of as I stood watching her was how treacherous the world is for a thirteen-year-old girl. Especially one like my daughter, whose parents are divorced, whose mother works full-time, and who has aspirations of becoming a serious actress. Anything could shift her into melancholy. Just as anything might shake her out of it.

"Hon?"

She turned. Her face was in shadows and I couldn't read her expression.

"Dinner's ready."

"Okay, I'll be right there."

I could hear the worry in her voice. As much as I wanted to ask her what was wrong, I held back. The direct approach didn't usually work with Dulcie, just as it hadn't worked with her father and, in most cases, didn't work with patients. Most people don't know what's wrong unless they've been educated through therapy to identify their feelings, express them and work through them.

Being the daughter of a psychotherapist, Dulcie was better than most teenagers at dealing with her feelings and naming the issues, but she still preferred to talk around her problems and let them surface on their own.

Back in the kitchen, I gave the heady garlic-and-basil-scented concoction one more turn, then dumped the pasta into a colander. Quickly—I always take too long and the pasta gets cold—I emptied the colander into a wide ceramic bowl, added the sauce and the chicken, tossed it and scooped it on two plates.

I was just putting everything on the table in the kitchen—we are luckier than many New Yorkers, who live without eat-in kitchens—when Dulcie came in and sat down.

I poured her a glass of milk and myself a glass of wine and joined her at the table. She took the first forkful and her nose wrinkled slightly. This came as no surprise. I'd probably burned the pesto, or hadn't gotten it hot, or there had been too much water in the pasta. Rather than ask her, I took a bite.

Something really was wrong. It definitely didn't taste right. The meat was sour and salty and didn't work with the pesto. I put my head down. It's usually faster for me to smell what's wrong.

How had I missed it? Had the scent of the garlic in the

pesto overpowered everything else? Or was it because I was on the phone when I'd been cutting up the food? Because I'd been thinking about the sexual frustrations of women in relationships? Because I'd been wondering why Nina Butterfield was suddenly pushing me to make a bigger name for myself? Unlike my father, who lived in Palm Springs with his second wife and was simply satisfied that I was productive and healthy, Nina had aspirations for me.

"Mom—what is this?"

"I was on the phone…" I started.

Dulcie was stifling a laugh. She was such a good kid; she was trying so hard to hold it in.

"It's awful. What is it?" she asked.

"Instead of chicken, it's filet of sole cooked in soy sauce."

"Soy sauce and pesto?" Dulcie couldn't hold it back; she was laughing out loud and I laughed with her. I think I would cook badly on purpose to make my daughter laugh like that. There wasn't very much that could bother me when she was happy.

"Peanut butter and jelly?" I asked.

"Let me help you. Or else it might be peanut butter and mustard."

We scraped the food into the garbage can and started from scratch. And while we made the sandwiches, I watched her from under lowered lids to see if the shadows fell upon her face again. But they didn't. Not that night. We were safe. For at least a little while longer.

Four

The usual two-inch stack of mail was waiting for her when Betsy Young sat down at her desk in the newsroom at the *New York Times*. She threw her worn brown suede jacket on the back of her chair, popped the top on her can of diet soda, took a long drink and started going through the letters.

She was tall, and her wiry body fit her high-energy personality, but at forty-six she was fighting the years. Her streaked hair was cropped to hang in a flattering curl, hiding her slackening jaw line, and her blue-tinted glasses concealed some of the tired lines around her eyes. There were younger people in the newsroom, but there were also reporters and editors older than she was. These were mostly men.

She left off perusing the mail to watch a breaking news report on the TV monitor next to her desk. A newscaster announced the jury had returned a verdict in a murder case that had been in the headlines for weeks.

"The jury has come back with a vote of guilty for Mary Woods, who, for the last six weeks, has been on trial for the murder of her brother, Daniel Woods. Women are less likely to be convicted of murder..."

"Blah, blah, blah," Betsy responded, to no one in particular.

Robby, a twenty-something crime reporter new to the *Times* from Florida, whose desk was next to Betsy's, looked over at her. She caught his eye and they laughed. He was still looking at her ten seconds later when she slit open the large manila envelope that had been next in the pile of mail. She was used to young reporters watching her, knew they admired her Pulitzers and wanted to soak up whatever they could by observing her. She thought about telling them that much of it wasn't talent but the sheer luck of having been in the right place at the right time, except she didn't really believe that. If luck was involved, it was because she made her own.

She didn't know what it was about her reaction to what she pulled out of the envelope that made him get up out of his chair, walk to her desk and peer over her shoulder. Normally she'd be observant enough to know if a man was sniffing her perfume.

But this time, she didn't. The eight-by-ten-inch glossy made her forget everything.

The corpse was lying on a simple metal gurney, his skin so white it was almost pale green. A halo effect of shimmering light forced her attention to the man's black pubic hair and shrunken penis.

Your eyes couldn't help being drawn there, she thought. And not just because of the lighting. The shot had been designed to emphasize the man's genitals. You were viewing the cadaver from between his legs, staring up past his crotch so that the perspective was skewed. The man's head was diminished. His sexual organs exaggerated.

"Oh, God," Robby whispered.

"There is a famous painting of Christ that shows him

from exactly this perspective—his feet to the viewer, the rest of him foreshortened. It was painted by Mantegna." Betsy held the photograph at arm's length and squinted at it.

Gingerly, she laid the photo on her desk and picked up the next one.

This photograph had been taken from a more traditional angle, from overhead, looking straight down. The man's penis was still dead center so her eye went there first, but everything else in this picture was in proportion and she could see the man's drawn face.

He appeared to be about thirty-five and in excellent physical condition. His naked form showed muscle and sinew but no fat. His hands were crossed on his bare chest, his eyes were closed. He might have been asleep if not for the pallor and pose.

The third shot focused on the soles of the cadaver's feet, each with the number 1 handwritten in bright red marker.

"I've seen awful things but these are just…" Robby shook his head. Although he was a prolific writer he couldn't find the right words for how these photographs shocked him.

"I know. There's something about the finality and pathos of a corpse—even in a flat photograph—that you don't ever get used to."

Robby looked down at the envelope the photos had come in. Betsy saw him making sure it was addressed to her, and she smiled. She knew if it hadn't been, he thought he'd have some shot at the story.

But it had been.

"The best you can hope for is that this will be so big that I'll need some help," Betsy told him. "Maybe there will be sidebars—"

"Except you're so tireless, you'll probably do them all yourself," he said sadly.

Behind her back, they called her "the pug," not because she was unattractive but because she was tenacious. In her dozen years at the *Times,* she'd won two Pulitzers, even if the last one had been more than five years ago.

"Do you think this guy looks familiar?" Betsy finally asked.

Robby stared at the man's face. "Yes. But not enough to place him."

Betsy examined the photo with a magnifying glass.

"So, are you going to go to the police?" Robby asked.

"Of course…but not this very minute."

"Won't you be an accessory if you got this and they didn't—"

"Robby, I said I was going to go to the police. But first I am going to do some reporting. Just enough to get a handle on this. Just enough so that no one can take it away from me."

They both looked back at the photographs on her desk. In death, the man's features were slack, but his nose was prominent and the mustache that graced his upper lip was still glossy and lush.

"He really does look familiar," Betsy mused. And then she snapped her fingers. "Got it," she said, her voice eerily gleeful. "Philip Maur. Chief operating officer of Grimly and Maur. The Wall Street firm. He's been missing for a week. We ran his picture last Tuesday."

She picked up the empty envelope, examined the label, then turned it over and investigated the seal. Suddenly, she stuck her hand back inside.

Betsy pulled out an ordinary household sandwich bag containing a two-inch-long, dark substance.

Two seconds went by. Three.

She let out a short breath and dropped the bag on her desk.

"Oh, my God, it's his hair, isn't it?" Robby asked in horror.

Betsy nodded.

Five

Detective Noah Jordain sat at the counter in a Japanese restaurant with his partner, Mark Perez. Both had plates of sushi in front of them. Jordain dipped a piece of *uni* into the soy sauce and then smeared it with wasabi.

"How can you eat so much of that without burning your sinuses?"

"You are a wimp," Jordain said in his slow New Orleans drawl, and Perez laughed. Since they'd been working together, Jordain had introduced his partner to all kinds of exotic food.

Jordain loved to cook and to explore New York's endless supply of ethnic cuisines. A Renaissance man, he not only cooked, but played piano, wrote jazz, collected antiques and managed not to get ribbed for any of it by a single cop in the department.

There was just one reason.

In police work, God was in the details.

They all knew it.

Jordain lived it.

And they respected him for it.

Jordain's cell phone rang. Pulling it out, he looked at

it as if it were an insect, put it down next to his green tea, speared another piece of sushi, dipped and smeared it, popped it in his mouth and chewed. The phone rang a second time.

Perez, who was as reactive as Jordain was laid-back, glared at his partner. In the two years they'd been together, Perez hadn't gained any of Jordain's patience.

"You want me to get that?"

Jordain swallowed, smiled, shook his head and slowly reached for the cell, answering it on the fourth ring.

As he listened, he ran his hand through his thick silvery hair. And then he did it twice again. Perez noticed and became alert. He'd learned to tell how bad the news was by how many times Jordain brushed the wavy hair off his forehead.

"Okay, give me a number," Jordain said as he reached for his notebook. He wrote the number down and read it back. Jordain was dyslexic. It hardly affected him now that he was an adult, but he was bad at retaining numbers in his head, and sometimes he reversed them when he wrote them down. Reading them back alleviated that problem.

The learning disability had been embarrassing in grade school, made reading tougher for him than for most kids, and kept him from excelling at spelling bees, but otherwise he hardly ever thought about it. However, it had made him listen harder and be more observant. He noticed sights and heard nuances other people missed. Even other detectives missed. Even the best ones.

"Well, this is one sorry mess," Jordain said as he snapped the phone shut.

"What?"

"Looks like a missing-persons case just erupted into a murder investigation, with a dash of fetish thrown in for good measure."

"Who called it in?"

"That might just be the best part."

Jordain took the last piece of sushi from his plate, dipped it in the soy sauce, spread the wasabi on it, looked at it and finally put it back down in the middle of his plate. He laid the chopsticks beside the fish. "Betsy Young."

"The crime reporter at the *Times?*"

"We know and love any other Betsy Young?"

"What does she have?"

"Death-scene photos of the victim. Came in her mail this morning."

"And the fetish?"

"Little twist that's a new one for me. The photos came with a lock of the victim's hair. And there's one other thing." Jordain took a long drink of his green tea, which by now was cold.

"Which was?"

"The body has the number 1 written on the soles of his feet."

"Number 1?"

Jordain nodded. "Yeah, and you know what I'm worried about?"

"You bet. If there's a number 1, there's bound to be a number 2."

Six

"You can ask her anything you want, but this is our story," Harry Hastings said. "I want that to be clear. We want to keep our lead and ensure exclusivity. So in exchange for cooperating with you, we want first dibs on anything you find." He pulled a cigarette from the crumpled pack. Even though the *Times* was a smoke-free workplace, sometimes he broke the rules. No one had ever complained. Especially not when they were in his office.

"Is that clear?" he asked the two detectives.

Jordain eyed the stocky man. Even though they were ostensibly on the same side, the *Times* editor was on the offensive. Jordain wouldn't respond. He'd leave that to Perez. They were in good-cop/bad-cop mode.

"Crystal," Perez said with a little more attitude than he felt.

The two detectives were seated at the round table in the middle of the managing editor's office. Opposite them, Betsy Young drank from a can of diet soda. So far she hadn't said a word. Her boss was done laying out the ground rules, which neither detective had any intention of adhering to.

"Why you?" Jordain asked Betsy. He'd worked with her twice before, and while he never expected a reporter to make his job easier, Betsy had been so desperate to get her story that she'd come close to compromising both cases.

"I don't know what you mean, Detective," she said. Although she was technically answering Jordain, she was looking at Perez.

Jordain knew exactly what the reporter was doing but ignored it. He didn't care what kind of game she was going to play. He and Perez would handle her, but inwardly he sighed—why couldn't it ever be easy?

"Why, of all the reporters at the *Times*...why, of all the reporters in the city at any paper, do you think you are the one whose name was on that envelope?" Perez asked, taking over.

She smiled wryly. "Why not me? I've covered some of the most important crime stories in the city."

Jordain cut in. "Do you know, or have you ever known, Philip Maur? Had any dealing with his firm? Anyone at his firm? Did you write the story about him being missing?"

He was watching her eyes, but again she was avoiding his and looking instead at the photograph. Behind his desk, Hastings bristled but didn't say whatever he was thinking. Jordain knew that the managing editor had been around long enough to know that, while not pleasant, this line of questioning was par for the course. The police had to find out if the reporter was in any way involved.

"Betsy, please. The more you resist the less time you get to work on the story. Do you have any connection to Maur?"

"No," she said curtly.

After a half-dozen more questions that led nowhere, Jordain looked at Hastings. "We're going to need to see the story before you run it."

"We're not going to run our stories by you, Detective."

"I think that you're going to have to. We need to keep some details out of the paper. Leverage, you understand. Why don't you just make this easy? We have a murder to solve, Hastings. You don't really want to hinder our investigation, do you?"

Hastings weighed this. He hated to give in but was also anxious to get Betsy back to work. She had a story to file. "Why don't we decide here and now what you want us to keep out of the story."

Betsy was gripping a pencil so tightly that her knuckles were white. "I really don't like the idea of withholding any part of this story, Harry."

"Neither do I. Let's hear them out, though. Detective, what do you want us to keep out of the story?"

Jordain and Perez examined the photographs.

"You can run this one," Jordain pushed the shot of the cadaver's foot forward. "But not these."

His gaze moved to the plastic bag with the hair clippings.

"And let's keep out any mention of the hair—" Perez started.

"No." It was out of Betsy's mouth before the detective had even finished his sentence. "No. The photos make sense—besides, we can't run the nude shots. But the hair is too important. Why did the killer send the cuttings? What does it mean? Is it symbolic of something? It's disturbing and perverse."

Jordain stood up. Perez followed his lead, and they gathered up all the materials, putting each item into an evidence bag. When the two of them were done, Jordain directed his comments to Hastings.

"I don't want this to be a battle. I'm asking you not to force me to throw the department's weight around."

Hastings lit a cigarette, inhaled and blew out the smoke. "We don't want that, either, Detective."

"Fine. I'm glad to hear it. So I won't be reading anything in the paper about this lock of hair?"

"No. You won't. And, in exchange, we expect to hear any information that you have before any other papers."

Jordain frowned at him. He wasn't going to bargain. And he wasn't going to give in. He didn't have to offer the paper anything and he was tired of the adversarial attitude. He'd encountered it in New Orleans and now here. "I am not going to make promises. We'll do our best to keep you informed. That's as far as I'll go. There are fingerprints all over the photos." He looked at Betsy. "Are your fingerprints on file?"

She nodded and tried to stare him down. It didn't work.

He and Perez were done. They started for the door, but Perez stopped and looked back at Hastings. "Because of the number 1 on the victim's feet, there's a strong possibility there is going to be a second victim. We're going to send someone over to talk to your mail room guys about how to sort through the mail for the next week or so. And you, too, Betsy."

Jordain and Perez walked out of the newsroom without talking. They were quiet on the elevator. You never know who's listening. You keep silent until you are alone, out of earshot. Especially when you're in the offices of the *New York Times*.

"Let's do a background check on Ms. Young," Jordain said once they were back on the street. "This might be nothing, but I want to make sure it's nothing."

Perez agreed. "Assuming it is, why would someone want the newspaper to have this before the police?"

"To make sure it's in the papers in all its glory. To prevent us from keeping any of it out of the public eye. To take control. To keep control. Take your pick."

"What's your pick?" Perez asked.

"All of the above," Jordain said.

Seven

I was sitting in the makeup room of the *Today* show on that Friday morning in early October, nursing a cup of strong black coffee while a young woman stroked my face with a wet sponge, adding a warm tone to my pale skin. It was seven-thirty and I still had to have my hair done. I wasn't due on the set for another forty minutes, but that wasn't why I was nervous.

Even though I knew the topic we'd be discussing, I didn't know exactly what the questions were going to be. Whatever I wanted to impart to the public about when to see a sex therapist and why, I'd have to do it in less than five minutes.

I drank more of the coffee and stared into the mirror, watching the makeup artist work her magic on my face.

No matter how well you understand how fear works, how adrenaline flows into your bloodstream and how it makes you feel, it's still unnerving to know you are going to be on national television, and that your face and voice and words are going to be seen and heard by more than eight million people.

I would have rather been almost anywhere else, but I

was there for one of those eight million people: a thirteen-year-old girl who was sitting glued to a TV screen at her father's apartment, waiting to see her mother on television.

Daily, Dulcie had been asking me about nervous reactions. While the debut of the Broadway production was months away, there was a preview in a few weeks, in Boston. We talked about stage fright often, from the chemicals your body releases when you are in a situation that gives you the jitters to dry mouth, and various remedies like slow, steady breathing. Dulcie needed me to show her that, with no training and no desire to be onstage, I could do it. "If you can when you don't even want to, then I can do it, too. After all, Mom, I'm the one with the passion for an audience."

The makeup artist told me to close my eyes, and I felt a brush follow the line of my eyelid.

My mother had gone through this every day. It was part of what had seduced her. Acting. Accolades. Attention. Applause. Starting when she was sixteen, she co-starred in a popular TV series. *The Lost Girls* was a drama about two orphaned teenagers who were taken in by a married couple—both professors at an Ivy League school in Boston.

The girls always got into terrible trouble until one of them—either my mother or her co-star, Debi Carey—would solve the problem and save the day. Meanwhile, the charming but clueless elderly couple never guessed how close the girls had come to danger, and sometimes death.

When the show went off the air after three years, my mother's career stumbled. She turned first to marriage and motherhood, and when neither satisfied the ache from missing the limelight and she failed to land another substantial role, she turned to drugs and alcohol and affairs to fill the emptiness.

My mother died of an overdose when I was only eight. Her star had lit up early and then burnt out too fast: her greatest legacy being the damage she did to her loved ones.

Where are you going? When are you coming back? I used to ask her when she went out smelling of roses, lemon and lavender, dressed up in her high heels and short skirts. She was so beautiful, no matter how sad and sick she was. She was one of *the lost girls* even if she was a woman with a child.

A lost girl.

Not the first one I had tried to save.

Not the last one I would fail.

Now I was faced with her granddaughter's stage lust. History was not going to repeat itself. I was going to keep Dulcie grounded even if her star lifted off and shot her out into the stratosphere.

The makeup artist added a final stroke of blush, brushed on more mascara and finished up with an apricot-colored lipstick. I was soothed by the sensations of the sable and the soft powders. Another woman combed out my hair and sprayed it in place.

In the mirror I saw a small woman, coiffed and made up, who only resembled me. A doppelgänger, more sophisticated and embellished than I ever was.

Done, I was escorted to the greenroom, where a half-dozen people milled around, nibbling on the elaborate array of fruits, cheeses and breakfast bakery goods. I refilled my coffee.

The producer came in to get the next guest—a willowy novelist named Lisa Tucker—and checked on the rest of us, asking if we needed anything.

I watched the show on the monitor for a few minutes, and when the screen went to commercials I picked up the newspaper that the novelist had left on her seat. Unfolding it, I scanned the front page.

There was a photo of a politician who'd made a speech at the UN, another photo of a sports figure who'd broken a world record, and a shot of the destruction left behind after a freak storm had hit New Jersey. But it was a small shot of the soles of a man's feet, with the number 1 written on them, that drew my eye. The headline read: Financier Assumed Dead.

Even before I started to read the story, three words popped from among all the black-and-white type. A name in the last paragraph of the article. The name of a man. Detective Noah Jordain.

I sighed and read past the headline.

Philip Maur, 41, the youngest chairman in the history of Grimly and Maur, the prestigious Wall Street investment firm, is assumed to be dead after a series of photographs of his body were delivered to the offices of this paper yesterday morning.

Maur's wife, Cyn Maur, said that her husband had been missing for five days. "He went to work on Friday morning and told me that he'd be home late because he was going to be attending a dinner meeting."

Maur was in his office all day Friday and left at 6:00 p.m. His secretary said he did not tell her where he was going and had not asked her to make any reservations for him that evening, which was not unusual.

Cyn Maur contacted the police on Saturday morning after not hearing from her husband all night. She'd tried his cell phone repeatedly but he had not answered, which she said was not like him. "He's a very responsible father and husband. He's never out of reach for more than an hour or two. Our daughter has juvenile diabetes and Philip is devoted to her. He'd never just go away without telling me. He's never stayed out all night before. I knew something was wrong."

A missing-persons report was filed at eight-thirty Saturday morning. There was still no information as to Maur's whereabouts on Tuesday morning, when the photographs were received by the New York Times. The photograph shown above and two others, which are now in police custody, were not accompanied by a note. There was no information alluding to the whereabouts of Maur's body.

"I don't have any comment at this time except to ask anyone who might have seen Philip Maur on Friday evening, or at any time since then, to contact our office," said Detective Noah Jordain of the city's Special Victims Unit.

The fact that Jordain is heading the investigation implies that there is a sexual component to the murder. The graphic photographs this paper received reinforce that suggestion.

The police have requested that we not print all of the photographs, due to the ongoing investigation.

My pulse was racing. My hands felt clammy and I cleared my throat. Seeing Jordain's name on the page had done that to me. I tried to slow down my heartbeat by concentrating, but the name had been like an electrical shock.

I hadn't known I was still that susceptible. It was silly. But it was the truth.

It had been four months since I'd seen him. Four months since I'd stood him up and then called him—when I'd known he wouldn't be home—and left a message on his answering machine, apologizing and explaining that it was just too soon after my divorce for me to think about dating anyone.

That had been a lie.

It had not been too soon.

I was scared of the detective and what I felt when I was with him.

Noah Jordain had walked into my office one afternoon and my heart had skipped a beat. His searching blue eyes had looked right into my dark brown ones and he'd dared me to look away. A police trick, I'd thought. Did he even know he was doing it? I dared him to look away first. A therapist's trick. He didn't. We were evenly matched. He held out his hand and I shook it, aware of it being large, pleasantly dry, but not too rough. I could tell he had enormous strength in his fingers but that he was aware of it and was being careful. And then the impact of him hit me. Like a blast of steam. For a minute nothing mattered and I lost my bearings. This had not happened to me with anyone I'd ever met, and it shook me to my core. I know better than to attribute instant attraction to anything but past psychological association—someone who looks like someone else whom you liked a lot—or a hormonal, pheromone, chemical reaction between two mammals.

It hadn't been that simple for us.

Faster than seemed possible, better than any shrink could have, he'd psyched me out and gotten under my skin. And that scared me. I don't like things I can't put a name to, or explain by some science or therapeutic logic. We might have been good together but, more likely, I think we would have destroyed each other. Neither of us was willing to keep from going too deep into the other's psyche. It all happened too fast and…I ran.

After that I'd promptly forgotten about him.

So seeing his name that morning in the greenroom, I was surprised at my reaction. Obviously, he'd made a stronger impression than I'd thought.

Bullshit.

I'd known exactly how strong an impression he'd made. That was why I'd run. He was overpowering. Sure of himself. A little arrogant, but kind. Caring. And. And. And. Sexually powerful. Jordain made me think about getting naked, about skin on skin, about lips locking. I looked at him and remembered his lips on mine, on my breasts, pulling on my nipples, nuzzling between my legs. I leaned into him, smelled him, and couldn't think of anything but putting my hands under his shirt, undressing him and doing whatever he wanted me to do. I wanted to surrender to that power. To let it take me over and see where it would lead. I had never thought about those things before I'd slept with him.

I had heard them from patients. I had dreamed them. I had even been thankful I did not feel that with my husband. It was too absorbing. I didn't want to surrender to any emotion, to any passion. Ever.

Jordain had too much intuition about me. About what I thought. About how to touch me. About how to make my body curve to his. About how to blow on the spot where my neck met my collarbone with breath so hot I had to close my eyes and hold on to his arms with tightened fingers.

He would have weakened me.

And that was not the worst he could have done.

A flush of heat warmed the back of my neck. My celery silk shirt was suddenly sticking to my back and my olive gabardine jacket felt as if it was a whole size too small.

Turning from the paper, I took another sip of the coffee, which by then was lukewarm. And another. I looked down at the ring on my right hand—a butterfly made of white gold, paved with tsarvorite in the wings and just a few tiny diamond chips in the body. It had been a birthday gift from my daughter and her godmother—my surrogate mother, Nina. I touched the tips of the wings, which were almost, but not quite, sharp enough to hurt. They had surprised me with the present just days after the Magdalene Murderer had been apprehended.

Just days after I'd almost been killed, along with one of my patients.

Just days after the last time I spoke to Detective Jordain.

"Dr. Snow? You'll be on as soon as this news break is over. Would you come with me, please?"

The air was freezing in studio 1A and I shivered as we walked down the hall, aware that I was cold over a layer of heat that was, like a memory, holding its own beneath the surface of my skin.

This was the last thing I needed to think about minutes before the camera focused on me.

"Do you need anything before you go on?" she asked.

"No, I'm fine."

But that wasn't true.

Eight

"**I**'m not here to talk about going into therapy myself. I'm here on behalf of a group of women who would like you to conduct private group therapy sessions for them," Shelby Rush said.

More than twenty-five phone calls had come in on Friday afternoon, following my appearance on the *Today* show. The receptionist at the Butterfield Institute, where I practiced, said that all but one had asked what kind of health insurance I accepted and what my rates were. Five of them had said they would call back to schedule appointments after they checked with their insurance agents. I wasn't planning on taking on all of them as patients. My schedule was already tight. But I'd meet them and evaluate them so that I could refer them to the right therapist at the institute.

One woman had asked for an appointment without inquiring about either my rates or the insurance, and now she sat opposite me in my pale yellow office, on the other side of my desk. Shelby was in her mid-thirties, attractive and articulate in a way that many women in Manhattan are. Her expensive clothes were unremarkable. Taupe slacks, white silk shell and black blazer. High-heeled Chanel shoes and a Gucci handbag—taupe fabric with interlocking Gs.

I dressed pretty much the way she did—but less expensively. The look was the same though: classic, tailored, chic. The New York City uniform for women over thirty. Not an expression of individuality so much as a way to win the fashion war that most of us were tired of once we left our twenties.

You can't read us by these clothes. Our shoes and bags, our suits, shirts and slacks all mean nothing. Our secret souls aren't exposed by the name on the label inside our jackets. They are not even visible on our faces.

Some therapists claim that they can get a glimpse of their patients' real selves in their eyes, but I wasn't sure of that anymore. Maybe it was because so many of the successful business professionals I worked with had learned the art of concealment and false impressions for work. Maybe it was because my talents lay more in getting people to open up, because they trusted I wouldn't judge them. I don't believe in popular psychology or fast fixes.

"What kind of organization do you belong to, Shelby? Why do you think I'd be the right therapist?"

She uncrossed her hands and looked down at her nails as if she'd find the answer to my question cribbed on the pale pink ovals.

I took her emotional temperature. She didn't fidget, but she bit her bottom lip and held the skin between her teeth so long it seemed as if the action was actually preventing her from speaking.

"Shelby?"

"This is a little complicated, Dr. Snow."

I nodded, encouraging her. She bit her lip again. I could wait as long as it took her to decide she was ready to tell me. I glanced at the two high arched windows on the south wall of my office. Beyond them was a three-foot-wide ledge—which, in Manhattan, many would call a terrace. It was only big enough to stand on and look down at the sidewalk or up at the sky, but I'd crammed the space with planters containing flowers and bushes that attracted butterflies.

When I'd first created my city garden, everyone told me I was dreaming, that there were no butterflies in the city apart from those in the butterfly exhibit at the Museum of Natural History.

But I knew there were masses of monarchs in Central Park. They settled on flowers in the Shakespeare Garden, in the Conservatory and in the Rambles. And since the Butterfield Institute was only a block and a half from the park, I thought they might come.

The first year they didn't, but they showed up the second and have been coming ever since. Lovely red-orange monarchs, cabbage whites and pop-art zebra swallowtails find their way to my small garden and grace me with their short-lived loveliness. Winged creatures that exist to reproduce and, in the process, help flowers to do the same.

By late September the butterflies were usually gone, but this year it was still so warm that they had not yet started their migration. A monarch, as deeply orange as the leaves on the maple trees, flitted from petal to petal while Shelby struggled to figure out how to reveal her secrets.

Aristotle had named butterflies *psyche,* the Greek word for *soul,* and I understood why. Their metamorphosis reminded me of the way patients work so hard to become free of what has kept them fettered in the past.

Finally, Shelby let go of her lip and began. "Our society—we call it a society, the Scarlet Society—is a secret.

Sounds so melodramatic, doesn't it? But it is. No one outside of the membership knows about it. We don't do anything illegal. Or dangerous. But it has lasted, in one form
or another, for the past forty years without anyone finding
out about it except the people we wanted to know."

I did the math. The society had formed in the early six-
ties.

Shelby had stopped talking and was biting her lip again.

"Can you tell me any more than that?"

"Yes. Of course. Our membership is made up of single,
married and divorced women, many of whom work for a
living. Everyone is fairly well off. Our dues are high."

She stopped. I waited. She didn't offer anything else.

"That doesn't really help me all that much. Is there
more?"

"Yes, much more. But first we need to reach some kind
of agreement, and I'm not really sure how to proceed here.
We've been so careful. Our members don't even know one
another's last names. You are the only one who knows
mine. Can you agree to help us? Then I can tell you more
of what you need to know."

"I can't do that until I know what you need and why."

Shelby frowned and looked back down at her hands.

"Okay. How about this? We are a group of women
who have similar interests. Nothing we do is dangerous.
Or illegal."

It was the second time she'd made those two points. So
I knew one thing: what they did was in some way dangerous. And possibly illegal.

We all lie. We learn when we are small children and see
an overweight woman in the pool and cry out—*Mommy,
look, there's a fat lady*—and our mothers tell us that isn't
nice, that we shouldn't say things that can hurt people's

feelings. Because in some cases it's kinder to lie, we are taught to ingest moral cyanide in the name of civility. And then one day we get to a point in our lives—perhaps the point that Shelby Rush was at that moment—when the truth is the only way we can begin to help and heal, but still we obfuscate and hide because it is what we are used to doing.

"Okay, if you can't tell me any more about the society, tell me why you think I'm the right therapist for you."

"Because you're a sex therapist."

I nodded but was frustrated and Shelby knew it. "I could explain it all if you would just agree to work with us."

I leaned forward. "Shelby, here at the institute, we make a serious effort in matching therapists to patients. We're professionals. I can't just assume that I'm the right therapist for your group."

"Almost everyone agreed that you'd be right."

"Who didn't agree?"

"One of our members who doesn't think we need a therapist at all. Another who wanted us to hire her therapist, but I didn't think that would be a good idea."

"Why me?"

"A friend of mine who isn't in our society recommended you. She was a patient of yours four years ago. Ellen Kenneth?"

I nodded. Shelby continued. "She told me you are non-judgmental and that you will listen to us talk about sex and the things we do sexually and that you won't tell us we should stop or warn us that we're all screwing up our relationships. That you will understand when we tell you we aren't, that we're keeping our relationships alive."

I felt the first stirrings of excitement that usually kick

in at the start of a good therapy session. "What is it a therapist would be judgmental about?"

Shelby sat up straighter, smoothed her pants and flicked her hair behind her shoulders. She was preparing for battle. "What do you think normal sex is, Dr. Snow?"

"I don't qualify sex as normal or abnormal. Each of us has boundaries. What might be acceptable for you, might not be for someone else. Not because the act itself is acceptable or unacceptable, but rather because of your own reaction to it."

"Isn't there anything you think is abnormal?"

"Are you asking me where I draw the line between what is healthy and unhealthy?"

She nodded.

"When your own sexual desires or actions cause serious pain or danger to either yourself or someone else."

Shelby sat silently, nodding, it seemed, to herself. "We need a therapist who is trustworthy. I know every therapist is supposed to be, but we need to find someone who has been tested. And we know you have been. I did some research on the Magdalene Murders. You never betrayed your patient. You never told the police what you knew."

I nodded in acknowledgment. Shelby continued.

"We need a therapist who will understand what it is like to be a successful woman making her way in a world that is still male dominated. Who won't be shocked or disturbed by what we have to say. And we want it to be a sex therapist, not because we need help with sexual issues but because the sexual component of our society is so intrinsic to it that we don't think anyone else would be able to understand what we have to explain."

Shelby had told me she was a divorce lawyer, and while I found most of her conversation devoid of legalese, this last speech was too convoluted for me. I wondered if she had done that to confuse me or was really having a hard time coming out and telling me about the Scarlet Society?

"On the *Today* show you talked about how, as women become empowered and gain more recognition and prominence in the work force, their success becomes sexualized, and how that is creating a sexual crisis in many relationships today."

I nodded again. This was also the basis of the paper Nina had asked me to deliver at the psychiatric conference next August. I waited to hear what connection this thesis had with the society.

"Our club is built on the idea that being sexually aggressive is not alien to women but something we've been taught to suppress in order to protect the male position. Male-dominated institutions, businesses, religions and philosophies have perpetuated the myth of the powerless woman. But there are women who want something else. Who don't want to be dominated. Who don't want to be chosen. Who don't get off on any of that."

I leaned forward. She smiled, knowing she had me. I knew it, too, but that was okay.

"Dr. Snow, our chapter here in New York is having a problem, and we don't know how we should handle it. I'm afraid…a lot of us are afraid that if we don't do exactly the right thing now it might rip us apart or threaten what we have. And that would be awful because women have a right to exercise their free will. Not just in the marketplace. Not just by being single parents. Not just reproductively. But we have a right to our own sexual free will. We have a right to be stronger women and enjoy men on our own terms if that's what pleases us."

"What are you afraid of?" I asked Shelby.

"We're afraid for our lives."

Nine

On Tuesday afternoon at 4:00 p.m., Betsy Young rushed out of the lobby of the *New York Times*. She had an interview uptown and didn't want to be late. A strong wind was blowing leaves off the trees, littering the sidewalk, and it was raining. Other people pulled their jacket collars up and opened umbrellas. Even though Betsy was in too much of a hurry to notice the weather or the leaves, she saw the blue sedan that idled outside the office.

But she didn't have time to do more than run into the street and hail a cab. Jumping in, she gave the driver the address of an apartment building on Park Avenue and slammed the door shut.

As the taxi peeled away from the curb, Betsy pulled a sheaf of papers out of her tote bag: research she'd pulled off the net about Philip Maur's wife and her family. Before she looked at it again, she turned and looked out the window, and saw that the blue sedan had pulled out behind her cab.

Was she being followed?

Well, it was possible. The police could be watching her. After all, she was the one who had gotten the photographs.

The only one. But she'd worry about that later. Now she had to focus on the exclusive interview ahead of her.

Earlier that morning, she'd taken a chance and called Maur's wife, who was also the daughter of a high-powered New York politician. Cyn Maur had been so confused and distracted that Betsy wondered if she actually understood she'd agreed to an interview. If she had, then Betsy wanted to know why. Even though her job depended on people talking to her, she was always astonished when anyone opened the doors to his or her private hell.

Betsy could not imagine showing her own scars and shame to the public.

Number 1235 Park Avenue wasn't the Maurs' apartment. It was the home of Cyn's parents. And that was why Officer Tana Butler didn't recognize the address when the reporter's taxi stopped there.

Betsy walked into the marble lobby, gave her name to the doorman, and told him who she was there to see. The doorman called upstairs and announced the visitor. He listened, then hung up.

"Apartment 15E, Miss Young. First elevator on the right."

Betsy walked into the interior lobby. As soon as she was out of sight, Officer Butler got out of the blue sedan and walked into the building. Flashing her badge, she asked the doorman who the woman ahead of her had asked to see. She opened her notebook and wrote down the name of Cyn Maur's parents.

Then she went back outside, got into the unmarked car and waited.

Upstairs, Cyn sat on the pale yellow couch in the living room and waited for Betsy's questions as if she were facing an executioner.

"Is this your first interview?" Betsy asked, trying to get the nervous woman to talk about how uncomfortable she was.

"I didn't want to do it, but it has been more than a week and the police still don't have a single idea of where my husband's body is. Not one lead on who killed him or why. And I have to know. I'm desperate to know."

"So you thought you'd talk to the press?"

Cyn nodded. Her mouth twisted into what Betsy thought was an ugly grimace. "You're vipers. You'll investigate ruthlessly. You're not hindered by the law. I don't care who finds my husband's body or his killer—the police or the press—as long as someone does. I am tired of crying from not knowing."

Even now, facing the reporter, the tears came.

"It's horrible. No matter where I look, I see the photographs the police showed me, those frozen images of my husband's body. I've even tried to pretend that he wasn't my husband. That the shots were of some other man. I even yelled at the detectives, told them that they had the wrong person. I pushed them, trying to get them to leave. But they knew what I was doing. So they waited and let me cry until, finally, I told them that, yes, it was Phil.

"He looked so cold in the pictures," she said, her heart splintering into pieces all over again. "I need to be able to close my eyes at night and go to sleep and wake up in the morning and pour orange juice for my children, and make them waffles. But I can't concentrate on anything. My husband was tied up and brutalized. He'd been photographed from the most lewd angles possible. Why? The pallor of his skin haunts me. His slack face and helpless hands obsess me.

"Phil had never been helpless in his life," she said, not sure if she was answering a question or not.

Betsy smiled sympathetically and leaned forward, her pen poised on a page of her notebook. "So, he was a strong man? Do you mean emotionally? Or physically?"

Cyn Maur heard something in the reporter's voice. Was it doubt? Confusion? Cynicism?

If she had slept even a little last night she might have picked up the subtleties in the reporter's tone. A warning bell might have alerted her that Betsy knew something that she shouldn't have.

Ten

My daughter was having dinner with her father that Tuesday night and I was home going through my office mail. Not exactly an exciting evening. Not social or illuminating or edifying. I had finished with everything but the manila envelope from Shelby Rush that had arrived that afternoon. Inside was a videotape cassette and a cream-colored note card.

> Dear Dr. Snow,
> It was good meeting with you. I'm sure that you are the right therapist for us and know you will be able to help us get through this troubled time. In the meantime, enclosed is a letter of agreement between you and the Scarlet Society. It's a confidentiality agreement. I'm sure you've been asked to sign something like this before. As I explained when we met, the society is very concerned about opening up to anyone on the outside. We're simply asking you to keep everything that we talk about in our group-therapy sessions in the strictest confidence—

I put the letter down and stood up. I didn't walk into the kitchen so much as stomp in. *Well no, Shelby,* I was saying to her in my head. *No one, in the six years that I have been in private practice as a sex therapist with the Butterfield Institute, has ever asked me to sign any kind of confidentiality agreement.* I couldn't even give her—or the society—the benefit of the doubt; I knew several of them had been in therapy before. They had to know that what happens between a doctor and her patients is privileged. Besides, I'd explained it to her. Damn, I'd almost gotten killed keeping the confidence of a patient last June, not going to the police when I thought she might be in danger.

My hand was shaking as I poured myself a glass of wine. I breathed in the fruity aroma as I took my first sip and, carrying the glass, went back to the couch in the den to reread the letter, finishing it this time.

> We are all grateful that you've agreed to help us and we are looking forward to our first meeting this coming week. By way of introduction, I've included a video. Like everything else about us, we are asking that you view it in private.
>
> I trust you, Dr. Snow. Just meeting you once, I know we've made the right decision.
>
> Sincerely,
> Shelby Rush

There was another sheet of paper in the envelope. The confidentiality agreement. I put that down without even glancing at it. I was intrigued by the Scarlet Society and by Shelby, and had been looking forward to the challenge of working with them, but I wouldn't sign legal papers for any patient. It was insulting.

Trying to let go of my resentment, making an effort to figure out why their request was making me angrier than it should have, I grabbed the video and slammed it into our VCR. Obviously, I wasn't letting go of the feelings.

A few seconds into the tape, the black screen gave way to a shot of an elaborate living room. Crystal sconces glittered, gilt frames glinted in the light. The room was filled with lush velvet couches, oversized chairs and exquisite Oriental rugs in subtle shades of blues and yellows. Opulent bouquets of roses and rubrum lilies sat on end tables. I could almost smell their sweet vanilla scent.

Loud rock music blared in the background. The harsh, driving beat of the Rolling Stones' "You Can't Always Get What You Want" was antithetical to the genteel decorations of the grand room.

The camera held steady until the French doors opened and a crowd flowed in.

It's funny how you see what you expect to see. I knew right away that I was looking at a tape of a costume ball—everyone was wearing elaborate masks that covered the upper parts of their faces. The women were ornately dressed, well coiffed and draped with brilliant jewelry—real or not, it didn't matter. Rubies and emeralds and diamonds glittered on ears and necks, fingers and wrists.

I was conscious that there was something different about what I was looking at, but it took a few seconds for me to realize that the women's gowns were not just cut low but designed to bare their breasts. Nipples were rouged, skin was powdered and often sprinkled with sparkles.

As the women continued making their way into the room, the camera moved in on them. Many of the gowns had slits up the front, revealing that they weren't wearing underwear.

The mood at the party was joyful. They greeted one another with air kisses, often whispering and then laughing.

The music segued into a Beatles song, "Love, Love Me Do," as tuxedoed male waiters furrowed through the crowd offering canapés and flutes of champagne.

Two women—one wearing a cat mask, the other wearing one decorated with peacock feathers—took drinks and then walked off together, arm in arm. While the waiter was wearing a tuxedo coat, white shirt, cummerbund and bow tie on top, I now saw that he was naked from the waist down and sported a semierection.

All the waiters were pantless. The camera focused on one in his thirties, trim, medium height, dark-haired, with a strong but ordinary face. A woman wearing a silver mask, with sapphires outlining the holes for her eyes, took a glass of champagne from him and then reached down and cupped his testicles, giving them a little squeeze.

I reached for my wine without looking away.

What was I watching?

In a hushed tone, almost as if she had been anticipating my question, a woman's voice started the narration and a title appeared over the scene:

The Scarlet Society's 40th Annual Gala
February 10, 2002

"Since 1962, the Scarlet Society has had a yearly gala to raise money. Both active and inactive members from all chapters are invited to attend, as are all of the men that the society has invited to play with us over the years.

"For some of us, who have moved away or for some other reason stopped attending the regular soirées, this is a chance for us to see old friends and slip into our dreams for one more night.

"At the 2002 gala, more than 130 members and 150 male guests were in attendance. We raised close to two million dollars, which will go far in helping us keep the society an active and vital organization. All of this money was given anonymously.

"This tape is a small thank-you for your contribution and a memento of the evening we shared. As we all know, it's not often that a camera is allowed into a society event, but since we were all so well disguised, the board thought it would be a wonderful record of our night of utter delight."

The narration faded, the music returned to its previous level and I realized what I'd missed up until then: the voice-over had said there were 150 men present, but other than the dozen half-naked waiters, I hadn't seen any men mingling with the female guests.

After thirty seconds more of the same footage, the camera zeroed in on a group of women and followed them through an open passage into a large ballroom.

I took ballroom dancing lessons when I was twelve. Krista, my father's second wife, insisted. Even though she was an iconoclastic sculptor who showed at a SoHo gallery, she thought the lessons were a rite of passage.

"If you don't learn, what will you do when some fabulous guy asks you to dance and a waltz is playing?"

Since I trusted and liked her—partly because she was smart enough not to try to replace my mother—I agreed to the once-a-week classes at the posh Pierre hotel on Fifth Avenue, just across from Central Park.

The girls were required to wear dresses and the boys to wear jackets and ties. The beginning of each session was the same: we stood on one side of the room and the boys stood on the other and we waited for them to walk across the parquet floor and ask us to dance. We learned more than the fox trot that year—the lesson of male power and female submission was reinforced for all of us every Thursday at five-thirty.

At the Scarlet Society's gala, the same paradigm was now playing out on the video: women were on one side, and men were on the other. But it was the women who were the aggressors here, gliding across the floor and choosing their partners from among the men in evening dress—none of whom stayed dressed for long.

The camera stopped on a tall blond woman. With her mask on, it was impossible to tell her age, but she was dressed in a stunning, low-cut lavender gown that was slit up the front to show off her long legs. She walked away from the group, champagne glass in one hand, smiling to herself and moving seductively to the music. When she arrived at the swarm of men, she stopped and looked them over.

Walking back and forth, sipping her champagne, assessing, examining, she looked for something about one of the men that spoke to her.

Finally, she stopped.

He was taller than she was, with wavy hair almost as blond as hers. He was fully and immaculately dressed in a black tux. As she looked, he lowered his head. Then she stepped forward until she was only inches from him, reached out, cupped his chin with her hand and lifted his face up to hers. Like her, he was wearing a mask, but a simple black one. Although his eyes, nose and cheekbones were obscured, his jawline was strong and his neck was muscular.

The woman nodded once at him and he began to strip for her.

I'd never seen a man undress so slowly, so seductively. There was something almost feminine in the way he took off his tie and his jacket and let them fall to the ground. His shirt, socks and shoes followed.

He interrupted the show for a moment once his chest was bare, and almost as if he was challenging her, he looked right at her, watching to see how she was reacting. Reaching out, she unbuckled his belt, pulled at the button on the waistband of his pants, undid it roughly, yanked down his zipper, and then took a step away from him. At that point, he continued undressing, until all of his clothes were in a puddle on the floor.

Naked, he waited and watched her from under partially lowered eyes, behaving like an obedient subordinate.

Ignoring his erection, the woman traced the muscles on his arms with one of her fingernails, delineating the sinews slowly. Dropping her hand to her side, she turned and abruptly walked away.

She must have said something to him that was inaudible over the music, or there must have been some sign from her that I didn't recognize, or there were rules in place for the proper behavior, because the man followed after her, like a loyal dog, out to the middle of the dance floor and then, making his second aggressive move, took her in his arms and danced with her.

I shut off the tape and sat in the den, staring at the screen, hugging my torso. We've all seen pornography. This was not that. Many people have videotaped themselves making love and then used the images to get turned on. Thousands have even released those X-rated home movies on the Internet. As a sex therapist, I often enter into the dark and secret places inside my patients' heads where I explore their imaginations and fetishes with them. What one man finds arousing troubles the next. What one woman craves disgusts another. Rarely can anyone articulate why one scenario stimulates and another disturbs. Nothing is normal or abnormal. In the folds of your brain, where your sexual fantasies form while you lie half awake, symbols, actions and activities come to you from a nether place that has no name and where there are no rules. I know those places.

I can be surprised by what I hear—I can even be shocked by it—but I cannot be undone. Passion has its own peculiar pathways and I had walked them with my patients. I'd studied them. I'd heard about them every day for the past six years.

And yet, I had just watched something not in my lexicon of psychological knowledge. I was unaware of any group of women who acted *en masse* sexually. Men? Yes. But women? No. Women did not gather in groups to engage in erotic activity for their own pleasure, just as traditionally women do not rape.

Scientific evidence presents a theory that the hormonal makeup of men and women is what causes aggressive or passive behavior. Women have more estrogen, which is the hormone that drives us to be nurturers. As a result of survival of the fittest, we are hardwired to be mothers. The best breeders—the more faithful women and those with the highest levels of estrogen, and the men who impregnated the greatest number of women and had the highest levels of testosterone—were the ones whose genes were passed on.

In the 1960s and '70s, feminists tried to raise boys who played with dolls and were not aggressive, and to raise girls who were aggressive and played with trucks. But it didn't work. Yes, yes, in individual cases it did. But not in general.

We are our hormones.

Except I was watching a video of women who were acting out male-pattern sexual behavior, and as a sex therapist, that interested me more than anything I'd heard about in quite a few years.

I clicked the tape back on and watched the ritual of other women picking out their dance partners. Their actions were not shy. The only bashfulness I saw was on the faces of the men who were on display, lined up, stiff in their tuxedos, waiting to be chosen and stripped.

If I had not met Shelby Rush, I would not believe that I was watching a real event, but rather an erotic film written and directed by women for the delight of women.

What was so stunning was the total reversal. Not one movement had been out of character for the aggressor. And there were more than a hundred of these women. Some tall and lovely, some short and round, others older, not beauties at all. But there was a freedom and lack of self-consciousness that graced each one's bearing.

It was a sexual dance of daring that I did not have the information to process.

It took courage to be that open about your desires. It must take enormous self-esteem and a willingness to act the fool. It takes a burning need to be satiated. I would not have been capable of walking into that ballroom, choosing a man and telling him what I wanted.

What must it feel like to not wonder if you are desirable? Not to consider what the other person was feeling or thinking or needing sexually, but simply to know that the act of demanding gave a man pleasure, and that his desire to please made him hard.

What would it be like to know that the fact of being in charge—no matter what I looked like or said or thought or did—was enough to make me desirable?

The tape was still running, but I shut it off and picked up the confidentiality agreement and read through it, looking at the blank space that was waiting for my signature. The first time I'd looked at it, I'd been furious that my professionalism had been questioned. Now I wasn't sure how I felt. And I didn't have any idea what to do.

Eleven

Paul Lessor was sitting in his apartment staring at the news on the television with the sound turned off, the light from the monitor the only illumination in the pigsty that used to be his living room. On the coffee table in front of him were piles of newspapers and plates of untouched food. Dried-out English muffins, butter congealed on the plate. Three-quarters of a banana now brown and rotting.

He had no appetite. That was one of the side effects of the medication, and was the least of his problems with the drugs.

What a fucking mess his life was. He was thirty-three. One of the most talented art directors at any publishing house in New York City, with more award-winning covers to his name than anyone else in the business. He'd gotten scholarships to Cooper Union and then the Yale School of Art. He'd had his photographic collages in four group shows. He got offers every year to jump ship from Pigeonhole Press, the small but prestigious publishing company where he worked, and move to the bigger houses, but he didn't go. He couldn't go. His boss, Maria Diezen, the fifty-two-year-old editor in chief, had told him that he couldn't. She told him often. He loved Maria. He loved how strong she was and how tough she was and how angry she could get at him when he didn't get it right.

And so he listened to her.

She'd been through twenty-four senior art directors in a dozen years when he'd started working for her three years ago. Now he held a record that other graphic designers in the city were in awe of. Everyone at Pigeonhole knew that Maria was a bitch: aggressive, demanding and crazy half the time. But Paul loved her. Worshipped her. Would do anything that she asked of him. Because when a woman like that, with that kind of temper and those kinds of standards, smiles on you, it's like the whole fucking world is yours.

There was nothing better than their lunch hours, when together they'd walk into the big, noisy, crowded Barnes & Noble superstore on Fifth Avenue and Forty-eighth Street, near the office, to look at one of his covers on the new fiction table. Nothing like getting a report back from the head of sales that the big buyers at B & N, Borders, Amazon and all the independents had upped their orders because "with a cover like that, there's no question the book is going to walk itself out of the store."

And more times than not, it had.

But as good as his work was, as much as he loved what he did and lived off the high that he got from it, he was fucking falling apart.

He'd gone to the psychiatrist six months ago for the crazy things that were happening in his head: manic mood swings—elation, depression, the sense that he could do anything, the realization that he was powerless.

They'd tried cocktail after cocktail of drugs to get him into some kind of chemical balance. The only thing that worked at all was Thorazine. Except for one little side effect.

He wanted to be able to live with it. Wanted to not care. Anxious to rise above the problem, he told himself that soon he'd get chemically balanced and then the doctor would be able to change the medication and find one that didn't make him impotent. He had to trust that.

Paul looked at the clock before closing his eyes. A year ago he would not have been home on a Tuesday night at eight o'clock, sitting on his couch, bored out of his brain by television. He would have been naked and fucking some Amazon who shouted out orders, telling him exactly where to put his cock and how to move his hands and what to do with his tongue.

Damn. Damn. Damn.

Not even reliving any of those incredible nights gave him half a hard-on. Not with the Thorazine coursing through his blood, softening his mind and his equipment.

No matter how hard he concentrated on remembering the high points of those months after he'd first been accepted into the Scarlet Society, it was the memories of his last two weeks there that tormented him.

It was depressing.

In its own twisted way, any depression was actually a relief tonight, because if he really was depressed, then the Thorazine wasn't working and they might be able to try something else. And if they did, then maybe, just maybe, he'd get his sexual energy back.

Now all he had was sexual shame.

The first night it had happened, no big deal. The woman he'd been with—a blonde named Anne—had tried her damnedest, shouting at him and roughing him up a little to get him hard again. But nothing worked.

It wasn't how the women had treated him, once word started getting around within the society that he couldn't get it up, that bothered him the most. There were plenty of them who didn't care that much about penetration and were perfectly happy to have him eat them or stroke their pussies. He thought he'd be able to ride out the soft-cock syndrome, at least until he and his doctor could figure out if the Thorazine was working and whether it was the best solution.

But it was how the men dealt with him that made it so fucking impossible. He was aware of every snicker and sidelong glance at his flaccid penis. He was nothing to them anymore. He was no one. He was back in high school, the skinny guy who wanted to paint and take photographs and be an artist. Who everyone called a fag. In New York City, Paul's artistic flair might have made him a totally acceptable kid. But in a public school in the sub-urbs of Detroit, it made him a wimp.

He felt the stare of every guy who watched him walk around the room with absolutely nothing happening be-tween his legs, and knew he was the fag again. It was mas-ochistic to keep going, but he couldn't stop. He kept hoping that he'd be okay, that the erotic stimulation would over-power the drugs.

He'd get back at them, he'd thought as he walked home from those embarrassing last nights of Scarlet Society vis-its. He planned what he might do to them to get his revenge. He was nothing if not creative. Hadn't everything that had ever happened to him been because of how creative he was?

He imagined all sorts of ways of retaliation, from the violent and absurd—literally slicing off the guys' dicks with a kitchen knife so they could experience what he was going through—to the ridiculous—slipping into the club with a camera phone and taking snapshots of them at their most embarrassing moments and posting the shots on the Internet.

Finally, a few weeks ago, he'd gotten so sick and tired of the guys' attitudes that he quit. For the first few days he was okay about it, even happy that he was finished with the society. But that didn't mean that he wasn't still the one they were laughing at.

To them, he was still the man who couldn't get it up. Who was soft and helpless. Like a baby. A wimp. They were probably still laughing about him when they got together.

Paul pulled the paper off the coffee table. He didn't have to search for the headline. His eye went directly to the upper right-hand corner, where the story and photo had been every time he had looked at it.

Every few hours for the last few days.

Philip Maur was dead.

Now they were starting to get theirs, weren't they?

Twelve

"Working with the Scarlet Society could dovetail perfectly with the paper you're working on," Nina Butterfield said the next afternoon as she pulled books off shelves. Three of the walls in her office were lined with bookshelves that had been built in the 1930s. The art deco theme continued with the large walnut desk, two Ruhlmann elephant chairs and a deep, overstuffed couch. A Chinese carpet from the same era covered the floor—brilliant blues and greens depicting a sailing ship. I always thought it was a great metaphor for what went on in her office.

That afternoon, the rug was covered with piles of books; by the time Nina was done, there would be more than a hundred ready for adoption by the staff of the Institute. This book cleansing was a twice-yearly ritual. No one devoured more literature about therapy, psychopharmacology and medicine than Nina did.

"You'll blow everyone out of the water when you make your presentation if you have a clinical case study like this backing it up. Women acting out in a sexual group situation! You'll be learning about sexual aggression. Role reversal. Female sexual power. Subjects that almost no one in the therapeutic community knows very much about. And you're not sure you should accept these clients? Morgan, what you will learn from this group will get you the attention you deserve. Finally."

"I'm not so sure I want attention, much less deserve it," I said, and then added what I hadn't said since she'd started on her crusade, but had wanted to. "Ever since the Magdalene Murders, you've been pushing me like crazy. Like suggesting me to that producer from the *Today* show. What's up?"

She turned, arched her reddish-brown eyebrows, and stared at me as if she were seeing me for the first time. But Nina had known me my whole life. She'd been my mother's best friend. They'd met when they were students at NYU and lived next door to each other in their Greenwich Village dorm. My mom only stayed in school for a year—she couldn't balance college and her acting—but she and Nina had formed a bond that lasted.

After my mother died, Nina had stepped in to help my father take care of me. Even after my father remarried, Nina remained the most important woman in my life.

"Don't deserve the attention? Why would you say that? You've done an incredible job with client after client. You saved a patient's life using nothing but your skill and your chutzpah. If you really don't understand how good you are, this might be an issue we need to work out. Is it?"

Nina believed that therapists and psychiatrists should periodically return to therapy for what she called tune-ups. Especially when they went through life crises. My four-month-old divorce and involvement with a serial killer definitely put me in the running, but I hadn't felt the need for counseling.

"Do you think I need therapy?"

"That's the question I asked *you*."

"No." I said, annoyed that she was playing therapist by answering my question with her own. Oh, I knew she was just trying to look out for me, like she always did, but this time it bothered me. I had a fleeting feeling that there was something I did need to talk about, deal with, but I didn't dwell on it. I was better at denial than any patient I'd ever had. I knew how to insulate myself from my feelings. "I'm fine, Nina. Sleeping. Eating. Not experiencing any over-whelming anxiety."

"Do you feel lonely?"

"Aren't most recently divorced women lonely?"

She nodded. "What about feeling apprehensive about Dulcie?"

"Nina, she's thirteen. What mother of a thirteen-year-old girl isn't somewhat apprehensive? This is about what it's about. No undercurrents. No hidden agendas. I'm just not sure that I want the kind of attention you think I should have."

"I'd prefer you did have a hidden agenda rather than be so self-effacing. Not every therapist should have a public persona, but damn, Morgan, you should. I want you to get attention because you are that good at what you do and de-serve more credit than you get."

From the way she pursed her lips, I knew there was something she wasn't saying. The one thing I especially wanted to hear. "And?"

She gave me a knowing smile. "And I want it because you would be a good face for the institute."

"If I'd wanted to have a public face, I would have gone on the stage. I would have—"

"Morgan, I'm not talking about you being an actress—

God forbid," she said with mock theatrics and a laugh. Whenever Nina's face lit up like that, it was easy to forget that she was sixty-two years old. Everything she'd lived through—two divorces, a scandal with the institute in the late nineties, being widowed by her third husband, Sam Butterfield—fell away, and she was just a sexy, incredibly smart and energetic woman with a great sense of humor who was enjoying herself and the people around her.

"Can we get back to the question at hand?"

"Yes, sweetheart. Sit down and tell me more about the Scarlet Society."

She put down the last three books she'd pulled off the shelf, stretched, ran her hands through her shoulder-length, copper-colored hair, and sat down on the couch. I sat on the chair opposite her, and described the part of the tape I'd seen.

Nina was all warm tones. She had tawny skin and bright amber eyes. Dressed in a pair of chestnut pants and a toffee-colored sweater, with a rope of amber beads doubled around her neck, she looked professional but easygoing and kind. And she was. Despite being so maternal, so caring, Nina had never had children. Because of my daughter and me, she claimed she never regretted it. We were her family, she always said, but she was also my boss, and it was important for us to keep our roles separate in and out of the office. We didn't always succeed.

Once I finished describing the tape, I handed her the confidentiality agreement. She read it. Leaning forward, she focused on me. "I believe, even more than I did before, that the Scarlet Society sounds like a perfect group for you to work with. I know you, so I know that nothing will be as satisfying to you as helping these women. And if in the process you wind up identifying a new trend, a syndrome, or a complex that no other therapist has noticed yet, it will give you even more gratification. This is what gets your blood moving."

I nodded. She did know me best. "But what about the confidentiality agreement? Isn't it insulting?"

"No, it's just naive."

"But they're going into this not trusting me."

"Do you blame them? If this organization is as you've described, what you learn could be explosive. Of course they are worried about confidentiality. Besides, Rush is a lawyer." She looked back at the piles of books. "Do you want to go through these? See if there is anything you want?"

I shook my head. "No, I have my own stack of books waiting to be read. Too many books, not enough time."

Nina scooted forward so she could put her hands on my knees. I could smell the spicy, Oriental scent she always wore. To me it was familiar and comforting, even if to everyone else it was sexy.

"Are you scared of working with these women, Morgan?"

I nodded. "But I don't know why." I was surprised that it came out as a whisper.

"You don't need to know why. Not yet. You do your best work when you are scared. Sign the paper," Nina advised.

Thirteen

The following Monday was exhausting. I'd scheduled back-to-back patients, and even with fifteen minutes between appointments—to get a cup of coffee, inhale a container of yogurt or return a phone call—I was still reeling from the information and emotion I'd dealt with. The most critical reason for those breaks was so that I could get up, stretch my legs, walk to the large windows in my office, look down on the street and change my focus.

Too often, I keep hearing the voices of my patients describing frustration that love has turned to hate, anger at how jealousy corrupts, fear about fetishes, obsession over a need to inflict or receive pain, self-loathing at an inability to become intimate, questions about a hunger that will not abate or an appetite that nothing seems to arouse.

I go over and over the conversations my patients and I have had, looking for alternative solutions, questions I need to ask during the next session, dark corners that need more light.

What I do is fulfilling. I am grateful that I have the kind of career that allows me to interact with people who need my help and want to lead more satisfied lives. But there is another side to my profession, even if I don't spend much time thinking about it, that can eat at my soul and corrode my own ability to connect to people in my life.

It's not that I am frightened of what can go wrong between lovers. I was married for a long time and, for most of those years, was content. I simply know too much. I'm too aware of how easily people break and how hard it is to make real, sustaining changes.

By six forty-five that night, I was so tired I regretted having agreed to fit the Scarlet Society into my schedule. In the fifteen minutes I had before they arrived, I got a fresh cup of coffee and called Dulcie.

She was just leaving rehearsal with her father, an independent film director. "Dad's taking me out to dinner and then to the opening of *An Hour Before Dark*." Breathless, she proceeded to tell me who had directed it and who the stars were.

As soon as I hung up, the receptionist buzzed to tell me she was sending the new group in.

I greeted Shelby, who started to introduce me to the other women with her.

"No, that's okay," I interrupted. "Let's get everyone seated before we do the introductions."

Everything that happens from the moment a patient walks into my office is potential information. I become a camera, watching and listening and trying to remember what I see, sense and hear.

During the day, when individual appointments are scheduled, my office feels spacious. I have a large desk in front of the bookshelves that line the east wall. In front of the desk is a chair. Against the west wall is a camel-colored leather couch, long enough for three people to sit, or for one tall man to lie down comfortably. Facing the couch is my oversized chair. When I have a group, though, I set up a semicircle of eight to twelve folding chairs and I sit so that I can face them. The large room gets smaller, but not uncomfortable.

A woman in a red suit was the first to take a seat, and she chose the one closest to my chair. Her clothes looked expensive, cut so the fabric hugged her slim body. She wore high-heeled black alligator shoes and carried a leather bag, which I recognized as Chanel: the leather and gold chain were unmistakable.

Shelby Rush, in a black pantsuit and high-heeled black suede boots, put her tote on the chair on my other side and then stood, hostesslike, making sure that everyone found a seat.

There were too many faces for each of them to make a distinct impression, but I was very aware of two women. One wore blue jeans, a white man-tailored shirt and a brown suede blazer, and carried a briefcase as worn as the jacket. Her eyes never stopped moving. She looked at me, at each of the others, at the windows, at the floor, at the artwork on my walls. When it came time for her to take a seat, she sat at the center of the semicircle, where she would have the best view of everything going on around her. Her attentiveness didn't appear to be nervous energy, but rather a need to observe. Her sexuality impressed me, too. She did nothing to hide it.

Like Shelby, there were several women dressed all in black—which is almost a uniform in Manhattan—but one woman was so blond, thin and pale that her black clothes overpowered her. She reminded me of a widow. Moving slowly, she appeared to have a hard time making a decision about where to go or which seat to take, and twice she stumbled over a chair leg. Her sunglasses probably weren't helping. Large black frames with very dark lenses, they completely obscured her eyes. Without having to ask, I knew that she was in hiding. I just didn't know if it was from me, from the other women or from herself.

As the rest of the seats filled up, it turned out that six of the twelve women wore sunglasses. One also wore a baseball cap. Another wore a scarf over her hair, tied in a retro "Jackie O" style.

I was used to treating groups who were strangers until I brought them together, choosing them carefully so that their personalities would play off one another. Week after week, I watched them become acquainted, exhibit personality and psychological traits and form a unit. But this was a preformed group, their dynamics already firmly in place. From what Shelby had told me, many of these women had been together in the society for several years. There was a lot of interaction I'd miss seeing acted out, making my work more difficult.

Even after they were all settled, they were oddly silent for people who knew one another well. Once, I had done grief counseling for a corporation where a tragedy had occurred. Even with that catastrophe overpowering them, there had been more conversation than there was with this group now.

As a therapist, I believe nothing is coincidental, no connection is unfounded. There was a reason that the members of the Scarlet Society reminded me of a bereavement group I'd had eight years before. I just had to be patient and discover what the correlation was.

Fourteen

"Let's go over the few rules that I ask everyone to follow when they're here. You all have a right to talk and an obligation to listen. We don't judge one another, but we do discuss how one another's comments make us feel. Even if those reactions are negative. Especially if they are. My job is to help you explore how you deal with one another. And consider behavior that is detrimental to the group as a whole and to its members individually—but I'm not your mother, your friend or your teacher."

I looked from one woman to the next as I explained how the group worked. There was an apprehensive energy in the room, which I was certain was not a reaction to my instructions. These women were scared of something and deeply disturbed; I could see it in the way they shifted in their seats, played with their hands or the straps of their bags, or looked around.

"When I ask you a question, there is no right or wrong answer. We're here for you to talk about your feelings or your problems expressing those feelings. For those of you who have been in a group-therapy situation before, this is probably familiar. For those of you who haven't, please ask me to explain anything that's unclear. Any questions so far?"

I waited, but no one spoke.

"Okay, why don't we go around the room so you can introduce yourselves to me and tell me a little bit about why you, personally, are here and what you hope we will accomplish." I turned to my right, knowing I would be frustrating the woman in the red suit to my left who, judging from her movements, wanted, expected and perhaps even needed to go first.

Before the woman on my right could speak, Shelby interrupted.

"Dr. Snow, I think we should just introduce ourselves and then I can tell you what the problem is. But first we need the confidentiality agreement I sent you with the videotape. You told me on the phone you would sign it."

I watched for reactions to Shelby's assertion of power: no one seemed surprised by her taking over. Responding to the group, rather than to Shelby, I said, "The entire relationship between us is predicated on trust. Just like any doctor, I am bound by doctor-patient confidentiality and will not disclose anything you say to anyone outside of this room. The only exception to that rule is if I have information that one of my patients might inflict harm upon herself. So if one of you talks about committing suicide and I feel you mean it, I will have to go to the authorities. The same holds true if one of you tells me that you intend to kill someone and gives me reason to believe you mean it, as opposed to just thinking or fantasizing about it. I should tell you, though, that in all the years that I have been practicing, I have never had to break a patient's trust."

Shelby nodded. "We all understand that, but I really have to insist."

Nina had known I wanted to work with this group, almost desperately, even if I wasn't sure I knew all of the reasons. Our talk had prepared me for Shelby's ultimatum. But it still rankled me. I got up, walked over to my desk, pulled the signed sheet out of a folder and gave it to her. She took it, glanced at it, folded it and put it in her bag.

I sat down, turned to the woman on my right and said, "Let's try the introductions again." I smiled at her.

Louise M. introduced herself and added, "I'm glad you are working with us. We need help."

One by one, we went around the circle. Ginny P., Shelby R., Martha G., Ellen S., Bethany W., Anne K., Liz B., Cara L., Aimee B., Gail S. and Davina C. I didn't remember all their names right away, but after listening to them for an hour and a half, I would.

During that initial go-around, I'd discovered the blond, slightly ethereal woman in black, who seemed so sad, was Anne. Liz was the woman in the worn brown blazer who was so observant. Ellen was the red-suited woman who'd wanted to be the first to talk.

"Do you all keep your last names private in the society?" Even though Shelby had told me that they did, I wanted to get them talking.

"Damn straight," Ellen said. I was not surprised that she answered. "We don't use our last names and neither do the men who join us. Our privacy is as important to us as getting what we want," she said, giving the last phrase an emphasis and energy that was slightly confrontational.

Shelby continued to explain: "Our entire organization—all of the chapters around the country—abides by the same rules. In fact, some of us don't even use our real first names.

We know one another only in one way, in one environment. We aren't friends outside of the society. It would be far too risky."

I saw Anne lower her head.

"How would it be risky?"

"We have families, spouses, children. We have careers. Some of us have public lives," Shelby said.

"But you are all a family, too, aren't you? A certain kind of family?" I asked.

Anne's shoulders heaved in a quiet sob. "Yes, we are," she said softly.

"We are a group of women who believe in fulfilling our sexual potential beyond the ways that society deems acceptable. We have refused to be afraid of what we want." Shelby said, taking back the reins.

I had to get the other women talking.

"What does it feel like to set the rules and the terms you want?" I asked, looking from Bethany to Liz to Davina, hoping to engage them.

Davina smiled. She was tall and shapely, with coffee-brown hair cut short to show off her heart-shaped face. Everything about her was lovely, except for fingernails bitten down so low there was dried blood on some of the cuticles. "It feels limitless," she said.

"Anyone else?" I asked.

Martha, who appeared to be the youngest member of the group, smiled at me. "It feels right to me."

No one else volunteered. It was becoming clear that I was going to have to work to find out what was bothering these women. "Can one of you describe the mission of the society?"

Shelby and Ellen both began to speak. They exchanged a glance. With a nod, Ellen acquiesced and Shelby began.

"Since its inception, the society's purpose has been to create an environment for women who want to be in power, where they can act out their sexual fantasies with men who are willing to be their sex partners."

"Why aren't any of the men here?" I asked.

"They don't belong to the society. It's our club and they are invited guests. We don't have relationships with them. We don't become their friends, or fall in love with them. They are just there to please us. Do you understand?"

I nodded, wondering why she was being so emphatic. I would have preferred she talk less so that the others could talk more, but it was also instructive to observe how the group deferred to her.

"What kind of men do you invite?"

"For the most part they are successful, highly respected and often powerful men, each of whom has gone through an extensive screening process. Sexually, the one thing they have in common is their preference to be submissive. Usually, we have about twice as many men on our roster as women—so we have about thirty now. All of them are invited to our weekly soirées. As long as a man accepts three out of every five invitations he remains active."

It appeared that she could go on talking indefinitely, but Cara, another of the women in sunglasses, interrupted. Her dirty blond hair was pulled back off her face, her olive skin stretched tight over prominent bones. Her voice was low and soft, and I had to lean forward a little to hear her.

"Last week we found out that one of the men who has been with us the longest had been reported missing by the partners at his company." She hesitated. "People wondered if he'd been kidnapped. None of us even knew his name until the article ran in the paper, with his picture."

Anne lowered her head once more and a tear fell into her lap. Martha covered her mouth with her hand as if to stop herself from talking. Shelby focused on Cara, watching her intently. Ginny, who hadn't yet spoken, took off her large silver-and-onyx ring and then put it back on, as if this action in some way centered her.

Cara had stopped mid-sentence but clearly had something else she wanted to say.

"Go on," I encouraged.

"His name was Philip Maur. It was bad enough that he was missing. Then last Friday the *New York Times* reported that he'd been killed."

I was shocked and hoped it didn't show on my face.

Davina, who had started to cry, asked me, "Did you see the article?"

"I did," I said, and clearly remembered that moment in the greenroom at the *Today* show when I'd read the story and seen the letters at the bottom of the page that spelled out Detective Noah Jordain's name.

"The problem is, how do we cope with this?" Finally, Ellen got to the point of why they were in my office. "Nothing like this has ever happened before. Men have left, but of their own volition. A few guys have gotten sick, but Christ, no one has died. What do we do? How do we cope with this?" she asked again, her voice tight and agitated.

Now that someone had exposed the problem, they all spoke at once, and I had to stop them and explain that they needed to go one at a time.

"A lot of us knew Philip really well. He'd been with the society for the past eight years." Davina said.

"We've all been with him, haven't we?" Martha asked, looking around the room.

Everyone nodded.

"We don't know what to do," Anne said. Her voice was musical and studied. I recognized its cadence and wondered if she was an actress.

Louise, who also wore sunglasses that covered more than a third of her face, and who had a faint Boston accent, said, "We can't talk about this with anyone outside of the society. It's driving us crazy. We don't know what to tell our friends or families about our melancholy. I burst into tears at the office this morning and my boss, whom I am incredibly close to, asked me what was wrong. I couldn't tell her. What am I supposed to do with all this grief?"

Around the room, with nods or murmurs, they all acknowledged that this was what they wanted me to help them with.

"There's something else," Ellen said. She looked angry, and tucked her hair behind her ears as if she was getting ready for a fight. I noticed the large ruby studs in her earlobes. "From the story in the paper, it doesn't sound like the police have any leads. What if his death has some connection to the society? What if one of us has something to do with it?"

"Don't you see? Any one of us could be involved with his murder," Martha whispered. "What if it's because he's part of the society that Philip's dead?"

Fifteen

Officers Tana Butler and Steve Fisher sat in an unmarked car parked on East Sixty-fifth Street between Madison and Park Avenues, across the street and four doors down from a turn-of-the-century limestone building.

"You wouldn't think to look at it that it's a sex clinic," Fisher said.

For the first time, Butler paid attention to the building's architecture: the elegant facade and decorative wrought-iron door.

"I guess not."

"And if you didn't know, nothing about the name on that nice little brass plaque would give it away. The Butterfield Institute could be anything, you know? A high-level think tank. An art school."

Butler looked at her watch. They'd been sitting in the car since 6:45 p.m. and it was almost eight. "You sure there's no back door to this place?"

"Nope."

"Well this doesn't make sense. She's been in there for more than an hour. And why was she wearing a wig?"

"Maybe she's doing some undercover investigation with

one of the therapists. Prctcnding to be a patient instead of a reporter. Makes sense. The case has a sexual component. Why wouldn't she do some follow-up with a sex therapist?"

"I guess. But how do you explain all the other women who went in there along with her?"

"It is a clinic, Tana. I'd bet most people go after work. Or maybe there's some group thing going and they all wound up going in at the same time."

Butler's cell phone rang. It was Jordain, and she gave him an update on where they were, how long they'd been there, and the odd detail of Betsy Young wearing the wig.

When she got off the phone, she filled Fisher in on Jordain's call. While they talked, they watched the Butterfield's front door. A young couple came out; the woman looked visibly upset.

"Have you ever been to a therapist?" Butler asked.

Fisher shook his head. "You?"

"For a few weeks after I—" She broke off. The door to the institute had opened again and Young walked out. She turned left, in the opposite direction of the car, and started walking toward Park Avenue.

Fisher turned the key in the ignition and pulled out of the parking space. The one easy thing about tailing someone in Manhattan was the traffic. Even at night, there were always a few cars on the street.

Even so, Betsy noticed the sedan trailing her.

Sixteen

The man was stretched out and tethered to the gurney with leather straps, but they were no longer buckled. He couldn't get up and walk away anymore. His eyes were shut. His cheeks were hollow. His skin was ashen. It was a color that was without color. One doesn't realize how many shades of yellow, peach and pink make up flesh tones until one has seen a body drained of all those colors.

Timothy Wheaton's skin was exposed to the air-conditioning and yet he didn't shiver or shake. He did not look like he was sleeping. A sleeping man has his head bent to one side. Or his fingers curled up under his chin. Or one of his feet twitches. This man looked dead.

It was midnight. Wheaton had been there for exactly four days. That was long enough. It was time to get to work.

The light exploded, illuminating the previously darkened room.

If a man was just sleeping, he might have sensed the brightness and opened his eyes, but Timothy Wheaton didn't, not even when the camera's flash went off for the second time.

The photographer smiled. After all these years of using a camera only for reference, it was satisfying to use it now creatively.

The process had been easier with this second man than with the first. The third would go even more smoothly. If there was a third. That was not yet decided.

It was a long walk to the darkroom, where one wall was covered with cork and more than a dozen shots of Phil Maur were pinned up in neat, even rows. Several of them had been sent to the *New York Times*. Others were too private to show to anyone. Every step had been documented: setting the stage, trapping the man, restraining him, preparing him and then rendering him helpless.

As each new, still-wet shot of Timothy Wheaton came out of the developer bath, it was added to the wall.

Both Philip and Timothy had been easy to seduce. Flattery and interest got them to settle down in the big comfortable chair, sip a glass of amber-colored liquor and talk about their sexploits. Neither of them had guessed that, along with the Scotch, they were ingesting liquid Thorazine.

They ignored the first relaxing effects of the drug because they were drinking and weren't surprised to feel a slight buzz. But by the time their eyelids became heavy, they had trouble lifting their hands and standing up. Once the drug completely kicked in, they were harmless.

The photographer had no trouble undressing them. In fact, Philip Maur had helped undress himself, thinking he was having a drunken adventure. He'd even been able to sprout an erection. That had been interesting: sex with a half-dead man who was helpless but hard.

But Timothy Wheaton had been impotent from the drugs.

Examining the bulletin board, the photographer wondered which of the new shots should be sent to the paper. That front-page placement of Phil Maur's photograph had been gratifying, even though there wasn't a photo credit. Obviously, nothing could be done about that. It was too bad the paper hadn't used those long shots of the beautiful naked body depleted of all its energy and vigor, but had instead used the simple shot of the man's feet. His numbered feet. Red numbers from the middle of the ball of the foot to the heel. A 1 on the right foot. A 1 on the left.

Now there would be a new photo in the *Times* with a 2 on the right foot. And a 2 on the left.

Everyone would assume there was going to be a 3 to follow.

Everyone.

Fear of being next had to be a powerful inhibitor, didn't it? They had to be thinking that if two of them had been killed, any one of them might be next, right? The photographer was counting on it.

Seventeen

Wednesday was rainy. A strong wind ripped the turning leaves from the branches and they lay plastered on the pavement, slippery but brilliant against the concrete streets.

Because of the weather, and because I'd scheduled a consultation with a new patient at 1:00 p.m. and only had a half hour for lunch, I ordered in vegetable soup and seven-grain bread and ate at my desk.

Nicky Brooks arrived on time, only minutes after I finished eating. Once he was sitting on the couch, I asked how he'd found me, assuming it was from the *Today* show, but it turned out Shelby Rush had recommended me.

"I told her I was looking for someone to help my wife and me. Shelby knows us. Knows what has been going on with us. What the issues are. She suggested you."

Nicky was in his mid-thirties, dressed well in a navy suit and sky-blue striped tie. He had a high forehead, thick chestnut hair, dimples and a determined chin. He looked like someone who moved through the world getting what he wanted.

"Have you been in therapy before?"

He nodded.

"When?"

"About six years ago."

"For how long?"

"About a year."

"You said that Shelby knew you and the kinds of issues you have been dealing with. I'd like to know what they are."

"My wife and I are separated." He looked around, taking in the room. I wasn't sure if it was interest in his surroundings or a way of avoiding looking at me.

"How long have you been married?"

"Eighteen months." He looked back at me when he answered.

"And how long have you been separated?"

"About four months. Couldn't even make it through two years." His voice dipped down, expressing disgust. With himself? With his wife?

"Who instigated the separation?"

"Daphne."

"Why?"

"We had issues."

"With what part of your lives?"

"Our sex life."

The way he said the word "our" made me wonder if, indeed, the problem belonged to both of them.

"I'd like to hear your take on what the problems are. If we go forward with the therapy, I'll be asking your wife the same question. Do you feel comfortable talking about the problems without your wife being here?"

He seemed surprised, as if it had never occurred to him that there might be anything wrong with talking about it without her. "Daphne and I met at the Scarlet Society almost three years ago. She was a member."

He was watching for a reaction, but I had been doing this for years and knew how to hide my feelings if I wanted or needed to. Nicky continued, "I'd found out about the society from a woman I'd been seeing who thought I'd enjoy it."

"And did you?"

"For the first time in my life, I was sexually satisfied."

"What had happened previously?"

"I've been uncomfortable with several of the women I've been with."

"Why, Nicky?"

"It's embarrassing. To explain what you like. It can turn some women off."

"What do you like?"

He sat back in the chair and crossed his arms over his chest. For the first time since he'd come into my office twenty minutes earlier, he was resisting going forward. His body language spoke more loudly than any words. His eyes darkened and narrowed. He lowered his gaze so that he was no longer looking at my face but rather at the cup of coffee that sat on the small end table next to my chair. He crossed one leg over the other.

"This isn't going to work if I don't tell you, right?"

"Right. You said you were in therapy before. Did this subject come up?"

"Yeah. But we never resolved it. And then I found the society and stopped therapy. I didn't need to resolve it."

"What about the society made that possible?"

He didn't say anything. It was time for some reassurance.

"I don't want you to worry about shocking me or embarrassing yourself. I've been a therapist for eleven years. The only thing I consider problematic is when a patient's sexual desires, or lack of them, gets in the way of how they want to live their lives, or if it endangers their partners."

He let out a long breath. "I'm not hiding anything dangerous. I just like to be told what to do. It's not such a big deal." He was arguing with someone who wasn't in the room with us. Someone who had tried to convince him that it wasn't normal for a man to enjoy being sexually submissive.

I nodded, encouraging him. "And the society offers you a place to do that without being judged?"

"I don't like the leather-and-high-heels dominatrix scene. I tried that. Dirty clubs. Expensive services." He shook his head. "I didn't want to be with those women. I wanted consensual sex with women who were like me. Not too far afield. Not taking my money."

I nodded again. He was finally talking in complete thoughts and I hoped he'd go on.

"I'm a wine merchant. I have more than one hundred employees. I tell people what to do all the time. I'm in charge all the time. So every once in a while, I like to give up being in charge."

"What is that like?"

He thought for a few seconds. "To have a woman standing there, hungry for you, telling you how to touch her…seeing her mouth part and her tongue slip out…and to hear her breath come faster and faster…knowing your job is to please her before you can please yourself…the wait of that…knowing that if you fail you will be punished—" He stopped, not sure he could describe it to me after all.

"How do you feel about the way you prefer to have sex?"

"Now?"

"Now or before."

"I'm okay with it. Wasn't at first. I was frightened by it. By the difference of it. For a while I wondered if it meant I was…gay. But this isn't about wanting to be with a man, or even wanting to be a woman. I just like having to perform. And being rewarded. I like the exchange and the parameters."

"Do you ever wish that you weren't turned on by being submissive?"

This took him aback. He didn't say anything. He recrossed his legs. He shrugged, but still he didn't answer.

I waited. The silence continued. I could hear the rain beating on the windows.

"I suppose my life would be easier if I weren't. But I need to be told what to do." He looked straight at me, unashamed.

I'd worked with men before who preferred to play a sexually passive role. Some were able to integrate it into their relationships—with wives or lovers—while others acted out with dominatrixes they hired or met in sex clubs. Two previous clients were only turned on by extreme S & M and I had referred them to another therapist at the institute who is an expert at behavior modification. But the Scarlet Society was a sandbox compared to a hard-core S & M club.

"How do your preferences work with your relationship with your wife? You said you met at the society and she was a member?"

"She was. And then we broke one of the society's rules and saw each other outside of the playrooms. That's what we call the apartment where the society meets—the playrooms."

I nodded. "And how was the sex outside?"

"We didn't do it outside until eight or nine weeks before we got married. We met to do all the things that we weren't allowed to do at the society. Talk. Go to dinner. To the movies. Hold hands. Sit in the park at twilight and discuss what we'd done that day. Daphne is a painter. Very successful. I posed for her during that time. Naked. She loved to paint me. And that was very erotic. It was as close as we came to having sex. But we saved that for the club. We were living these two lives—three really—and no one knew."

"Can you tell me about the three lives?"

"In one life each of us was just as we appeared to the world. A wine merchant and a painter. Then there was the secret life we shared at the club. Doubly secret because the society is secret to begin with, and when we were there no one knew that Daphne and I were breaking the rules. The sex during that time was better than ever—with her and with the other women, too. And there was our third life—the two of us together, dating." His tone of voice was wistful.

Even though I can explain to patients that nothing is a more powerful aphrodisiac than illicit love or illicit sex, I haven't always been able to extricate them from its grip. Once, a woman whose life was coming apart while she carried on a passionate affair asked me if what she was feeling was real. If that insane high she and her lover experienced when they were with each other was going to last. If the intensity of colors, tastes, sights and sounds she experienced during those first six months they were together was genuine.

It was real in that it was her reality. But no, it could not be sustained. The high thrived on its very impermanence. It was fueled by its own secrecy.

We want what we cannot have. Not because we cannot have it so much as because longing works like an opiate. It magnifies our lives and heightens our senses. Yearning has propelled artists to paint, sculpt, write and compose. Cities have been built out of desire, and governments have been toppled.

Some argue that nothing except the will to survive is as powerful as early secret passion. I don't know. But listening to patients, I have come to believe it is possible. The sexual union becomes almost mystical in these relationships. The connections that we make in the dark of clandestine assignations are elevated beyond other experiences. Men and women become gods when they steal away to luxuriate in each other. They talk and touch as if they've never done either before.

Longing has made this so. For many people, pent-up passion incites the most ardent encounter they've ever had.

"Why did you want to get married?" I asked Nicky.

"We figured that there couldn't be a better match for either of us. Daphne is very strong and verbal. She likes being in control. I need to be dominated. Plus, we shared a love of art, good food and wine. Everything fit. And we knew each other's secrets. We accepted them." He didn't say it, but in his tone I heard the "I thought." The doubt.

"What happened?"

Nicky looked away from me again and out the window. There were only ten minutes left, according to the clock on the end table next to the agate ashtray. We'd covered a lot of ground in the past thirty-five minutes. If he couldn't go further, I wouldn't be surprised.

At that point my phone rang. I glanced at the caller ID. I only took calls during sessions if they were related to my daughter. This one wasn't. I gave Nicky a few more seconds.

If he hadn't responded, I wouldn't have pushed him. But he began talking.

"Daphne got pregnant three months after we married. It was planned. Then she lost the baby. About a month and a half in. She barely mourned. She wasn't depressed. Or so she said. But she started working harder than ever, preparing for her next show. She threw herself into painting with a crazy energy. Day by day she became more and more fanatical about perfecting her paintings. Even though she said she wasn't mourning the baby, and that early miscarriages were easy enough to get over, I could see how upset she was in the paintings. They were dark—black, blood-red paintings of bundles of torn and ragged bunting. At that point she became preoccupied with death and started going to the temple. She's Jewish. We both are. Both nonpracticing. Suddenly she was intensely religious. Even studying Kabbalah. Soon she was talking about how we had to rethink our lifestyle. She wanted to try to have a baby again. But first we had to stop acting out sexually and give up the games, and she wanted me to quit going to the society."

"I don't understand. You'd broken the rules and you were still going to meetings?"

"No one had found out. Daphne just dropped out without giving any reason. No one even knew I'd gotten married."

"When did she stop going?"

"When we decided to get married."

"Whose idea was that?"

"Hers. She said that as much as she had enjoyed it, she didn't need it anymore. At that point she said she thought that she could handle me going. At least, before we got married, she thought that." A thick layer of resentment underscored his words now. "She claimed that it was okay for me to have different needs than she did."

"So she stopped going and you kept going?"

"Until she lost the baby. To placate her, I stopped, too. I had to. I couldn't stand how she was changing. I wanted the woman I was in love with back. And I wanted to start a family with her. I'd lived without the society before. I'd had traditional sex for years before I finally figured out what it was I enjoyed the most. I could make a sacrifice, couldn't I? A simple sacrifice. Not that hard, right?"

His eyes were filled with pain and anger.

"But you couldn't?"

He shook his head.

"Did you try?"

He nodded. "Like hell. I stayed away for six weeks."

"What happened?"

He shrugged.

"Can you connect going back to something that happened in your life?"

He shrugged again, but this time he followed the gesture with words. "I'd been traveling. Went to a large wine auction in England and made a killing. Had one of the most successful trips of my career, came back, got in from the airport and didn't even go home. Went straight to the society and spent three hours there."

"Did Daphne find out or did you tell her?"

"I told her," he said.

I wasn't surprised. You cannot be punished if you don't get caught. After his success, he needed to be reminded that, despite his power, he was powerless. If he stayed in therapy with me, with or without his wife, we'd work on his need for punishment—but only when he was ready.

"And now?"

"Daphne wants me back. I want to go. But she's given me an ultimatum. I have to give up the society. Except I can't. I need help to do that. And she has to be one of the people to help me. She has to go back to treating me the way she used to sexually. She doesn't want to. Sex with her is deadly serious now."

"Is she willing to join you in therapy?"

He nodded.

"That's good."

His forty-five minutes were over. I leaned forward, just a little, to be inclusive at the very moment when I had to tell him our time was up.

"Nicky, I think you've been brave to come here. And very forthcoming. I also think you're smart and intuitive. So if you want to work on this—with or without your wife—I'd be happy to help you."

As he stood, he became the calm, successful man who had walked into my office almost an hour earlier. His armor was back on. He'd lost the scared look he'd had only minutes before.

"You'll love Daphne," he said. "She's the most creative person I've ever met."

Eighteen

Noah Jordain poured chicken broth into a saucepan, added two tablespoons of oil and a cup of uncooked rice. While he waited for the mixture to come to a boil, he poured himself an inch of Maker's Mark and took a sip.

Carrying the glass, he walked out of the kitchen and into the living room, where he put a CD in the expensive Bose stereo system. Jordain lived in a much nicer place than most NYPD detectives could afford, but he had a sideline: he played and wrote jazz, and some of it was good enough that he'd been able to buy his Greenwich Village loft and some original arts and crafts furniture with his ASCAP royalties.

Back in the kitchen, he checked the stove and covered the boiling rice.

Cooking was therapeutic for Noah, as it had been for his father, who'd been one of the toughest cops in the New Orleans police department. Jambalaya had been his specialty, and whenever Noah made it he thought of his dad. André Jordain had been a well-respected policeman and a thirty-year vet when someone set him up.

He and his partner, Pat Nagley, had busted a cocaine

ring. It looked like an easy collar until the defense presented evidence that André and Pat had been on the take, accepting payoffs from the dealer for five years and finally turning him in when he refused to increase the payoffs.

Noah and his family knew the accusation was bogus. Yes, his father had been a flirt; yes, he had too much to drink sometimes and had let his temper get the better of him. But a bad cop? No way. *Someone* had been on the dealer's payroll, but it hadn't been André Jordain. And Noah had vowed that one day he'd clear his father's name. That's what had brought him to New York four years earlier. He'd heard the dealer was tied to someone high up in the NYPD.

After another gulp of bourbon, Noah lifted the lid, smelled the fragrant stock and spices, and stirred the mixture. Then he went to work on the rest of the ingredients, putting andouille sausages in a frying pan and turning up the heat.

He sliced bright red and green peppers and a bunch of scallions, chopped some tomatoes, then removed the sausages. While they drained on paper towels, Noah threw cut-up chicken into the pan, stirred it and finally added the vegetables.

Jordain breathed in the smells and felt the first kick of homesickness when his phone rang, the sound clashing with the smooth Dizzy Gillespie jazz CD. No matter how much he wanted to, he couldn't ignore the phone. That was the one thing Noah resented about being a cop.

It was Perez.

"Noah, I just got a call from Betsy Young at the *Times*—" He didn't have to finish.

"Number 2?"

"Yes."

"Do they know who it is?"

"They are saying no."

"And we've had, what, a hundred, two hundred missing-persons reports in the past few days?"

"At least."

"What was in the package?"

"Same as last time—three photos and another clump of hair."

"We're not going down there. Ask a uniformed cop to go get Young and the evidence and meet us at the station house."

"No prob."

"And call Butler. Have her waiting for Betsy and get the photos to the lab ASAP."

"Want me to pick you up?" Perez asked.

Jordain looked at his watch. It was eight. "Did you eat yet?"

"No."

"You hungry?"

"What are you cooking?"

"Jambalaya."

"I'm hungry."

"Good. Come on over. We can eat in ten minutes and then go meet the press. It's always better sparring on a full stomach."

"She is going to hate that we made her wait."

"We are not making her wait. Have Butler talk to her."

"It's going to screw up her deadline—" Perez stopped midsentence. "Right, that's what you want, to keep the story from running tomorrow."

Jordain hung up and sighed. The first story, announcing the murder to New York and the rest of the world, had been an embarrassment to him and the rest of the depart-

ment. For the paper to have gotten it first was unacceptable. And to make it worse, they still didn't know a single
damn thing about what had happened to Maur. But now
for there to be a second man? And for the *Times* to know
again before they did?

He eyed the Maker's Mark lovingly but didn't pick up
the glass again. He was officially back on duty.

Usually the SVU is not the last to know. Whoever was
behind these murders wanted a *Times* reporter to get the
story before the police.

Why was that?

They finished up their second helpings of the food—
without the beers they wanted because work was waiting—in fifteen minutes. Long enough to make the reporter
cool her heels.

They'd wolfed down the spicy rice mixture as if it might
be their last meal. At least, their last good meal. And well
it might be. There was no telling how much information
they were going to get tonight. They might not come up
for air for a day or two.

"If there are two of these killings…" Jordain said as he
and Perez walked out into the damp night air, climbed into
Perez's car and headed uptown to the station house.

"Don't say it," Perez begged.

But Jordain had to say it. He had to give weight to it and
make the words real. "If there have been two of these killings, there might be three. The last thing we need is another
multiple on our hands. We're still reeling from the last
one."

"Maybe this is just a copycat of last week's murder."

"Maybe you are dreaming," Jordain sighed.

Nineteen

❧❧❧

"I don't want you to open another envelope, if you're sent one, until one of us can get there," Jordain told Betsy Young.

It was 8:45 p.m. The two detectives sat opposite Young and Officer Butler in an interior room of the station house—a drab room with a beat-up table and eight chairs that varied in condition from old but still comfortable to very old and almost unbearable. There were no windows, and the once-white walls were stained and yellowed like the teeth of a person who had smoked too much for too long.

Foam cups of coffee and cans of diet soda rested on the floor beside their chairs. The evidence Young had brought with her was spread out on the table's surface.

"Waiting for you guys to show up might compromise my story," Young said, eyeing Jordain aggressively. It took him by surprise. She was challenging him, and not only in a professional context. The sexually predatory gleam repelled him.

Ignoring his personal reaction, he leaned closer to her, matching his body language to hers, even forcing his lips into a smile for the first time that night. "But when you open these envelopes and look at this material first, it compromises our investigation."

Betsy didn't respond. Instead, she stared down at the three glossy eight-by-ten photographs in the middle of the scarred wooden tabletop. Jordain had reviewed them a dozen times, but he did so again. Betsy had identified the man as Timothy Wheaton, and it hadn't taken much work to confirm that she was correct; his wife had supplied them with photos of him when she'd made the missing-persons report.

Wheaton was in his early- to mid-thirties. Short but well built. His eyes were closed. Slight bruising decorated his wrists and ankles. He was as still as the stone angel that stood over Jordain's father's grave.

This man had been laid out exactly as Philip Maur had been, and the angles in both sets of photographs were identical.

Three shots. One of the man's feet, each with the number 2 drawn on the sole in red ink. A second focusing obscenely on the man's penis. And a third showing his whole body.

Alongside the photographs, there was something else on the table: an innocent plastic bag. Inside was only one thing: a lock of sandy blond hair about an inch and a half long.

Betsy leaned back just a fraction in her chair, moving away from Noah. "Well, I suppose there's a deal we could make. Let me follow you around while you investigate the case. Put me in your fucking hip pocket. Let me hear and see everything that happens. Just me. No other reporters."

Jordain's first thought was to say no outright. The idea of spending his days with this pushy woman annoyed him.

"Will you fax us your articles the night before they run? Just as a heads-up. No editorial input."

Negotiating, Betsy nodded.

"Okay," Jordain said.

Perez did not make a move, but Jordain saw his partner's eyebrows arch ever so slightly. Meanwhile, Betsy's eyes gleamed. Her lust for the story chilled Jordain. The way she imitated the worst traits in a man made him pity her. Why did she force her toughness? Didn't she know how much more powerful women were than men, even if they were wearing pink sweater sets? He was surprised that in the midst of this complicated and disturbing meeting, with the upsetting photographs in front of him, he had stopped to think about any of this.

"One more thing," she said. "My job is to break the news. That's harder and harder to do with twenty-four-hour cable news shows reporting all day and all night. I need assurances that if I let you in the newsroom to work on this case as it breaks, you will not issue statements to other members of the press once you walk out the door."

As much as Jordain hated to admit it, he understood her problem, but he wasn't used to bargaining with a newspaper. Then again, he'd never come across this particular situation before.

Out of the thousands of missing people, two men had turned up dead within days of each other, in exactly the same way. There was absolutely no evidence of where they had been or what had happened to them. Damn. Damn. Damn. The case was cold from the get-go. They didn't have anything to go on. Not a single lead. Two men. Dead. He went over it again. Why photographs? Why hair clippings? Why these two men? What was the connection? Who were they to their assailant? And why was the only communication from the killer being sent directly to Betsy Young at the *New York Times* instead of to the NYPD?

"How did you figure out the names of these men?" Perez asked Betsy.

Jordain knew what his partner was thinking. Was the reporter holding something else back? A letter? E-mail? Nothing had come with the photos and the hair that would have identified the victims.

"We'd run a story on Philip Maur when he was reported missing. He had a big job. I saw it. I remembered his face." She shrugged.

Jordain didn't like the way she'd said it. A little too glib. He filed it away.

"And how did you know who Timothy Wheaton was?" Perez asked.

"Same thing. He's the son of a very well-known author. When the missing-persons report was filed, we saw it."

"Did you report on it?"

She shook her head. "Me, personally? No."

"The paper?"

"Yes, but not as prominently as Maur."

"Except you recognized him?"

"Not right away. I pulled up all the stories we'd done on missing people in the past few weeks, taking a guess I'd find something."

"And you did," Perez said.

"I did." Her words were clipped.

Perez looked over at his partner—indicating he was finished with his questions. Jordain only had one left.

"Betsy, do we have a deal?"

"You'll give me total exclusivity?"

"I won't give out any statements to the press until you've run your story."

"Except to me."

"Except to you when appropriate," he corrected.

"I don't like that last part," Betsy said. "Deal's off."

Jordain had consulted with the department's legal counsel on the way to the station. The *New York Times* didn't have to agree to any of the department's requests. The mail was being sent to Betsy Young, not to the police, and while there were court orders the NYPD could obtain to intercept Betsy Young's mail, the lawyers felt it would be better if Jordain could get the paper to cooperate. "The *Times*," the lawyer had said, "is the newspaper of record for the city, the state and, in fact, many feel, the whole nation. It would be better if we didn't have to go up against the Gray Lady. That would make the news in itself, and the killer might just stop sending mail completely." It was not what Jordain had wanted to hear. But he knew he had to deal with it. Or deal around it.

Jordain stood. Perez was only seconds behind him. "We've done what we can to work with you. If you won't agree to what I've asked, you'll push me into getting a court order to intercept your mail."

Betsy pulled out a cell phone, dialed a number and said only two words: "No deal."

She listened, then she handed the phone to Jordain. "My boss would like to talk to you."

Jordain took the phone.

"Good evening, Mr. Hastings. We seem to be having a problem here. Ms. Young can't wrap her head around the fact that we have a killer loose and we need you to cooperate with us on our investigation. I really would prefer that to getting a court order demanding that you do so."

"There is every chance you could get such an order, Detective. And every chance it would be denied you. Ms.

Young is asking for something well within your rights to grant her. Exclusivity in exchange for us opening our doors to you."

"There are lives at stake here and you're bargaining?" Jordain said, finally unable to keep the anger out of his voice.

"I'm running a newspaper and trying to be accommodating."

Jordain spoke into the phone but looked right at Betsy. "No. You are asking for more than anyone would agree to. Here it is, Hastings. Once more. Last time. We'll have an officer there to go through the mail in the morning. Anything suspicious he finds, he will make two calls. One to me or Detective Perez, the second to Ms. Young. And she'll wait until we show up before opening the mail. And I want you to agree to hold off running the story until we tell you it's okay."

"How much time?" Hastings asked.

"I can't tell you that. I won't know until I know what we need to do."

"If you take too much time we could lose our exclusive."

"Not likely. If anyone else gets a lead they will have to call my office to confirm, and we won't do that until after we've given you a heads-up."

"I don't like that," Hastings said.

"And I'm not surprised, but this isn't just news, it's murder. And it's complicated. And we don't have anything to go on except what you are getting."

"The thing that bothers me with this nice-nice cooperation between us and the *Times*," Perez said to Jordain after Young had left, "is that the killer is getting exactly what he wants and what is going to feed him. He's sending those photographs to the *Times* instead of us because he wants to be in the paper. And we're allowing that to happen."

"We're not allowing that to happen. The Constitution of the United States allows that to happen."

Perez nodded. They had both been policemen long enough to know that their jobs were not always made easy by the civil liberties in place in the country. "There's nothing we can complain about—no one to complain to. We have to work within the law."

"Except in situations where there is no law," Jordain said.

Perez heard the smile in his partner's voice. "What are you talking about?"

"I don't think there is any law that says we have to remember to call Betsy Young and fill her in on everything we get. There is no law that we have to report to the reporters. And there is no law that says we have to rush to give the *Times* the okay to run the next story. Or, God forbid, the story after that."

"They won't like that," Perez said.

"I can live with being disliked."

"They can retaliate."

"They can, but they won't. The NYPD has a relationship with the paper. I don't trust Young, but Hastings won't risk losing our cooperation on every story he's got, especially when he knows in his gut that what he's agreed to is the right thing to do."

"So one day when we remember to, we'll call Young and tell her our plans and invite her to come along on a raid and keep her sitting in a car on an empty street corner after the moon's gone down but before the sun's come up."

"Right. And in the meantime, let's get the lab working on this hair sample and these photographs. And pray that there is some information here that Young hasn't compromised."

Twenty

The call came the next day at exactly 6:47 p.m. She obviously had been to therapy or knew enough about therapists to know that patients always left at forty-five minutes past the hour. She identified herself as Betsy Young and said she was a reporter for the *New York Times*. I recognized her name from her byline on the story about the event that had brought the Scarlet Society to me.

"How can I help you, Ms. Young?"

"I was wondering if you could answer a few questions." Her voice was low and intimate and just slightly familiar, but I couldn't place it.

"In reference to what?"

"The Philip Maur murder. Did you see the photograph that ran in the paper when we broke the story?"

Could it be a coincidence that the *New York Times* was calling me—the therapist working with the Scarlet Society—for comment? Of course not, but who had leaked my involvement?

Shelby Rush had sent out a memo to everyone connected with the society, introducing me and the Butterfield Institute, and suggesting that anyone in need of grief counseling could contact me. Was it possible that a member of the society had sent that memo to this reporter and that was why she was calling?

Of course. Anything was possible, but I could hardly ask Ms. Young without possibly breaking confidence.

"I did see the photograph and read the story, but I don't know why you are calling me for comment."

"Based on photographs that we received but didn't run in the story, there are suggestions this was a sex crime and—"

"You'd have to talk to the police about that, Ms. Young."

"I have. They, too, believe it's a sexual crime based on those details. Can I tell you the indicators?"

"I really don't think I'm in a position to—"

She interrupted me, launching into a description of Maur's body. "The corpse had bruises around his wrists and ankles as well as bruising on his testicles. In addition, another shot completely emphasized the man's genitals. Do you think that is important?"

"I can't comment. I haven't see the photos."

"If I had a set sent over to you, would you study them?"

"No, I'm sorry—I don't think so."

"Detective Jordain suggested I get a second opinion."

"From me?" Hearing his name unnerved me. I had to force myself to focus on what the reporter was saying, not on what had happened four months earlier.

"You worked with the detective on the Magdalene Murders, didn't you?" she asked.

"I can't discuss those cases."

I didn't want to think about the murders or the detective who'd handled them. Especially not while I was talking to a reporter on the phone. Dealing with her required all my concentration; I couldn't afford any missteps. "Ms.

Young, did the detective suggest you call me? I don't think you told me that."

I heard her let out an annoyed breath. "It was reported that you had worked with the only survivor of the murders. There were even rumors that you saved her life and helped lead the police to the killer. And since you are a sex therapist and this new case suggests some sexual abuse of some kind, I thought you'd be a great place to start. So, Doctor, can I ask you two questions?"

"You can ask but I can't promise that I'll answer."

"In the article that ran in the *Times,* did you notice that Mr. Maur had the number 1 written on the soles of his feet?"

"Yes, I saw that."

"Would that suggest, from a therapist's point of view, that there are going to be more victims? A number 2, 3 and so on?"

"Yes. But not from a therapist's point of view—from common sense the numbers suggest that."

"And can I quote you on that?"

"If you want to, I suppose that you can."

"Thank you. Now, can you give me an idea of what kind of sex play might be involved if there is bruising on a man's wrists, ankles and testicles?"

"Black-and-blue discoloration often indicates S & M. Restraints can heighten both the sense of control and submission in sex play. But you know, there could be other reasons for Mr. Maur to have been restrained that would have nothing to do with S & M."

"Thank you, Dr. Snow," she said, and hung up, leaving me sitting by the phone. My thoughts zigzagged from Betsy Young and her motivations to Noah Jordain, and as soon as that happened, I stood up suddenly and pushed back my chair.

I needed to talk to Simon Weiss, I decided. About a patient I wanted to refer to him. I knew he'd be in his office; I'd just seen him walk by. It was important. To get away from my desk, my papers, my phone. To stop my thinking from going where it was headed. To do anything to keep my mind off the detective and the time I'd spent with him.

It didn't occur to me to wonder why Betsy Young was doing another story on Philip Maur. But I'd be finding out soon enough.

Twenty-One

~~~~~◦◦◦◦~~~~~

The next night, I left the institute at eight-thirty, after my last session. The night air wasn't cold and my black leather jacket was enough to keep me warm. I looked at the people walking on the avenue, on their way home or out to dinner. I window-shopped the boutiques that offered up designer goods more expensive than I could afford. There was a tempting pair of tall black boots in one store, a simple but elegant navy silk suit in another. No matter how much I ever made at the institute, these items would still be obscenely expensive.

I took my time that night because Dulcie's father had picked her up from the studio and I was on my own. She'd be staying with him for the next four days. Usually it was a week every month plus every other weekend, but he had a shoot that was taking him out of town when she was due to stay with him next, so we'd rearranged the schedule.

I'd worked harder at an amicable breakup with Mitch than I had at anything I'd ever done, never forgetting that awful year when my mother had left my father and the two of us had lived in the small, pathetic apartment in a walk-up on the Lower East Side until she died, leaving me to think I hadn't been smart enough to save her. But I'd tried. That whole year.

My mother was often sick. And when she was, I did for her what she did for me when I was sick: I told her stories—the only ones I knew by heart. I sat by her side on the lumpy couch in the living room that she used for a bed, held her hand, fed her saltines and ginger ale, and re-counted each episode of her TV show, playing all the parts myself. And when I ran out of the real ones, I made up new ones.

I always ended by delivering my mother's co-star's fi-nal line. "And what happened next?"

"They all lived happily never after," my mother would say in a faraway voice.

No matter how bad off she was, she always remembered her sign-off. I have a recurring dream where she finally changes the line to: "They all lived happily ever after."

But that was just a dream. She didn't. And by the time I was old enough to understand that my mother hadn't been ill most of those nights, but drunk, and that my words probably hadn't even made sense to her, it was too late. I already knew I'd failed her. I hadn't been able to save her.

I was on Madison Avenue and Seventieth Street when my cell phone rang. I kept walking as I pulled it out of my bag. If it weren't for Dulcie and my concern for her well-being, I doubted I'd ever answer the damn thing. It's wrong that we can never escape from people who want to reach us.

Instead of a name on the LED display, the screen read "private caller," and because there was a chance—albeit a slight one—that the call was about Dulcie, I answered it.

"Hello?"

I had reached the corner just as the light turned red, and as I waited I heard a man's voice say my name.

"Morgan."

It was as if he was trying it out, letting it slide from a thought into a word, as if he had not heard it or said it in a long time and was unsure that he was pronouncing it right, as if it were the name of a foreign spice in a store that has many things you have never heard of.

I looked around for somewhere to go. To get away from the voice, because I really didn't want to hear it, but there was nowhere to go. There never is when the problem is inside your own head. "Hello, Noah."

At the other end of the phone, I heard the detective take a breath. Suddenly, I was picturing his face, close up, the way it had looked the one night we'd spent together, months before. How could a man I had not talked to for months cause my hand—the one holding the phone—to tremble? He was just a police detective from New Orleans. Except he played exquisite jazz on the piano, cooked like a five-star chef, made love like some crazy kind of dream come true, and intuited more about me than I wanted anyone to know.

"How are you?" Noah asked.

The sound of his voice reminded me of his fingers stroking my face. Of his arms holding me. How his lips felt. I stopped the deluge of impressions and forced myself to talk. "I'm okay. Overworked."

"If you are admitting it, even a little bit, it must be extreme."

I laughed. Had we only known each other for a few weeks? *Stop thinking,* I said to myself silently. *Find out what he wants, then get off the phone.* "So, how can I help you, Noah?" I asked, cringing. Why when I spoke to him did I always wind up sounding like I was flirting?

I was impatient for him to state his reason for calling

so I could get rid of him as fast as possible. I was instantly exhausted.

"I was wondering if you have some time to meet up with me. Either at my office, yours, or if you happen to be as hungry as I am, for dinner."

"I meant to call you back," I blurted out, not realizing it was a non sequitur.

"No, you didn't," he said.

I couldn't argue and so I said nothing.

"Morgan?"

"Yes?"

"Where are you? Let's grab some dinner."

I'd stopped walking and was leaning against the red stone wall of St. James Church. The night sky had turned from electric cobalt-blue to a blue-black velvet, and I had the feeling that if Noah kept talking, I'd keep standing there until stars came out and not even notice that any time had passed.

"I'm here." No, that didn't make sense. "I'm on the street, actually, Seventy-first. I just left the office." Not good, I thought. I didn't sound like I was in control.

"So, where can you meet me? I need to talk to you. I need to ask you in what way you are involved with Timothy Wheaton's death."

Twenty-Two

Twenty minutes later the maître d' showed me to a round table for two in the back corner of Nicola's, an Italian restaurant that had been a staple for people who lived on the Upper East Side for the past thirty years. I'd had dinner there with my father and Krista at least once a month since I was a child. It was a noisy, friendly, unpretentious restaurant decorated with the autographed book jackets, album covers and photographs of their better-known patrons.

I'd suggested it because it was the least romantic restaurant I could think of in the minute I had on the phone.

Noah had somehow gotten there first and, equally amazing, considering the size of the crowd waiting at the bar, secured one of the few quiet tables. It occurred to me not to ask him how he'd done it—I didn't want to appear impressed.

As I took the last steps to the table, he looked up from a stack of papers he was reading. His eyes locked on mine. And held. It was a look that went right through me the way a blast of heat does on a winter night.

The waiter pulled out my seat.

"It's awfully nice to see you," Noah said in that slow

drawl that made each word sound much more exotic than it was. I could see that he'd ordered a bottle of red wine because a glass, already poured, was waiting for me.

"You, too." I could hear how clipped my own voice sounded. As cold as that winter night. He either ignored it or didn't notice.

"Have some wine." He gestured to the glass. "Have some garlic bread." He held out the basket. "I bet you didn't eat today. Except for maybe a container of yogurt. Or half a bagel."

I didn't want to give him the satisfaction of knowing that he was right.

"How's Dulcie doing? How's the play?" he asked. "It must be opening soon."

I sipped the wine. Then drank again before answering. "It's opening in January. And she's working hard. Too hard, as far as I'm concerned, but she loves it. They're going to Boston in two weeks for a preview."

"Is she as nervous about it as you are?"

I'd met him in June and seen him only a half-dozen times, most of them professionally as he tracked down a serial killer, and yet he knew exactly how I was feeling. I hated that about him.

Part of my job with my patients was to keep my emotions in check—not to let anyone guess what my reaction was to what they were saying—and I was good enough at it that not even my ex-husband, whom I'd been with for sixteen years, could figure out what was going on behind the unremarkable expressions I kept plastered on my face.

But Noah knew.

"She is scared. But excited, too. It's an enormous role. She's in all but two scenes. She has three solos and six more numbers that she performs with other members of the cast." I shook my head. "I don't know what I want to happen. If she does well I'm afraid she's going to want to stick with it, and I hate the idea of the theater—or worse, film—eating up her childhood." I took another sip of the wine, which was so smooth it felt like velvet in my mouth. "And I'm equally afraid that if she doesn't do well it will hurt her terribly. She's at such a vulnerable age. Not yet grown up, but not really a little girl anymore."

He listened intently, reading my face, my expressions—paying attention to what I was saying and what I wasn't. That's what he did. He listened to me. It was how he'd seduced me, by asking me questions no one had ever asked me: about how I felt listening to patients all day long, about what it was like taking in all their pain and confusion and processing it. And for a while, I had luxuriated in his questions. Talked and talked. Frantically. Wildly. Like a butterfly that had been caught in a net for hours and then suddenly let go.

Afterward, I knew if I ever allowed myself to see him again, I wouldn't be able to hold back anything, and that was such a disquieting, foreign feeling.

It was like getting a box of rich, dark chocolate truffles, and rather than putting them away and having one every once in a while, savoring them, I had thrown the whole box away, because I didn't trust myself to go slowly. And I had not regretted it.

Or so I thought. Until tonight in Nicola's.

We looked like all the other couples around us. Men and women who'd had separate days, coming together at night to go over what had happened to them and figure out how to deal with it.

Except we weren't a couple.

He was a detective in New York's elite Special Victims

Unit who wanted information from me. I was a sex therapist who was not at liberty to discuss anything that tran-
spired in my office.

What made the conversation even more complicated
was that I didn't even know what I had to keep silent about.

The waiter arrived and Noah ordered shrimp scampi, a
side order of linguini and escarole with garlic and olive
oil—all without taking his eyes off me. When my turn
came, I ordered veal piccata. As soon we were alone again,
Noah opened his briefcase, pulled out a fax and handed it
to me without saying anything.

It was a news story. One and a half pages long. I read
the headline.

Picture of Death

And then I read the subhead.

**Missing New Yorker Timothy Wheaton Feared Sec-
ond Victim**

The byline credited Betsy Young—the reporter who
had called me earlier that evening.

I looked up. "What is this?"

"It's a story the *Times* is running tomorrow."

"Why do you have it?"

"I'll explain all that after you read it."

Yesterday afternoon, the New York Times received
a package that included three photographs of
bestselling author Les Wheaton's son, Timothy
Wheaton, senior vice president at the MLM adver-

tising agency. Wheaton, thirty-nine, was reported missing over the weekend when Linda Ravitch, his wife, said he failed to come home after a business meeting.

I reached for the wine. Took a sip. Looked up from the paper, found Noah's eyes, then continued reading the article, which went on to explain that the police had examined the photographs and were withholding comment at the present time. Wheaton's body, like Philip Maur's, had not been found.

Detective Noah Jordain of New York's SVU said that the department is investigating the case as a related incident and is currently speaking to several suspects.

"Is that true? You have suspects?" I asked, interrupting my reading.

Noah shook his head sadly. His strong jaw was set in defiance. I'd seen him look like that during the worst days of the Magdalene Murders. "We don't have any idea what's going on." He motioned to the paper. The next paragraph caught me by surprise, despite my expectation that it would be there.

Dr. Morgan Snow, a sex therapist who works at the Butterfield Institute and who was instrumental in solving the recent Magdalene Murders, said that there are signals in photographs the paper has chosen not to run that these might be crimes of a sexual nature. In one, an unseen photographer shot directly between the victim's legs. There is black-and-blue bruising on the victim's wrists, ankles and testicles. This, said Dr. Snow, strongly suggests a sexual component to the crimes.

"Black-and-blue discoloration often indicates S & M. Restraints can heighten both the sense of control and submission in sex play," said Snow.

I turned to the next page of the fax. There was no copy. I was staring at a grainy photograph, about three inches square, of the soles of a man's feet. It was almost identical to the photo of Philip Maur's feet that had previously appeared in the paper.

The difference was that instead of the number 1 on each sole, now it was the number 2.

I put the papers down. Noah reached across the table, took them and put them back in the folder that looked as if it was filled with other photographs, and even in a restaurant with hundreds of food smells wafting in the air, I identified the specific sharp scents of the chemical emulsions used in photography.

"Now can you understand why I wanted to talk to you? You're quoted. You've talked to the reporter who is covering this story. Why?"

"She called me."

"And you saw her."

"No."

He didn't say anything, but his neon-blue eyes flashed at me.

"What is going on?" I asked him. "Why am I here? Because I talked to a reporter?"

He took a drink, then broke off a piece of garlic bread and chomped on it. Noah loved food, loved to eat it, to cook it, and to plan on what to have and where to have it. In the brief time I'd known him, he'd once taken the contents of my pathetically unstocked refrigerator and prepared a meal that was as good as anything I'd ever had in a restaurant.

"I'm going to tell you what we know and after that ask you a few questions. I trust you'll answer them." His drawl made each word sound musical, even those that were brutal, ugly or demanding.

"To the best of my ability."

"Okay. In the past two weeks Betsy Young, the reporter you talked to, has received two unmarked packages. The first contained photos of Philip Maur's body. The second contained photos of Timothy Wheaton's body. In both cases, the family or friends of the victims contacted us with missing-persons reports a few days before Young received the photos. Everything we have past those missing-persons reports, we've gotten from Young. And that stinks."

"Why do you think the killer is sending a reporter evidence of his crimes instead of you?"

Before he could answer, the waiter arrived with our food and Noah stopped talking until all the plates were placed on the table. I could smell the buttery garlic sauce and the scent of the sea.

Picking up his fork, he speared one of his shrimp but, before he put it in his mouth, stopped to ask, "Aren't you going to eat? It's hot, Morgan." He motioned to my plate.

I'd been waiting to hear what he was going to tell me about the murders, but I picked up my knife and fork, cut a piece of the veal and put it in my mouth. It was delicious and so tender I barely needed the knife. While I chewed, I watched Noah. The way he ate reminded me suddenly of the way he'd made love to me that one time. He'd devoted himself to the experience. He'd relished it. Remembering it so vividly, I shuddered, and hoped Noah hadn't noticed.

"Because the killer wants to make sure, without a doubt, without any possibility, that the news of these killings appears in the newspaper. What do you think?"

"I think that's a logical conclusion," I said, forcing myself to concentrate.

"How is your veal?"

"Delicious."

"Good. So are the shrimp. Do you want one?" Without waiting for my answer, he speared a pink curl and held it out to me. I tried to take the fork but he didn't let go of it: he wanted to feed me. I could have resisted but instead pulled the offering off with my teeth. The garlic and butter delighted my tastebuds.

"Morgan, what other reasons do you think, from a psychological point of view, that the kidnapper could have for sending the shots to Young?"

"He could have an attitude about the police and could be punishing you. Wanting to embarrass you."

He nodded. "Anything else?"

"Not that comes to me this second. Can I see the photographs you have in that folder? Are all the other shots there?"

"Not all of them, no."

"Can I see what you have?"

"I don't think so."

"Why?"

He didn't answer that but instead asked, "Morgan, what do you know about Timothy Wheaton?"

"Nothing."

"Why are you quoted in the article?"

"I told you. The reporter called me."

"Why you? Out of every therapist in New York City, why you?"

"Because of you."

His eyebrows arched.

"She said she called me because you were handling this case and you'd handled the Magdalene Murders and I'd been involved in them, so it made sense to her to call me on this."

"Did you believe her?"

He was looking at me. Eyes holding mine again. More questions in them than he was asking out loud.

"I didn't have any reason not to."

While we ate and drank we continued speculating about why else Betsy Young might have called me and why someone would reveal his crimes to the paper instead of to the police. It occurred to me that Noah suspected Betsy Young of committing the crimes, but when I asked him about that, he danced around the question without really answering it directly.

"I don't think a woman's behind this."

"Because women traditionally are not serial killers?"

"Women commit crimes of passion, sure, but cold-blooded, planned-out, multiple killings like this? No, that's usually men's work."

After we were finished, we both ordered espresso. The waiter was walking away when Noah called him back and added one zabaglione to the order.

When it arrived, he made me taste it, feeding me the strawberries drenched with the thick, sweet sauce from his spoon. I tried to ignore the intimate way he once again offered me the food. And I tried not to pay attention to the way he was looking at my lips as I took the sugary concoction, or the pressure as he pulled the spoon out of my mouth.

He would have let anyone taste his dessert, I told myself. It was not an invitation. Not a suggestion of anything.

Except I knew it was. And that frightened me because Noah was stronger than I was. And his strengths made me realize my own weaknesses. I didn't want to be reminded of them. Not by him. Or by anyone.

Twenty-Three

Out on the street, the wind swirling around us, pushing us toward each other, I dreaded how we were going to say good-night.

"Is Dulcie home?"

Surprised by Noah's directness, even though I shouldn't have been, I shook my head before I could stop myself.

"So you don't have to go right home?"

"No, but I should. I have an early patient."

"Too early for you to come to the station and look at the photographs that we asked the *Times* to withhold?"

Then his mouth moved, the corners going up, and his eyes twinkled in the light of the street lamp and he smiled. All-knowing and seductive. A laughing smile without any sound. He'd got me. And he knew it. He'd probably done it on purpose. Teased me into thinking he was asking one thing but offering something else entirely. Was he getting me back for not returning his calls last July?

Torn between wanting very much to see the photographs and being embarrassed, I took a deep breath and inhaled the crisp night air. In it, I smelled something familiar. But what?

And then I knew, it was Noah's cologne: rosemary and mint.

Looking away from him so he couldn't read what I was thinking or feeling, I told him yes, I'd like to see the pictures.

It could have been 10:00 a.m. instead of 10:00 p.m. at the station. We walked through the busy lobby and crowded halls, up the stairs, down the hall, around a corner and into the office Noah shared with Mark Perez.

The room was unexceptional. Institutional, well-used furniture, windows that needed to be washed, scratched-up tables, worn wood floors. But despite the drab anonymity, the room crackled with the detectives' energy. A row of jade plants and ivy in colorful pots sat on the windowsill—green and healthy looking, though I couldn't imagine much sun made it through those windows. There was a Mardi Gras mask hanging from the silver lamp on Jordain's desk.

But the focus of the office was the south wall. It was covered with photographs, notes, maps and reports: a collage of images and papers, some sections enlarged so much they were just patches of color, mosaics without meaning.

But they did mean something.

Noah took my arm in an impersonal way and led me to the far right section of the wall.

"Start here."

Two shots were side by side, each taken from an identical angle. It appeared the photographer had stood about two feet in front of the bodies. This specific point of view distorted the perspective of the corpse so the feet were larger than normal, as was the penis, but the chest and the head were diminished.

"You okay?" he asked.

I nodded but wasn't sure; these men had not just been killed, they had been sexualized. The bruises around their wrists, necks, ankles and testicles, which Betsy Young had described to me, were vivid purple, black and blue. Shades of violence and abuse. For relief I looked at the background, which was plain gray and smooth. Not a wall. There were no bumps or cracks, no suggestion of windows, doors or ambient light. I thought that I should know where they were but I couldn't focus.

"Where are they?" I asked Noah.

If he thought it was strange that my first question was about the walls, he didn't say so.

"We don't know yet, but we think that gray expanse is a studio backdrop. Many photographers have rolls of different drops in their studios, and depending on what they need, they just pull down the effect they want."

I nodded. I knew exactly what he was talking about. When Mitch was starting out he'd worked as the assistant to a director who shot food and tabletop commercials. I'd seen backdrops like that.

"By pulling it down and all the way out he's covered the floor, making sure to conceal any clues," Noah continued.

"It would be far too obvious to assume the killer is a photographer, right?"

"No. Nothing is ever too obvious. But we had a professional look at the shots, and he said the exposures are somewhat amateurish and the developing is uneven. He feels that whoever took them is at ease with a camera and understands composition but isn't someone who shoots for a living."

I sat down in the chair opposite his desk, facing the collage, unable to stop staring at the pictures.

"That means the photographer is self-taught or someone who studied photography somewhere. After all, he's developing the shots himself."

"That last part fits the profile," Noah said. "Serial killers are loners. They feel isolated, disconnected from society. Misunderstood. The killings can even be a misguided way to connect to people. Either to the victims or to the people who are going to be distraught over the deaths. They work alone, and I'm pretty sure that this guy didn't take these shots into the corner One-Hour Photo. He's probably got his own darkroom."

"Can you say that's he's a serial killer with only two victims? Maybe there was a reason he needed to kill the two of them and now he's finished. It might be all over." I was still staring, riveted to the images of the pale corpses.

Noah answered me, but I didn't hear him; I'd noticed something in one of the photographs.

Twenty-Four

The coffee was extremely hot, but Paul Lessor wasn't paying attention and burned his tongue so badly he slammed the cup down. The liquid flew up in an arc and splashed down on the front page of the *New York Times*, just missing the article he was reading. The coffee seeped into the paper and spread. Was it an omen that the stain stopped just at the edge of the story about Timothy Wheaton?

The pain inside his mouth was intense, but Paul couldn't be bothered with that now. He read every word and thought about all the men from the Scarlet Society who were also reading this at their desks, at their breakfast tables, on the subway, in their chauffeur-driven cars, in their taxis. They were probably shitting in their pants.

Two men. First missing. Now lifeless bodies with pathetic numbers on the soles of their feet. Number 1. And now number 2.

For the first time in his life, Paul Lessor understood the expression "rubbing your hands together with glee." This was the best feeling he'd had in a long time. This was revenge. This was comeuppance. Ha. If he couldn't come anymore, at least he could get gratification thinking about how this was screwing with the head of every man who ever visited the society and every man who had ever looked at him with pity.

So what if he couldn't get it up? They wouldn't be able to get it up anymore, either. Thorazine wasn't the only thing that made you impotent. Fear did it, too. Every one of those men must be choking on their croissants, spilling their orange juice, breaking out in a sweat, feeling a cramp in their stomachs or a loosening of their bowels. They were questioning their little hobby, now weren't they? Wondering what they could do differently from Philip and Timothy so they could go back to the society but escape the fate of these two. Except even if they braved it, overcame their fright, how good would the sex be now, really?

Under his robe, Paul put his hand around his penis. Squeezing, rubbing, hoping that the elation he was feeling at seeing the article and thinking about the other men suffering would translate into another kind of elation.

If he could be this happy, wouldn't he be able to get hard?

Nothing was happening.

He tried harder. His mind focused on the image of a woman demanding he undress for her. Of a woman pushing her breasts into his hands and telling him how to touch her. Of a woman standing over him and shoving her pussy into his face.

His flaccid dick betrayed him, and as if it were burning his fingers the way the coffee had scorched the inside of his mouth, he jerked his hand away.

Think about something else, anything else.

He looked down at the newspaper and started to read the article again, savoring the picture of the man's feet. And the number 2. Envisioning another photograph of another man's feet with the number 3 on them. And then another with the number 4 on them...

There was no telling how many would meet their fate this way.

He smiled, knowing even if he couldn't get every kind of pleasure, at least this pleasure was not being denied him.

Picking up the cup of coffee, he drank from it. Bitter, black and lukewarm. It didn't matter, the only thing he tasted was the sweetness of revenge.

Twenty-Five

Nina and I were walking up Fifth Avenue on the west side of the street, where there are still cobblestones and if you wear high heels they can get trapped in the cracks. We took walks often during lunch, most of the time without a destination, just a direction. The object wasn't where we would wind up, but the excursion itself.

"I saw the article in the *Times* this morning about Timothy Wheaton, with your quote in it," she said.

"I think he might have also been involved with the Scarlet Society."

"Why do you think so? Have you met with the group again?"

"Not until Monday. But there are marks on his body that are exactly the same as those on Philip Maur's. Marks that aren't mentioned in either article."

"Did the reporter tell you about them? Why would she?" Nina asked, confused.

"No. The reporter didn't say anything."

"Who did? Who told you about the marks?"

Damn, I never should have said anything. Now I would have to explain to Nina that I'd seen Noah the night before, and she didn't have any faith in the police.

In 1996, when her husband Sam was Butterfield's director, the NYPD suspected the institute was a front for an illegal prostitution ring. They had placed a detective inside who posed as a sex therapist and who found enough evidence to put Sam in prison. The case was under appeal when Sam died of a heart attack.

Rather than blame Sam, who had indeed been guilty as charged, Nina used the NYPD as her scapegoat, insisting that their undercover sting had been too much of a shock for him and that if they had been aboveboard he wouldn't have died.

I'd experienced Nina's irrational anger at the police for the first time when I'd gotten involved with the Magdalene Murders and met Noah. Now I braced myself for another explosion of it.

"Noah Jordain called me. He told me about the photos."

"Oh?" She didn't look at me, but I could sense the barely perceptible cooling of her tone.

"He saw this morning's article yesterday before it went to press, read my quote and called to find out what my involvement was and why the reporter had interviewed me, out of all the therapists in the city."

"What did you tell him?"

"There was nothing to tell him. I don't know why the reporter called me."

We'd reached the Metropolitan Museum on Eighty-first and Fifth. There were always food carts on the street and it was our lunchtime habit to stop and indulge in a New York City delicacy: Sabrett hot dogs with sauerkraut and mustard, enveloped in warm buns.

We got our food, sat on the wide stone steps leading up to the museum, ate and talked about a therapist we both knew who wanted to come to work at the institute. I was glad Nina had dropped any discussion of Noah.

Except she hadn't. We stood up, and as we brushed the crumbs off our clothes, she asked, "You didn't say anything to imply to Detective Jordain that Philip Maur belonged to any kind of group, did you?"

"How can you ask me that?"

"The rules get murky sometimes."

"Not for me. And you know it."

"No. Not for you. Not yet. But sweetie, you're human. You went through a traumatic experience last June and Noah Jordain came to your rescue and you might—"

"He didn't. I was not in any danger by the time Jordain showed up."

"Okay." She didn't sound convinced.

"None of that has anything to do with anything, Nina. This is one of those times when you are getting mixed up, not sure if you should be my boss or play mother. You are confusing your roles. What are you really worried about? Me? The institute? Our clients?"

We walked to the bottom of the steps and headed back down Fifth. Neither of us said anything.

"You're right," Nina finally offered.

I smiled at her.

"It would just be easier if you didn't see the detective again. It's a loaded situation. It's too tempting."

"He's not married, you know."

She laughed. "I didn't mean that kind of temptation. But it's interesting to note where your mind went."

I didn't think it was funny at all. "Don't shrink me, Nina. Just tell me what you want to tell me."

"Okay. Fair enough. What I meant was that if you get involved with the detective, then when it comes to telling him something that might make his job easier, even if it means compromising your own professional ethics, you will feel tempted to do the wrong thing to help someone that you care about."

"Haven't I proved myself?"

"None of us is made of steel. We don't face every situation the same way. What happened last summer was one thing. What happens next time will be something else."

"Well, you don't have to worry about it. I'm not getting involved with him."

"Okay. So this is settled?"

"Yes," I said. And at that moment I was sure that it was. Nina was right. She had to be.

Twenty-Six

I don't make house calls except in very unusual circumstances. Since Nicky's estranged wife was suffering a severe case of agoraphobia, I'd made an exception and had agreed to see them at her house in Greenwich, Connecticut.

Nicky said his wife, a painter, normally spent long periods of time alone and so he hadn't noticed the phobia creeping up on her, neither did he know what had triggered it. But since he'd moved out to an apartment in the city, he didn't believe she had left the house. Forty minutes away from Manhattan, she'd imprisoned herself on a twenty-acre estate that had been in her family for three generations.

Once a week, my colleague Simon and I drove to an upstate New York prison to work with incarcerated prostitutes. Usually he drove us, but if I was going to help Nicky and his wife, the best time to do it was on Thursday after my stint at the prison. So I'd rented a car, done my work with Simon, and then driven to Fairfield County.

A black mailbox identified number 26 Pondview Avenue. As per Nicky's instructions, I made a right and drove for five minutes on a road that had been cut through a forest. Tall weeping pine trees on both sides cast a dark blue-green shadow that blocked the sun and created a sudden evening, although it was only midafternoon.

After twisting and turning for a few hundred yards, the road ended in a clearing. The house was directly ahead of me, and in every direction there were fields and more forest.

I pulled into a parking area where two other cars were parked. The silver Mercedes SUV didn't have a speck of dirt or dust on it, but the celery-green Jag looked in need of a good wash.

Getting out, I stretched my legs and looked around. The grounds were meticulously cared for and picturesque. In the distance was a pond and beyond that were rolling hills as far as I could see.

The scene dictated quiet, but there was work being done somewhere on the property, and the drone of a mechanical monster was out of place and annoying. If birds were chirping, as I was sure they were, I couldn't hear them, and the bucolic view was marred by the sound. The air was filled with the perfume of the pungent pine trees and scents of fall. Somewhere close by, wood was burning in a fireplace.

Living in a very crowded city for my entire life, the idea of so much space and such solitude seemed both an enviable luxury and a frightening prospect.

The uneven stone path to the front door was edged on both sides with an English cottage garden. I noticed how many of the plantings were popular with butterflies: bee balm, violets, English lavender, passionflower, columbine, asters and buddleia bushes. Except for the purple, white, and lavender buddleias, the flowers were all past bloom. I had some of them growing in the planters on my own small balcony. It had been a warm fall and there were likely still some butterflies that came to feed in this garden, but I didn't see any as I walked by.

I rang the bell and heard a long chime sound inside. Footsteps followed and then Nicky opened the door. He was wearing a pale blue shirt, black cashmere V-neck sweater and pressed jeans. He smiled warmly, shook my hand and told me how grateful he was that I'd agreed to come all the way out there.

"Daphne is inside," he said as he led the way through a main hall, the living room and out onto a patio that had been enclosed as a sunroom. Majolica cachepots graced the end tables. The couch and chairs were oversized, deep-cushioned and covered with a cabbage-rose chintz. The walls were pale, pale blue with white trim. The tile floors were partially covered with almost threadbare, but exquisite, Oriental carpets. Everything bespoke old money. And a lot of it.

As I entered, Daphne stood and extended her hand.

I knew better than to think that something like agoraphobia would show on someone's face, but I didn't expect the woman who greeted me.

She was blond, long and lean, and offered a strong, firm handshake. An elegant neck supported a heart-shaped face that was well tanned. From the Cartier watch to the tweed slacks, leather boots, lemon-yellow sweater set and the string of lustrous pearls, everything fit the image of a Junior Leaguer.

I looked into her eyes as I introduced myself. They were a pale green-gray color, intelligent but stormy and defiant. Not the eyes of a woman afraid of going out of the house. Or afraid of anything else, I thought.

And then she gave me a soft smile that defused her hardness. "It's so nice to meet you, Dr. Snow. Nicky's told me a lot about you. He's very enthusiastic about this process. Would you like some tea or some coffee? Something cold?" Her voice matched her prettiness, not the defiant eyes, and sounded like honey and silk.

"No, I'm fine. Thank you."

She motioned for me to sit, and as I did, she did, too. "I really appreciate that you would come out here to work with us. It won't be for long, though. I'm working on the agoraphobia with my own therapist and we both feel I'm getting close to a breakthrough."

The chair was too big for me; I felt lost in it and missed my own office. The estranged couple sat on the couch facing me. It was a good sign that they had chosen to sit together.

"Who are you working with?" I asked, in case I needed to consult with her therapist at some point.

She hesitated. Was she apprehensive about telling me for some reason? A breeze blew in from an open window. It carried Daphne's fragrance toward me. Lilies of the valley. Fitting. But the perfume wasn't the only thing I smelled; suddenly, there was something else in the air, too. Clean, sharp and astringent. But I couldn't place it.

"His name is William Klein. Here in Greenwich. I've gone to him on and off since I was a teenager."

I wanted to ask her why she'd gone to a therapist when she was a teenager, but it was too soon. I filed the fact away. "How long have you and Nicky known each other?"

She looked over at him before she answered. I couldn't see her face and so couldn't read her expression. I asked a few more questions that didn't matter very much except to get the session started and establish a rapport.

"Do you want to work out your problems with Nicky?"

Her answer was quick, and extremely vehement. "Yes. More than anything I have ever wanted. I'll do anything to make our marriage work."

"Well, not anything," Nicky countered.

"Anything that I'm capable of doing."

"Daphne, can you tell me about the problem the two of you are having?"

"Didn't Nicky tell you?"

"Yes, but that was his version. I'd like to hear yours. And then I'd like you to tell me what you think the problem is, Nicky."

"We already went through that at your office," Nicky said impatiently.

"Yes, but I want each of you to hear what the other thinks."

"The only thing standing in the way of our having a good relationship is Nicky's fucking inability to leave the Scarlet Society."

Her use of that one word seemed out of place in this genteel house. Was she being rebellious or angry?

"He's told me three or four times that he's quit, but he can't stay away. I'm willing to accept that he has an addiction and work with him on it, but I can't just shrug my shoulders and let him go there two or three nights a week, play the pussy pansy and look the other way."

If she wanted a reaction to that expression, I wasn't going to accommodate her. "Do you think shrugging your shoulders is a solution?"

"It's Nicky's solution. He wants to be married to me and have a family with me, and on the side get naked and be treated like a—"

"Let's focus on you and what you want," I said. "We'll let Nicky speak for himself when it's his turn."

In her lap, Daphne fussed, clasping and unclasping her hands. Her nails were short, unpolished, not manicured. The skin was rough and red. Seeing me look, she smiled and held up her hands to make it easier for me to see. "Painter's hands. The turp does damage."

That must have been what I'd smelled.

"I'd like to see your work."

"Are you an art lover?" she asked.

"I am, albeit an uneducated one." That was true, but it wasn't why I wanted to see her paintings. I was curious about what they would reveal about her.

"That's the best kind. Someone who just looks at the work and decides if she likes it or not based on how it touches her, not based on what some asshole professor or critic tells her to think."

Hostility now. I was curious to pursue that line, but couldn't afford to go that far afield from Daphne and Nicky's relationship in the first session. I turned to him. "Nicky, would you tell me if you agree with Daphne's assessment of what's going on between the two of you?"

He nodded. "I can't give up what she wants me to."

"Do you want to?"

"I can't."

"Are you willing to try?"

"I have."

"Are you willing to try again?"

Before he could answer, Daphne did. "No—he's not. He thinks it's up to me to change. He thinks that since I was once part of that vile club, I should be understanding. But I want my husband to be faithful."

"I am faithful, Daphne. What goes on there is not about love or even affection."

"What is it about?" I asked him.

"Sex."

"Sex isn't about love?"

"It can be. But it can also just be sex. It's a physical activity. Like playing tennis, or going swimming."

Daphne let out a long peal of laughter that surprised me with its nasty edge. "He is so full of shit. I know what he wants and—"

"Time out," I interrupted. "I don't want either of you to assume what the other wants. Just answer for yourself. Daphne, tell me about the Scarlet Society. How long ago did you join?"

"Years ago. A friend of mine was a member and she told me about it."

"How often did you go?"

"About once or twice a month. Usually with her."

"What did you enjoy about it?"

"I don't see why this shit is important to—"

"Because it has to do with your marriage. The society is what you say is getting in the way of you and Nicky having a good marriage. I need to find out more about that."

She thought for a minute, and in the quiet of the room I heard the steady drone of machinery along with the beat of a hammer, hitting its mark every five to ten seconds.

"What did you ask me?"

Was she buying time or had she really forgotten what I'd asked?

"I asked you what you enjoyed about being a member of the Scarlet Society."

"It was like painting in another artist's hand. I do very realistic paintings. It was as if suddenly I could paint like an abstract expressionist. I wasn't myself there. Or at least not the self I'd always known."

"How did that make you feel?"

"It was exciting…also confusing. For the first time in my life, I was in an environment where no one knew who I was, who my parents were, what kind of life I had. We don't talk about ourselves. You know that, right?"

I nodded.

"There was a real sense of freedom. Until then, I'd only known a world where there are right ways of behaving. And wrong ways. Everything about the Scarlet Society was the wrong way of behaving. It was the best damn thing that ever happened to my art."

I hadn't expected that. "What do you mean—the best thing that happened to your art?"

"My father was a Supreme Court judge. My mother was a member of the Junior League and the DAR. I am one of three sisters. By the time I was twenty-five, they were both married with kids. And they're younger than me. My painting was an indulgence that my parents thought I'd outgrow. It was fine that I studied art—as long as I did it at Radcliffe. It was all right that I painted as long as my studio was in the apartment they'd bought for me on Park Avenue. The society was something that would have freaked them out. They would never have approved."

"And you only did what they approved of?"

"It never occurred to me to cross them. You just didn't do that."

"When you were very young, how did they handle it when you did something that angered them?"

Her answer came fast, delivered in a low voice that was almost a whisper. "They stopped talking to you. Completely. Depending on your crime, for hours or for days. You were treated like you were invisible. Until you apologized. Until you repented."

"Did you feel guilty about what went on at the society?"

"No. I wasn't me there. I didn't even use my real first name. It was totally separate from the rest of my life."

"Some people might find that difficult. To balance two such different lives."

"Really?"

There was something very naive about that question, which alerted me to watch out for other instances of an ability to distance herself from reality.

"For some people it might be."

"Well, it wasn't for me. And it was good for my art. That was the best part." She clasped her hands tightly together.

"How so?"

She smiled and her face was transformed from a serious, troubled visage to a child's face, full of wonder. "It would be easier to show you." She stood.

I wasn't sure we should interrupt the session at that point, but her enthusiasm was important.

"Is that okay with you?" I asked Nicky.

"Hell, yes, it's fine. I told you I wanted you to see Daphne's work."

I followed Daphne as she led me around the sunroom, showing me four still lifes of flowers and fruit that she said she had done in her early twenties. They were bright and bold and very well done. A combination of Matisse's colors and Cézanne's blocking but without either's originality or verve. So unremarkable that I hadn't even noticed them while we were sitting and talking.

"This was the kind of work I was doing after college. Competent. Uninspired. I couldn't get the attention of any serious downtown gallery. A safe, old-fashioned Madison Avenue gallery took me on." She laughed. "But that turned out to be because my parents had guaranteed the sales for each of my shows."

"When did you find that out?"

"A few years ago. My mother died and I inherited this house. All of the paintings that I thought had sold to clients from all of my shows were still in their shipping crates in one of the rooms in the basement."

"How did that make you feel?"

"It was such a kind thing for them to do. I felt grateful."

"No anger?"

"I suppose it might have made me angry if I hadn't broken out by the time I found them. I don't need any help selling my work now. There's a waiting list for my paintings."

There was a tone in her voice—this wasn't self-confidence; it was bragging. Was this her usual way of talking about her work, or was it for my benefit?

"Take a last look around, Dr. Snow." She waited a few seconds. "Now, let me show you how I evolved as an artist."

Daphne led the way out of the room. We walked back through the living room and foyer. In front of us was a large and curving grand staircase. Daphne walked toward and around it.

Behind the stairs was a hallway with a glass-paned ceiling. We walked through a breezeway into a large artist's studio in what seemed to be a separate building.

The walls were painted a stark white. Large skylights flooded the room with natural light. Here, the smells of turpentine and oil paints, which I had only been slightly aware of in the sunroom, were more intense.

In the middle of the room was an easel. The painting on it was facing away from us. Daphne sauntered over to it and turned the easel around.

The canvas was more than four feet wide and at least

as tall. The colors were deep and luminous. The paint was thick and heavy. I was looking into a cavelike room. The light source was beyond the edge of the canvas but it lit up the painting, warming the skin tones of the naked man who lounged on a velvet couch, sporting an erection. Strangely, he had been feminized in a way that suggested submission rather than homosexuality. It was subtly done—I certainly didn't know how she'd done it.

I forced myself to look away from the erotic painting and back to its creator. She was smiling, her eyes shone and her lips were parted. The pleasure she experienced watching me encounter her work was palpable and sexual.

I looked back at the painting.

That the woman standing next to me, of the pearl and the horse-country set, had created the painting would have been hard to believe if not for that edge to her words and the glare in her eyes. She was a fine painter, but what gripped me and kept me staring at the painting was its very real sexuality—as provocative as the video of the society that I'd watched ten days earlier.

You see an expression on a man's face like the one Daphne had captured only in the privacy of your own bedroom. You try to memorize it because you know it isn't one you will see often. Many people never get to see anything exactly like it, ever.

That she had painted it said much about Daphne. It was past voyeurism to paint this portrait of this man. It was almost sacrilege to portray the inner depth to his want.

Actors making love in movies do a good job of expressing passion, and if you get caught up in the story on the screen you don't notice the subtle false notes. They aren't important.

But the expression that Daphne had caught in this man's

face wasn't an act. He was gazing at a woman with such desire that it pained him, and he was willing to do anything he had to do—no matter how much it demeaned him—in order to get what he wanted. And he wanted it right then, urgently, and for a whole host of reasons both right and wrong.

"It's amazing, isn't it?"

This not from Nicky, but from the artist herself. It surprised me, too. It was not arrogance. Not bragging this time, either. She had separated and become a spectator looking at a stranger's work.

I answered carefully but honestly, watching her reaction. "Yes, it is very powerful."

"Before I joined the society I'd never understood much about sex. It was dark and removed and secretive. I learned about need and perversion and fantasy, and even though the sex stayed secretive, I was able to at least understand it. I tried out so many ways of expressing myself sexually, and that impacted me. It fed my work and made me creative in a way I'd never been. It became part of me. Or I became part of it."

"And you still needed to keep going there?"

"To see this kind of look on the men's faces. Over and over."

I wanted to know where she was still seeing this kind of look if she had stopped going to the society a year ago. Who was she painting now? Who posed for her this way? But it was not the right time to ask that yet.

I turned to Nicky to gauge his reaction to what his wife had said. He was looking at Daphne with the same naked expression as the man in the painting. Obviously, he was very attracted to his wife. Either because she was no longer available to him, or because she was talking about her sex life before she married him, or just—and this was not only the simplest but also the least possible of reasons as far as I was concerned—because he was in love with Daphne, in awe of her talents and wanted to be with her.

Twenty-Seven

On the drive back to the city, I replayed the mental tape I'd made of the session, knowing that there were more questions raised than answered. And there were several things disturbing me. Most important of them all, I wasn't certain that Daphne was telling me or her husband the truth about the agoraphobia.

I returned the rental car to the garage and got home by four-thirty. I had to be downtown at the rehearsal studio at seven for a meeting for all the parents and young actors, but I had some time. In the kitchen, I made coffee in the French press—this being one of the very few food preparations that I did not mess up—and took a mug into the den.

The tape that Shelby Rush had given me was on the bookshelves, behind a row of psychiatric textbooks that I knew Dulcie would never look at. I pulled it out, slipped it into the machine, hit the play button, then the mute button, and sat in my comfortable east-side apartment watching a few dozen women act like predators.

I found what I was looking for within minutes.

Daphne *was* on the tape. I hadn't known who she was

when I'd first watched the video, but she'd looked familiar to me when I walked into the sunroom. Here she was
at the gala, in a teal-blue gown, with a sequined blue mask
covering her eyes. But the hair was not hidden. The long
lean body and the heart-shaped face and the stunning neck
weren't disguised.

She stood in front of a line of tuxedo-clad men, appraising them and finally making her choice. Putting one hand
on a tall black man's shoulder, she nodded to him, turned
imperiously without looking back to make sure he was following her, and walked off screen.

The tape played on as I sat and sipped my coffee, mesmerized by the sex play.

Even though I could list every perversion and fetish,
had heard men and women sit in my office and admit the
most intimate details of their sex lives, had instructed sex
surrogates on how to do their jobs, had studied hard- and
soft-core pornography, I had never seen real people play
these kinds of sex games.

I didn't relate to the women's aggression, but I was affected by the men, by their willingness to perform, by
their lack of self-consciousness at being treated in this
way, by the striptease from tuxedo to underwear to full nudity in front of such a big audience, for no other reason
than that they knew it was what the women were demanding of them and they wanted to please their audience. That
their pleasing aroused them aroused me.

I had never ordered my husband to strip for me or
walk around a room naked or get down on his knees in
front of me. I had never demanded anything of him sexually. We had made love without any role-playing and
our sex life had been satisfying without being obsessive,
mysterious or spiritual. I'd never minded. Firsthand, I'd

seen that kind of passion break and cripple people, destroy relationships.

The more I learned about sexuality in graduate school, and in therapy after that, the more I realized that my own sex drive was average and that my fantasy life was not very fertile. But we don't try to solve things that we don't perceive as problems. Since I was never sexually frustrated, I never thought about being bored with Mitch. I didn't focus on my own libido.

I'm not proud to admit this, but I worked with so many patients who were disturbed by some aspect of their own sexuality that, if anything, I was pleased that mine was low on the list of issues I focused on. I even felt slightly superior about it.

I know now that I was wrong, but for so many, many years, I really believed that if I did not care too much about sex, I'd never be disappointed by it.

That lasted until Mitch and I separated.

In the months after that, I realized how little effort either of us had made to explore each other. For two people who were so creative with their own careers, we were dull to the point of being destructive with our relationship.

I didn't know why. It was something I had yet to figure out. When I had the time. When I wanted to deal with it. When I wanted to rehash the past to see what I could learn that might help me in the future.

That time hadn't come yet.

The screen had gone to black and I was about to hit the stop button when a new scene came up on the monitor. I hadn't watched past this point the first time I'd viewed the tape. I hadn't known there was any more.

I turned up the sound and watched a room lined with books fade in. There were six rows of chairs filled with women whose backs were to the camera. A makeshift stage stood at one end of the room. There, Shelby Rush stood behind a podium.

"And now we have number 3—Tim," she said.

From camera left a man walked onto the stage. He was shirtless and shoeless, wearing only a pair of faded jeans. His shoulders were broad and his chest was buff. He stood, humbly, his palms face out.

"Tim, would you take off your jeans?" Shelby asked.

As if he fully expected the request, he complied without any sense of embarrassment, and within seconds was stripped down to his underwear.

"Would you please make yourself hard?"

Without any trepidation, Tim obeyed. Reaching down, he rubbed his crotch through the cotton briefs. Watching the audience watching him, he smiled slightly as his hand kept up its steady motion.

It took less than thirty seconds for the bulge to appear and the underwear to tent out.

"And now, show us."

Tim stepped out of his underwear.

His body was beautiful. Strong and sculpted.

"Does anyone want to test Tim before I start the bidding?"

"I would" came a voice from the audience. A short red-head stood up.

In a culture where so many men, and now women, relied on an array of prescription drugs to replenish desire that had disappeared, been destroyed, or was pushed down so deep they were afraid to find out what was inhibiting it, the raw and real appetites of these women was mesmerizing.

What was different about them that allowed for a suspension of social mores? Wanting to be part of a couple regardless of how unfulfilling it may be, so many women I've worked with have chosen a life of compromises over the alternative. They deny, even in the privacy of their minds, their most creative fantasies, choosing instead to borrow from the sex scenes they read in soft-focus fiction. They are afraid to search the twisting tunnels of their own ids to discover what would be arousing—be it talking out loud, role playing or pursuing pain.

And yet this group had overcome all inhibition to indulge in their cravings. To create a solution despite how unconventional it was. Was what they craved unusual? Yes. Was it dysfunctional? It might be for some of them and not for others. Judging them wouldn't help me to understand how they could be in touch with the darkest and most private parts of their sexual selves. But I could wonder at it. Especially here, in my own home, watching them act out their fantasies for one another to see.

On the monitor, the naked man walked off the stage and toward the woman, whose back was still to the camera. The camera pushed past her pale gray gown, angled down and zoomed in for a close-up of her manicured fingers reaching out and testing the heft of Tim's testicles. Then she wrapped her hand around his cock, holding it as if it was a leash, and led him out past the all-female audience.

The video cut to a darkened bedroom. Tim's bare back filled the frame and the woman's now-naked legs were visible on either side of his body. Her toenails were painted a deep blood red.

"Don't go fast," her disembodied voice demanded. "Take your time." Her fingers clutched at his back, pressing into his flesh, leaving deep, moon-shaped marks.

Soft, ambient light gleamed off his back as he moved in a slow-motion dance.

"You understand this is not for your pleasure. I don't want you to have any release. Not now. Not at all. Do you think that you can hold back?" Her words weren't just instructions; she was excited hearing herself speak. "Can you stay hard for me? For as long as I need it?"

"Yes." His voice was thick and low. Obedient. Without any trace of theatrics. He seemed sincerely respectful.

The only sound for the next few seconds was the stinging noise of his skin slapping against hers.

"Tell me how you can hold off. Doesn't it feel good?" She whispered so softly I had to lean forward to hear. I could see the sweat on his shoulder blades now, and the way his buttocks flexed, relaxed, and then tensed again.

"It does. It feels too good. But I want to please you."

"Why?"

"Because I want my reward."

"The longer you can wait, the more you can give me without giving anything to yourself, the more I'll reward you. Is that what you want?"

"Yes," he answered. "Please."

"Won't it make you crazy when I start to buck under you? When I start to come? And you can't?"

"Yes, it will."

"But you'll be able to hold off?"

"Yes."

I sucked in my breath.

"How will you hold yourself back from coming, from spewing out, from shooting into me?" She was lost in her own sex play, speaking now not for him at all, but to heighten her own delight.

"Because it's what you want me to do."

As her breath came faster, she made small sounds of delight. His breaths were shallow. The muscles in his back were tensed and delineated. The effort was obviously painful.

Meanwhile, the camera held, motionless.

The man moved in rhythm to the woman's moans and sighed softly. She shouted out, "No. No. Do you hear me?"

I held my breath.

"Yes," he whispered. "I'm sorry."

"Are you sure you can do this?" Her voice sounded urgent.

"Yes."

A long, slow arc of sound escaped from her and, before it was over, the scene changed and we were back in the library. Tim was on the stage again. Still erect. With his head bowed.

"Now that Tim has passed his first test, let's get the bidding started."

I was in an erotic fog, but before I could understand why, I was overwhelmed by a wave of sadness. There was no one I could expend my energy on. No one I could even confess to about how watching a group of women assess a man and test his prowess had gripped me with a want completely unfamiliar to me.

No. That wasn't why I was melancholy.

There was someone. Even though I'd been with him only once, I was certain—even in that very hazy moment—that Noah Jordain would have understood what I was experiencing. That if it were possible for me to tell him about the video and my reaction to it, he would give me his slow smile that looked the way his voice sounded, take his hand, put it on the side of my face, look right at me, and tell me that he'd play a game with me if that was what I wanted. Any game I

wanted to try. That yes, he'd even be happy to stand in front
of me naked and do my bidding.

Like a burst of unwanted morning light when you are
craving more sleep and darkness, I saw Noah, not in my
daydream, but standing in front of that wall of hideous pictures at the station house. All the feelings stirring and swirling through my body and brain were wiped out with one
sudden realization.

The man I'd just been watching on the tape, who had
stripped down, made himself hard, preformed on command, and then allowed himself to be auctioned off, was
the second victim of the killer Noah was hunting.

Tim. Of course. Timothy. Timothy Wheaton. Healthy,
bronzed and almost unrecognizable as the gray corpse in
the photos at the police station.

With a shaking hand, I pressed the rewind button on the
remote, listened to the whir of the tape spinning back-
ward, hit Stop, and then Play. I'd overshot the section so
fast-forwarded, all the while watching the sensual footage
running by too quickly like bad slapstick.

Finally, I found the section I was searching for.

Tim, standing bare-chested in his jeans, posing for the
hungry women.

Tim taking off his pants, and after that his underwear.

Tim showing off his erection, leaving the room with the
unidentified woman.

I shut my eyes to recall, as clearly as I could, the photographs on Jordain's wall. I pictured the face of the man in
the shots the newspaper had not run. He was pale, naked and
without any life in him, but he was absolutely the same man
who was on the tape.

It had been terrifying that one man who had been connected to the Scarlet Society had been killed.

But two men?
That could not be a coincidence.
Two men had to be a pattern.

Twenty-Eight

~~~~~~~

It was still light when I left the apartment and headed downtown for the parents' meeting at the rehearsal studio. As I walked from Madison to Lexington to get on the subway, I watched the sky deepen. The twilight was thick and colorless that night and the skyscrapers blended into the gray of the evening, their tips disappearing in the cloud cover and ensuing darkness. The autumnal gold and red leaves were like bursts of fire against the dusky evening.

On the ride, I obsessed over the video, but as I walked into the lobby I forced myself to let go of Dr. Snow's problems and just be Dulcie's mom.

Young stars and parents alike sat on metal chairs in the makeshift auditorium, sipping soda, bad coffee, or even worse wine, listening to the director talk about the upcoming out-of-town preview. He handed out schedules that included the name of the hotel the theater company had commandeered for the weekend, the directions, the times of the performances and other pertinent travel arrangements. Then he talked about the kind of stress the kids were all facing and what we could do to help our children as they approached this momentous performance.

Dulcie sat between my ex-husband and me and shifted in her seat, unable to find a position to hold for more than a minute or two. Her glance never left the director's face, and several times I noticed she was chewing the inside of her cheek, something I hadn't seen her do in years. Her nervousness was escalating.

Afterward, the three of us had dinner at the Time Out café, an easygoing but trendy restaurant two blocks from the rehearsal studio. She had a soda; Mitch and I both had wine. It was much better than what had been offered at the meeting.

We got along well, this man whom I'd been married to for almost half my life, and I. After all, we had a common goal—to be the best parents we could be to our daughter. Dissolving a union is never easy, but our experience was sad as opposed to brutal, and neither of us felt animosity toward the other. We'd managed to stay friends through the proceedings, which I credit entirely to Mitch. He was generous and thoughtful.

If I am going to be truthful, I will say that part of my reason for being so reasonable was because Mitch and Dulcie have a very special relationship. They are more alike than she and I are. They share the same love of theater and film, of books and of physical activities such as skiing and mountain climbing. They have the same tall, lanky frame, the same near-sightedness, and the same taste in food, preferring their meals less spicy than I do.

I have, at times, been jealous of the bond they share, forgetting that Dulcie and I are also close. But having lost my mother so young, I worked too hard at connecting to my daughter and sometimes, in a moment of clarity, knew it did more to push us apart than bring us together.

We were on dessert. Well, Mitch and Dulcie were, each

of them working on a slice of cheesecake. I was making do with an espresso. I'd been watching Dulcie all night, waiting to see the nerves relax even a little. But they hadn't. Something was up.

"You okay?" I asked my daughter.

She nodded and then looked at Mitch.

I knew that look. I'd been seeing it for years. My daughter's way of working out her problems never changed: she went to Mitch first and after that the two of them brought the dilemma to me.

When I'd talked it over with Nina years ago, she'd told me that it wasn't unusual for the child of a therapist to be wary of that parent's insight. That bringing in the nonpsychologist parent first gave the child a ballast and a buffer. Nina had helped me to accept the alliance, but that didn't mean it made me happy.

"Morgan, it's about the trip to Boston," Mitch said, translating Dulcie's look.

"Okay. Spill," I said to her, trying for a lighthearted tone, hoping I could signal that I would just listen first and not react. But inside I was instantly worried. Instantly afraid. Some of this was my own projection about what she was going through, but more of it was coming from Dulcie.

Since she was a tiny baby, I had always picked up on her pain, both physical and emotional. Often, I'd be doing something miles away from her and get a sudden pain in my throat, or stomach, or hand, only to find out when I arrived home that she'd gotten sick or cut herself.

Other times, I'd felt a pang of homesickness or fear and found out that while she was on her sleepover or at camp she'd missed us and wanted to come back, or that in school some other kid had been mean to her.

Earlier that night, I'd felt nervous. I'd written off the feeling as what I'd assumed was her normal stage fright.

"I'd like Daddy to come with me to Boston."

I felt relieved. "Of course he can come, honey. We're both coming. You don't even have to ask. Does she, Mitch?"

My ex-husband returned my gaze, warning me with his expression that I wasn't hearing what Dulcie was saying.

"That's not it, is it?" I asked her.

She was holding her lips pressed together, not wanting to explain, leaving it to me to do the work for her. It was easy enough. "You want me to stay home?"

She nodded and rushed into an explanation. "It's not that I don't want you to come. I just don't want you to see the mistakes. I want to get all that out of the way first. I don't want you to see the play till we open in New York. Till it's right. Till it's perfect."

I nodded. Something that had been bothering me was suddenly making sense. "Hon, is that why you usually tell me to pick you up at one time, only for me to get there and realize I'm about ten or fifteen minutes later than the other parents? You don't want me to see the rehearsals?"

She bit her bottom lip. "I just want you to see the play. On opening night. All perfect."

There was something else she wasn't saying, but I knew from the way her blue eyes had clouded over that she wasn't going to tell me any more than that. She had inherited some of Mitch's negative traits, too. That stubborn shutting down being one of them.

I picked up my glass of wine and took a long sip and tried to separate my hurt from a real clinical assessment of what my daughter was doing and why. But all I could think was what had I done to my daughter to make her think that I wanted—or needed—her to be perfect?

Putting my hand on hers, I leaned toward her. "Sweetheart, I don't need your performances to be perfect. I'm not judging you."

Tears came too quickly. "If I can't do it right, you won't let me keep doing it."

"What makes you think that?"

No words now, just a shaky shrug of her shoulders,

"I love you, Dulcie, whether you get up there and belt out the songs like Judy Garland or flub your lines, or sing off-key. As for you continuing with acting, that's a family decision. One that we'll all make together when the run of this play is over. We'll look at your schoolwork and what kind of stress you're feeling and we'll decide together."

She nodded, but I didn't know if I'd convinced her. Later, when I was alone, I'd deal with everything I was thinking. Right now all that mattered was saying something that would alleviate my daughter's distress.

"I promise I am not going to stop you from pursuing this if it's what you really want. You believe that, don't you?"

She nodded.

"What about Boston?" she said with a slight catch in her voice. "Can Dad go with me? Can you wait to see me till it's the final show?"

"If it matters to you that much…" I let the rest of the sentence drift off.

"It does. The rehearsals always go bad. Lots of the other kids have convinced their parents not to come watch."

I glanced at Mitch. There were no answers in his eyes.

Twenty-Nine

I waited until after we got home. And then I waited until after Dulcie had done her homework. I waited until after we sat and watched an episode of *Seinfeld* together, both of us laughing even though we knew all the jokes ahead of time. And finally I waited until after she got undressed and into bed and fell asleep.

Still I didn't do anything. I put a pot of water on to boil. Waited for a cup of tea to brew. Waited for a teaspoon of honey to melt. And then there wasn't any excuse I could give myself to wait anymore. Even though I didn't have any solid information that I could give him. Even though I couldn't break any confidence.

I could tell him that one thing I'd noticed in the photographs at the station house that hadn't made sense at that time did make sense now, couldn't I?

Didn't I need to?

No one in the Scarlet Society group had told me anything about it. Shelby hadn't mentioned it when we'd talked in private. It was something I had noticed on my own.

I picked up the phone.

And then hung up.

What if my talking to Jordain would make a difference to his investigation? What if the information I had dovetailed with facts he'd found out but hadn't quite fit into place? I went over the argument again in my mind. Going to the police with information that had to do with any patients wasn't something you just did. There was nothing more sacred in our business than the confidentiality between me and the people who came to me to help them.

I fell asleep after lying in bed for what seemed like hours, going over both sides of the argument, trying to tackle it with logic, without coming to a solution. The apartment was quiet except for the occasional sound of a car on the street five stories below. Where was he? The man who had killed Philip Maur and Timothy Wheaton. Was he on the videotape that Shelby had given me? Had any of the women I was working with in the group had sex with him? What was his connection to the Scarlet Society? And what was my responsibility?

I got up, throwing off the sheets, and walked barefoot through the dark hallway to Dulcie's room. The door was open halfway and my eyes had adjusted to the gloom while I lay in my bed, restless and worried.

My daughter was lying on her back, one arm under the sheets, the other thrown across her chest. Her face was smooth and peaceful. I couldn't see the shadows under her eyes that I'd noticed that night at dinner. All I wanted to do was keep her safe. Keep her happy.

Somewhere beyond these walls was a man who had already killed twice. I didn't know why. And I didn't know what I could do about it. But I knew that the men he had killed had children who would miss them, whose lives would never be the same again.

Lost girls. Lost boys.

Could I really keep what I knew from Noah Jordain?

Thirty

At lunchtime the next day, Nina asked if I wanted to take a walk.

"Yes, if you'll come with me to run an errand. I have to go to Tiffany to pick up a present for Dulcie."

She nodded. "I'll get my jacket."

The temperature still hadn't dropped; it was a sunny sixty degrees out. The walk should have been delightful but I was preoccupied and tired, and she knew it.

"What's bothering you?" she asked as soon as we were out on the street.

I didn't deny that I was troubled. Nina had known me too long and too well.

There were two things on my mind, but I was only ready to talk about one of them. I still hadn't figured out how to deal with the information I had about Timothy Wheaton and Philip Maur, but Nina and I had already fought once in the past few days about my talking to the police, so I chose the safer issue and told her about my daughter's request that I not go to Boston for the preview.

There was a lot of pedestrian traffic that afternoon since it was one of those energizing fall days when everyone who lives in cities like New York and Paris and London takes to the streets. If only it could stay like this, we all say to one another about the bracing air and vibrant trees.

"Being a motherless daughter makes me question every damned decision," I said as we walked downtown on Madison Avenue, too engrossed in the conversation to do any window-shopping.

"Is that it? You didn't have a mother for long enough, so you don't know what to do?"

"Why can't that be it?"

"Well, even if you'd had a mother for your whole adolescence, you still wouldn't be prepared for this particular problem."

"I'd have road maps."

"You might. But that's too obvious. I think something else happens when Dulcie exerts her will like this."

I sighed. I really couldn't expect less of her, could I? Nina was first and foremost a therapist. "What?"

"Morgan, when Dulcie told you that she didn't want you to go with her, do you remember how you felt?"

"I just concentrated on how to react. On what to say to give her support and make her feel that I would take her seriously, that I love—"

"Stop. You can make me so mad sometimes. Are you listening to yourself?"

We'd gotten to the gray granite building on the corner of Fifth Avenue and Fifty-seventh Street. The art deco lines, clean and sleek, were from an older time, and the familiarity was comforting. The parts of New York that never change are landmarks for those of us who have lived here all our lives. The hamburger shop on Madison Avenue and Sixty-third Street where my mother took me when I was six was still there. So was Saks Fifth Avenue, where my father used to take me on my birthday for shopping sprees. The Christmas tree that arrived every year at Rockefeller Center brought back memories of each Christmas when I took Dulcie to the lighting. There were other places, too, but some were gone, torn down to make room for new buildings. I missed those signposts of the past.

I sighed. "Do we do this on the street, right now, Nina?"

"No. Right now we go into the store and act very civilized and enjoy the rarefied air, but we continue this after we've picked up your gift. What is it, anyway?"

To celebrate Dulcie's lead in *The Secret Garden*, I'd ordered a monogrammed gold key on a chain, symbolizing the one Mary Lennox found that led her into the hidden space that had been abandoned for a decade.

"A necklace."

We walked through the glass doors and into the quiet hush of the jewelry store. Little blue boxes from Tiffany, with their white satin ribbons, were a luxury that I wanted Dulcie to enjoy as much as I had when my father had given them to me. My sweet sixteen present, my high school graduation gift, my college graduation gift, had all come from Tiffany. As had my wedding ring. And Mitch's. Dulcie's baby rattle and her first baby cup.

Nina stood by while the salesman showed me the gold key, carefully pointing out the inscription on the back: the date of the opening along with "To Dulcie. Love, Mom and Dad."

On our way back to the office, Nina and I stopped at an espresso bar, where we sat at a small table that had just been vacated. We ordered cappuccinos and small sandwiches.

"Okay, let's get back to it," she said after the waitress had left.

"Do we have to?"

She nodded.

"I don't remember where we were," I lied.

"I know you too well for that, Morgan. You have never forgotten where you were in an interrupted conversation in your life. What I asked was how you felt when Dulcie told you that she didn't want you to go to Boston with her."

I started to think. Nina interrupted.

"No, no thinking. Just tell me. Fast. How did you feel?"

"That she didn't want me."

"Who didn't want you?"

"That my mother—" I stopped. Shocked. Even with everything I knew about psychoanalysis and with all the psychotherapy I'd had, I hadn't made the connection myself.

"Dulcie going into acting is bringing more of your memories of your mother to the surface, isn't it?"

My throat tightened. I nodded.

"She loved acting so much," Nina said, her voice softening as she, too, thought about her old friend.

"I remember how she used to get dressed up to go to tryouts. I'd sit on the edge of the bathtub and watch her meticulously apply her makeup and spray on her perfume. I'd wait for her to come home, too. She was always so excited when she got back, telling me about everything that had happened and how sure she was about getting the role and that when she did, we'd move into a bigger apartment but..." I was remembering too much now and didn't want to go on. I'd thought of something I'd never realized before. "Nina, she wasn't going to tryouts, was she? She was going to bars, right? She was trying to pick up guys so they'd pay for her drinks and her drugs."

She nodded.

"And they lived happily never after," I said, repeating

the line that had made my mother famous for a few heartbeats and that ultimately had done more damage than good, spoiling her for a life that would never live up to what it had been before. She'd been seduced by her brief stint at stardom and nothing ever came close: not her marriage, not her family, not her friends, not even me.

And I was letting my daughter step into that same spotlight.

I shuddered.

Nina took my hand. "Dulcie isn't your mother, sweetie. She's your daughter. And she has a mother. She has you."

Thirty-One

The following Monday evening the group from the Scarlet Society was silent and somber as they gathered in my office. It was our second meeting and I still didn't have a handle on them.

"Did you see the newspapers on Friday and over the weekend about Timothy Wheaton?" Shelby asked me even before everyone was seated.

I nodded.

"He was someone else we knew. From the society."

"Really? That's very disturbing. And probably very frightening for you." I had guessed at what she was telling me but acted as if I didn't. How could I explain prior knowledge? "I'm very sorry about Timothy. About your loss," I said, addressing the whole group.

Shelby nodded, accepting the condolences.

"Should we get started?"

No one said anything for a few seconds. They looked at one another. Anne spoke. "There's no way that this could be a coincidence." Once again she was all in black and wearing the oversize sunglasses that hid so much of her face.

"How does that make you feel?"

Ellen answered with a hostility that surprised me. She wore a forest-green suit that looked like Chanel, and a large emerald ring gleamed on her left hand. "How are we supposed to feel? We knew these men. Intimately. For years we shared something private with them. Something that was special. And amazing."

"In the paper, the police said that they haven't yet discovered where their bodies are," Davina said. Her voice was not as robust as I remembered it from the week before.

"That's just a matter of time," said Liz, who once again was wearing jeans, a button-down shirt, soft brown suede blazer and boots. Her briefcase was in her lap and her elbows rested on it.

Bethany, who had been mostly silent throughout the first session, spoke up. She had a slight southern accent and looked familiar to me from the tape now that I had seen it more than once. "You just don't have any emotional attachment to this."

Several of the other women sat up straighter in their chairs. Davina leaned forward. Ginny uncrossed her arms. They were preparing, but for what?

"Exactly what is that supposed to mean?" Liz asked in a voice laced with acid.

"That you don't care about any of this the way the rest of us do. You were angry with them all, anyway. You've been complaining for months," Bethany explained.

"Angry?" Liz laughed.

I didn't interrupt. This interaction was important—not just for them, but for me. I needed to have them act out their relationships so that I could learn how they related to one another.

"You told me you were," Bethany said.

"That was a private conversation."

"It might help if you talked about it with all of us, Liz," I suggested.

She didn't say anything.

"Why were you angry at Timothy and Philip?"

Liz remained quiet.

Ellen started to speak, "I think that what Liz means—"

"I think it would be better for Liz to explain herself," I interrupted, then refocused my gaze on Liz. "Now that we know you were angry, why don't you tell us why? I know it's very difficult to be angry with someone only to have them suddenly die. We're left with feelings that we don't know how to process. Regrets and guilt are difficult to deal with on your own."

"Regrets?" Liz's high-pitched laugh verged on hysteria. "Everything is fine with the whole concept of the Scarlet Society as long as the men want you. But when they don't, all the same old shitty problems of being a woman are right there, waiting for you, taunting you. It's no different than in society at large."

No one said anything for a minute.

"What are you talking about?" Anne finally asked in an empathetic voice.

Liz crossed her arms over her chest as if she was going into hibernation and didn't answer. I let a full thirty seconds pass.

"What if someone is stalking the men from our group?" Shelby asked, directing her question at me.

"Why are you changing the subject?"

"I think we need to talk about this."

"Why, Shelby? Do you think that's what is happening?"

Out of the corner of my eye, I saw that Liz sat immobile, her face rigid with anger.

"Well, I don't think it's a coincidence that two of the men who are part of our organization have been killed in the same way, do you?" Shelby asked.

"On more than one level, no. I don't believe in coincidences."

"And other than members of the society, no one knows who we are," Martha said. "Hell, we don't even know who one another is. Not really." She wore tinted glasses that evening, not dark enough to hide her eyes, but blue and large enough that they altered her appearance. She was dressed casually in black jeans, a pale blue sweater and a herringbone jacket. "How could someone figure out who the men were, short of them having revealed it?"

"Philip wouldn't have told anyone," Anne said. "He had a wife and children and a public life that mattered to him. He wouldn't have told anyone. The only way he could have both us and his career was to keep our secret."

"We all feel that," Davina said.

"All of us," Ginny echoed.

The room lapsed into a moment of silence.

"What are we supposed to do now, though?" Anne asked. "Should we keep going to meetings? Should we close the society?"

"No." Shelby was adamant, and shook her head as she spoke. "No."

Around the room others nodded, agreeing with her.

"You seem so certain," I said.

"We have to trust one another," Shelby continued. "Everything about the Scarlet Society is based on trust. We are stronger than any outside force. What we do is our right. No one can scare us into giving up those rights."

When she made statements like that, I could feel the collective body sway in her direction. They didn't look at her with blind devotion. Shelby was not a guru to them, but she was their chieftain. And they—women who were stronger than most in their hunger and their need for power—yielded to her.

"The newspaper didn't say anything about them belonging to the group," Liz said grudgingly. "How do we know that their deaths are connected through us? Isn't it possible for two men to have been killed in Manhattan without it being a conspiracy?"

"It might be helpful to talk about your individual feelings for Philip and Timothy instead of trying to figure out who perpetrated the crimes," I said, addressing the group. For one thing, I wanted to get them back on track. The purpose of our sessions was to help the women involved deal with their emotions over the deaths. Feelings that they had no other outlet for except in this room.

They waited, all of them, for someone to go first. And I waited with them. Finally, Martha spoke.

"I don't know how to do this."

"Just talk about them. About what was special about them. What you remember."

She stared at me for a time. "Philip could—" She broke off.

"What is it?" I asked.

"Whatever I say, it's all going to be about sex. About how he was so happy when you told him what to do, when you pushed him to hold off on coming, the longer you forced him—see? It's wrong. We can't talk about them like that, about what they were like to fuck."

"Why?"

"Because…" But she didn't have a reason.

Next, Shelby tried. "Timothy had very strong arms. He worked out. He could lift you up and keep you in the air and while he was doing that he would be high up inside you." She shook her head. "This is more complicated than I thought it would be."

"Why do you feel that it's wrong to talk about these men the way you knew them best? You had sex with them. Did you know them any other way?"

"I talked to them—both of them," Anne said. "Often. About what they liked, about why they liked it. That's part of how I was with them. To hear them talk about what it felt like to be powerless. To have me be the one in charge. But how do you talk about a lover after he's died when he wasn't in any other part of your life?"

"I think they were both full of shit," Liz said.

All heads turned to her.

"They were supposed to be willing to do whatever we wanted. But they couldn't. Not with all of us."

"It's awful for you to say that," Anne said.

"Why is it awful?" I asked. "Tell Liz why what she said bothers you, describe how it makes you feel. Don't judge her."

"You don't understand," Ellen said to me in a strident voice. "She's jealous of us. She thinks that since she's older than most of us, the men aren't interested in her. But it's not that. It's her attitude. The way she demeans them."

"I do not demean them." Liz's mouth had disappeared into a thin, angry line.

"Of course you do. To you it's not just about power and control. You ask them to be your slaves. You want them to cower at your feet. You want them to be afraid of you and some of the things you ask them to do are disgusting."

"How do you know what I ask them to do?"

Ellen smiled. Wickedly. It occurred to me that she had been waiting to say this for a long time.

"Mark told me. He said that you asked him to go into the bathroom with you and to—"

"Shut the fuck up!" Liz shouted.

Anne started to cry. Martha got up and took Anne in her arms. Ginny was saying something to Liz, but over the rest of the commotion I couldn't hear it.

"Everyone, please sit down. Shelby, Ginny, sit down. Let's wait till everyone can hear you—"

Liz stood, her bag slung over her shoulder, her briefcase under her arm. "Are you leaving?" I asked her. "We still have forty-five minutes left to the session."

"I don't know why I came in the first place. I'm an outsider here. They all play at this game. They don't take it for real. They think they are being powerful, but it's like little girls playing at growing up."

"Liz, it would benefit everyone if you sat back down and stayed. You all are going through this together and leaving isn't going to be helpful, not for you or the group."

She continued to stand, hovering above the rest of them. The light cast shadows on her face and the furrows in her brows seemed deeper. She certainly wasn't pretty. Her hard features were jagged and too large. But her eyes, which were deep green with long lashes, were catlike and mysterious. Her hair was blond, thick and curly, but for some reason didn't seem to fit her personality or the rest of her looks.

"These men debased themselves for us," she said. "They came to us because they wanted us to abuse them. Order them around. Treat them worse than they had ever or could ever treat any women. We like to pretend that what we do is fine. It isn't. It's perversion. I'm not happy about it, but it's the way I want my sex. I don't want to be grabbed—I want to do the grabbing. I want to tell a man to walk to me holding his cock in his hands and begging me to let him get closer. So what if I wanted to see what it would be like to have them as slaves? Isn't that what men have had women doing for them for years? Love them? Admire them? Eulogize them? None of us can do that. We used their hard cocks and versatile tongues. We didn't love them. We didn't get to know them. We made them do our bidding. They liked being surrounded by hot women wanting hot sex. They liked looking at tight asses and high tits. You don't know what it's like when you look at them and they look away." Liz focused on Ellen, then Anne, Ginny and finally Shelby. "You don't know what it's like when you see them hoping that you don't pick them because they aren't so sure that they can perform for you." She was choking back tears, not the way a woman does, but the way a man will refuse to allow himself the luxury of weeping.

The others watched, some with compassion on their faces, others with contempt. Only Shelby, who was closer in age to Liz, got up and went to her. She took her by the hand and, without saying a word, led her back to her seat.

"It doesn't matter. You belong here. With us. We have to hold on. Especially now. All of us."

Liz sat back down, but her glance remained focused on the briefcase she held in her lap like protective armor.

"There is going to be a memorial prayer service for Philip on Friday," Ellen said to me once everyone had settled down. "And some of us want to go."

"But we can't," Shelby said before I had a chance to respond. She seemed suddenly exhausted. "We have an honor-bound agreement. Showing up anywhere in public together—even two of us—would threaten the society."

She turned to me. "This is part of our problem. We simply don't know what to do. How to handle our grief. How to deal with the fact that we can't do something as simple as go to a memorial service. And it's not like we have months to spend to figure this stuff out. Is there some kind of intervention therapy you can do with us?"

"Let's use the rest of our time tonight to talk out those issues and focus on the memorial." I looked around the room. "Are any of you having a hard time accepting that you can't go to the service?"

"I am," Anne whispered. "We knew this man. We were an important part of his life. No one seems to think that matters, but I do. I think it matters a lot. I know how he smells." Her voice cracked as she corrected herself. "How he smelled. How the inside of his mouth tasted. I know how his bare arms felt around my back." She started to cry and stopped speaking.

"No. You're not the only one," Martha said. "I think it matters."

Anne looked surprised.

"How does that make you feel—that you can't go?"

"It makes her feel like shit. What kind of stupid question is that?" Ellen said.

"Ellen, it would be better to let Martha herself tell us all how she feels."

Ellen glared at me. I wasn't surprised by the level of aggression she exhibited. It was one of the more interesting things about this group that so many of them shared specific personality traits. While they weren't all beautiful, they were comfortable with their bodies. That in itself was unusual for a group of this many women, except when you considered the interest that they all shared. By the very nature of belonging to the society, they could not be shy or intimidated. Every one of these women was—at least sexually—aggressive. Even when I put together a group of sex addicts, I worked hard to ensure that each member of the group had different issues and handled their needs in unlike ways: that some were aggressors and others were passive.

"Martha?" I looked at her.

"What is confusing about this is that, while I know we have rules that dictate we only deal with the men at the society in a sexual manner, they are people, too. And two of them are dead. And they knew us. And we knew them. And one of them is having a memorial service and I want to be there."

"Oh, isn't that sweet," Cara spat out. She hadn't spoken at all before, neither in the last session or the present one. She had dark olive skin and flashing black eyes and wore an elaborate Hermès scarf tied over her hair.

"Comments like that are not really helpful," I said. "Tell us how you feel."

"This is ridiculous. We use these guys. They are hard bodies, willing hands, they are a way for us to finally get what we want with no strings. We work damn hard at making sure the men we let in want to be treated the way we want to treat them. This is not about feelings."

"You know, that is such a stereotype that it's almost laughable," Davina said. "Just because we use them doesn't mean we can't have feelings for them."

"Whether I should have feelings or not—the point is I do," Anne said to Cara. "And I am not embarrassed to say I do. And I want to go to the service being held for Philip and pray along with everyone else that his body is found and that he can be put to rest. I think it's horrible what's happened to him. I haven't been able to stop thinking about him laid out somewhere, dead. How was he killed? Why was he killed?"

"Jeezus," Cara muttered.

I looked at her. "Cara, what is wrong with Anne caring about what happened to Philip? Did you know him?"

"No, but I fucked him." She glowered at the rest of the room. "You know what is so damn hypocritical about this is that we are all consenting adults who belong to a god-damn fuck club. It's not a dating service. Most of these guys are married. We are not their mistresses. If anything, they serve us. They have crushes on us. We do not have feelings for them."

"Don't you have any feelings for any of the men you have been with at the society?" I asked her.

"No."

"How long have you been a member?" I asked her.

"Nine years."

"How often do you go to the society?"

"About two or three times a month." She leaned back in her chair.

"And do you always spend time with different men?"

"No. I have preferences."

"Based on what?"

"Based on their performance."

"Do you talk to the men you are with?"

"With the men I choose?" she corrected me in a clipped tone.

"All right. With the men you choose."

"Yes, I talk to them."

"What do you talk to them about?"

"What is the point of these questions?" she asked venomously.

"Why are you here if you have so much disdain for the

process?" Shelby asked. "I made it really clear when I suggested that we come to Dr. Snow that only those of us who thought that Philip's death was an issue for them should come."

Cara didn't answer her.

"I think that's a fair question, Cara," I said. But it was also too direct a question. I could have guessed as to what the problem was. But my being blunt wouldn't help anyone.

"I think that what Cara is feeling is confusion," Davina said, with amazing perception.

This wasn't the first time that she had tried to explain how someone else was feeling. My guess was that she was either a lawyer or had some kind of psychoanalytic training herself. All her responses and questions and reactions to what went on in the group so far seemed impersonal, as if she were looking at the proceedings from a distance that no one else but Liz exhibited.

"Cara, are you confused?"

"Only about why we are even questioning our original decision about not breaking our rules. They are very clear. We do not communicate with other members. We do not engage in social activity with other members. We don't try to contact any of the men or have any kind of relationship with them outside of the society."

"And have you kept to those rules over the entire time that you have been in the society?" I asked her, hoping that my instincts were right. While she'd been talking she'd uncrossed her arms and seemed to stretch them out, palms open to the room, almost in supplication. It had been a small movement but I'd noticed it.

"And have you kept to those rules during the time that you have been in the society?" I asked again.

She didn't answer. But Liz did.

"No, she hasn't."

Cara turned and glared at her. The look was vicious. Violent. Her eyes narrowed to slits, flashing even more brightly.

No one said anything for a minute.

"Cara, is there something you'd like to tell us?"

"No. Liz is lying."

Liz was smiling in the way a small boy does after he's put a frog in his teacher's pocketbook. There was something between these two women that we would have to deal with eventually. But for now, the group had other issues that I felt were timely.

"Cara, are you angry?"

"You're damn straight I am angry."

"At whom?"

"At her." She pointed to Liz.

"Why?"

"For lying."

"I am not lying. I saw you and—"

"Shut up, you fucking bitch. You're just jealous. You're jealous of every one of us and you know it. It's not easy for you anymore. You're always saying it. That age is a terrible thing. You can't exercise enough. You can't figure out how to stop the process. You don't like how the men react to you anymore and—"

"Cara, this isn't helpful. Throwing accusations across the room isn't going to do any good. Let's try to get back on track and deal with how you feel. About what you are going through."

"I don't feel anything right now except anger at the mistake that we are all going to make if any of us shows up at the memorial service." She'd crossed her arms over her chest again. There was not going to be any way to reach her now. My guess was that she had seen someone outside of the club, but I couldn't confront her about that until there was another opening.

For the rest of the session, Cara stayed silent and the rest of us talked about the service that was going to be held at the end of the week. In the end, everyone agreed that as much as some of them wanted to go, it wouldn't be right. It wouldn't do Philip any good, and ultimately they were honor-bound to uphold the commitment that they had made to him. And to each member of the group.

"We only have one thing that binds us to one another and allows us to be part of this, and that is our oath not to put any of us in jeopardy of our activities being divulged," Shelby said toward the end of the ninety minutes.

It had been a good session. They had talked about their sense of loss and worked on their confusion about how to deal with a man they had been intimate with in one sense but knew nothing about in another.

By the time they left, I believed that they would all keep their word, stay away from the service and keep silent.

Thirty-Two

By 7:00 p.m. on Monday night, Jordain and Perez's office was littered with used foam coffee cups and takeout food wrappers.

"Why the hell don't we have anything? How can you kill two men and hide the bodies for this long? And now a third? Shit. Where are they?" Perez said as he poured himself yet another cup of the strong chicory-laced coffee that Jordain had just made. It was their fourth pot that day.

"You really asking that?" Jordain asked.

Perez shot him a look. Obviously, it hadn't been an actual question. The two detectives were frustrated, tired and angry with the killer, who was so elusive.

"How much you think Delilah would hate it that we've given him a woman's name?" Perez asked.

They'd taken to calling the anonymous killer "Delilah" because of the locks of hair that had been sent to Betsy Young, along with all three sets of photographs.

Yes, three. The third had come in early that morning.

"He would despise it. An affront to his power. To his masculinity. We're really getting him but good by calling him that."

For the second time in less than five minutes, Perez shot his partner an exasperated look.

The phone rang, as it had been doing all afternoon, but all calls were being intercepted. Half of them were from the managing editor of the *New York Times*, who was waiting for the police to give him the go-ahead to run the next story in the series, which announced that there was a third victim. Grant Firth. Forty-two. Doctor of orthopedic surgery at New York Hospital. Father of three girls. Husband of Donna Firth, who was a medical reporter for the *Wall Street Journal*.

"You know that's Hastings on the phone," Perez said.

"Of course it's him. He can't stand it. Every minute that goes by is one more minute lost. And if he loses too many of them, he loses his lead story for tomorrow."

There was nothing about this case that pleased either detective, except perhaps watching Harry Hastings wait and beg. The paper could run the story when they said so. And not before.

The lab reports had all come back without a single break. The envelopes were a mess since they'd been through the postal system. There was no saliva on the inside flap or under the stamps. There were no stray hairs inside. Just the clippings put there on purpose.

There was one fiber in the second envelope. A small white thread, no more than an eighth of an inch long. Frayed at the end. Meaningless on its own.

The paper that the photographs had been printed on was standard and sold in almost every photography-supply store in the United States, as well as hundreds of stores online. Even if they found out where it had been bought, what were the chances that the photographer would have used a credit card?

It didn't matter. They had experts working on tracing the stock.

The nine-by-twelve manila envelopes were even more common than the photo paper. The postmarks were at least interesting. The first envelope had been sent from midtown Manhattan. The second from Port Chester, New York, about a half hour away from the city. And the third had been mailed from Harlem.

They were working on finding the pattern to those three locations. But it was too early for them to lock in on it.

The footsteps were light, but since both men were waiting for her they looked up even before Officer Butler walked in.

She was smiling, which Jordain thought was the most beautiful thing he'd seen in at least thirty-two hours. "What do you have?" he asked.

"The hair sample on Firth."

Both men had leaned forward and were listening hard. "Yeah?"

"There was some blood on it. And in the blood are traces of Thorazine. We checked with Firth's wife. No history of any prescription drugs. No antidepressants. No mood elevators. Nothing."

"Which means that he was drugged before he was killed," Jordain said. "Or the drug killed him."

Butler nodded.

"How hard is it to get Thorazine?" Perez asked. "And how hard is it to OD on the stuff?"

"I'm ahead of you on that," Butler said. "As soon as I saw the report, I put in a call to the M.E."

"And?"

"And I'm waiting for him to call me back."

"More waiting," Jordain said.

"There's something else," Butler said.

"Yes?" Both men looked back at her.

"There's another substance on one of the hair samples. The lab guys aren't sure what it is. A chemical. They're running more tests now. Should have some information in a few hours, if we are lucky."

"So far there hasn't been any luck on this case," Perez lamented.

"Maybe that's about to change," Jordain said.

Perez smiled at his partner the way a parent smiles at his child on Christmas Eve when the kid is putting out cookies and milk for Santa.

"It's nice that you can still dream."

"If you stop dreaming, you might as well stop living," Jordain said.

It was true. He believed that. Even doing what he did every day, even seeing what he saw, even knowing what he knew about the human psyche and the ability man had to be evil.

"It's that damn piano," Perez said. "You're a fucking romantic because of that damn piano."

In answer, Jordain put his hands on the edge of his desk as if it were a keyboard and moved his fingers up and down, miming playing. He scatted along with the action, his voice giving real life to a jazz riff that he'd written. Perez had seen his partner do this a hundred times, and so had Butler, but they still stared in wonder at the way Jordain's hands moved with a grace that wasn't expected, and the way his voice moved them even though they were tough cops and should know better.

Thirty-Three

My last patient on Tuesday left at 4:55 p.m.—ten minutes late because we had broken through a major issue and I was loath to rush her out. I hurried to the staff meeting in the upstairs conference room that usually began on time.

There were eight therapists at the institute, all of whom specialized in sex therapy, and our weekly conclaves gave us a chance to talk with one another about our patients and their treatments. Nina—and her husband before her—believed that one of the strengths of the Butterfield Institute was the combined expertise of several doctors and therapists under one roof. Indeed, for me, being able to consult with others had proved preferable to working alone, as most members of my profession did.

That night, the discussion was focused on one of Nina's patients whom she thought needed to begin working with a sex surrogate. She wanted our opinions—surrogacy being the last resort.

We'd been going around and around about whether there was any other impotency treatment Nina might try first, but no one offered any options that Nina hadn't already exhausted. She looked at me and said, "You haven't had much to add, Morgan. No ideas?"

"It sounds like you've covered pretty much everything but the surrogate."

She nodded but was frowning. "We moved off of that about five minutes ago."

I stared at her.

"We've been talking about which surrogate would be best in the situation."

"Sorry."

"What's going on with your caseload?" she asked.

It wasn't required, but it was expected that at some point in the meeting we'd each do an update on some of our most complicated cases. But the only thing I needed to discuss was the one thing I didn't want to discuss. I tried to think of every other patient I was seeing, to dredge up some valid question and get a conversation going and move Nina's attention—and her fierce eyes—off me.

"Morgan?"

I still hadn't said anything and she was waiting. This wasn't like me, I knew. Anxiety was making my blood race. I forced myself to just say it.

"I need to talk about going to the police," I said.

Nina's eyebrows arched. "I thought we covered that."

I shook my head.

"Going to the police about what?" Simon Weiss asked.

There were no windows in the conference room. Just dark green walls, comfortable black leather chairs, a verdant marble table, and antique prints of maps on the walls. From where I was seated, I could see a line of etchings of Europe on maps from the seventeenth century. The blue of the ocean was slightly faded, but the reds, browns and yellows of the countries were still fairly intense. I couldn't keep staring at the prints. Taking a breath, I launched into an explanation of what had been going on with the Scarlet Society, what I had seen at the police station, and what I felt I needed to do.

"The only thing Morgan hasn't mentioned," Nina said in a tone that was harsher than normal, "is that we already talked about this and I advised her not to talk to the police again."

"You did. But I just don't think that's the right decision."

"It's the only decision that you can make under the circumstances," she countered.

Around us, Simon and the rest of the staff must have been aware of the subtext of the conversation. Everyone knew of Nina's overdeveloped and irrational anger at the NYPD.

"Please, Morgan, can't you just trust me on this?"

I looked at Simon, my closest friend at the institute, imploring him with my eyes to step in. He did. Of course he did. I could always count on him, and I gave him a half smile before the fact to thank him.

"Nina, what's your objection? If the women in the group haven't given Morgan this information, if it's something she saw on her own, there's no reason she can't go to the police."

There were murmurs and assents from two other therapists.

"I don't think you can, Morgan," Helen Grant said. She was one of the older members of the staff and had been handpicked by Sam, even before he married Nina, to work at Butterfield. She was elderly then. Now she was approaching ancient, but she still came in five days a week and saw patients. "No. Morgan can't go to the police. She has a commitment to her group. There is nothing she can offer up that will help, if the society is as secret as she says it is." Her white curls bobbed with the intensity of her next words. "It is not our job to solve crimes. Haven't we gone through enough of that around here?"

Nina was looking at me sternly, differently from how she looked at any other member of her staff. She was frowning the way I'd frown at Dulcie when she pushed me to the point of exasperation.

"I am not a child," I said more stridently than I'd wanted to. "I am not unaware of the boundaries. I don't have any reason not to tell detectives Jordain and Perez what I saw in those photographs."

"Well. We're done for tonight," Nina said as she put her mug down on the table.

The crack was not as loud as it was unexpected, and everyone stared at the shards of white china and the tea that pooled on the table. No one moved except for Nina, who leaned over and started to pick up the broken mug.

"Don't do that—" I started to say, about to warn her of exactly what happened. She cut her forefinger on one of the slivers of porcelain. A droplet of bright blood appeared. She stared at it as if it were an intruder. With the blood starting to drip off her finger, she looked up and over at me.

"You understand that I believe you are about to make a serious mistake."

I turned and picked up a paper napkin from the sideboard where the coffee, tea, cups and a plate of cookies were. "Here," I said as I reached her side. "Your finger is bleeding."

She took it from me without thanking me. Suddenly, I became aware that the room was too quiet. I looked around. We were alone. The other members of the institute had slipped out.

"Why are you so dead set on doing exactly what I don't think you should do? Why would you bring that up here? It was between us."

"No, Nina, it wasn't."

"I told you the other day that—"

"This isn't a decision about me personally that I talked over with my godmother. This is about a therapist, a group of patients and two murders. I brought it up in front of the members of the Butterfield Institute because the institute needs to make a decision about it."

She looked stricken. As if I'd pushed her off a narrow parapet and she was afraid that she was falling.

"It isn't about the institute. It's not about your patients. You know it isn't." She then walked out, slamming the door behind her and leaving me by myself in the conference room.

Thirty-Four

I pulled on my black suede coat and left the building. Downstairs, I wasn't sure what direction to take.

Nina and I had never fought like that. She'd never walked out on me. She was the only woman I'd known for my whole life. I looked back at the building and could see that her office light was still on.

Should I go back? If I did, what would I say? That I didn't want her to be upset? That I hated fighting with her? I could tell her how anxious her suddenly impersonal tone of voice made me feel. But none of those things would matter if I couldn't also tell her that she was right and that I was not going to tell the police anything.

And I wasn't ready to tell her that.

I thought about calling Simon on his cell phone, but even continuing to discuss what Nina had done and how she had reacted seemed to be a transgression. This wasn't purely professional. It was personal. I had friends outside of the institute, but it would be a breach of professional conduct to talk to them, because to explain it I would have had to explain too much about the Scarlet Society and the photographs.

I was still standing on the corner, waiting for the light

to change, still trying to figure out what to do. Running down my options. Leaving out the most obvious one.

Well, I could go home. But to an empty house where I'd just sit and brood. Dulcie was with Mitch. Joint custody might be the best thing for my daughter, but I missed her when she wasn't home. My ex-husband's connection to the New York City independent film community was, at this point in my daughter's life, a constant attraction. And in the last few months the custody leaned in Mitch's favor.

I could go to a movie. No, I probably wouldn't even notice what I was watching.

The light changed and I crossed the street. The sky above was gray and crowded with storm clouds. There was a nor'easter blowing in and the leaves on the street swirled in fast circles. The shorter days and the cooler air had not crept up on us but rushed in. It had just been summer, hadn't it? Without making any conscious decision as to why, I turned left and started walking downtown. I'd gotten to Sixty-second when it started raining. I didn't have an umbrella and I didn't want to ruin my coat.

Looking at the street sign, I tried to figure out what to do. Barney's department store was only half a block away. At least I could buy an umbrella there.

I ran there and rushed in, brushing the water off my coat. The store was open until eight. I could look around and then buy the umbrella if it was still raining. Strolling past the glass cases, I stared down at glittering baubles. One-of-a-kind pieces rested on velvet, price tags hidden, waiting for someone to try them on.

I headed to the escalator. The umbrella could wait.

I knew just where I was going. The fourth floor. Shoes. That was something that would keep my mind from obsessing about Nina.

* * *

They were chocolate-brown suede pumps. High heels. I reached out and touched them. So soft and smooth, my finger left a slight impression. I knew that they were impractical. That I'd wind up buying clothes to go with the shoes since my wardrobe was made up of entirely too much black, but I'd like to get a brown suit. Something that was snug around my waist. That opened a little bit lower at the neck than I would wear to work.

A saleswoman interrupted my daydream to ask if she could help, and I gave her my shoe size, sat down, slipped off my flats and waited, watching the other women who were doing the same thing I was.

What were they shopping away? Fights with husbands, problems at work? Sons who weren't doing well at school? Daughters who were on diets that left their hair lank and stringy?

How many of us here really needed these shoes? Or the chocolate-brown suit I had in my mind. We dress ourselves and redress ourselves, obsess over how we can make ourselves look better, fool ourselves that there is nothing wrong with spending money as a reward for the things that are wrong in our lives.

The saleswoman arrived with the open shoebox, and despite myself, I felt a little jolt of adrenaline as she held the right shoe out for me to slip my foot into.

I stood up and walked the few feet to the mirror. My legs weren't bad and the shoes made them look better. I hadn't worn heels for years, until one of my clients recently inspired me to start again. What I had discovered when buying high heels and lingerie again was that I enjoyed shopping for lovely things. I wanted to look better. Oh, come on—I wanted to look sexier. To pass by a window on the street and see in its reflection a man taking a second look at me.

I handed the woman my charge card and waited for her to ring up the purchase.

The women in the Scarlet Society had not given up what I'd given up. They pursued sexual thrills despite a society that didn't offer an easy way for them to do that. They got what they wanted in business and they wanted to get it sexually, too. Was there anything wrong with that?

Shopping bag in hand, I walked away from the shoes and began looking at the clothes on the rest of the floor. I wanted to see if there were any chocolate-brown suits.

Nope. Nothing on four.

I went up another escalator and started browsing through the racks on five.

When I saw the brown velvet dress, I knew exactly why I wanted it and where I was going to wear it. To Dulcie's Broadway opening. With the shoes.

It had stopped raining by the time I left the store. The doorman glanced at my two shopping bags and asked me if I wanted a taxi. I nodded, waiting while he stepped out into the street, held up his hand and hailed one for me.

I fished a dollar out of my bag and handed it to him as he opened the door. Then, making sure I was settled in, he closed it.

I knew what the odor was in the first ten seconds. The driver had been smoking a cigar in the cab before picking me up.

"Sorry," I said. "Can you pull over? I'm sorry but I can't stand the cigar smell."

Cursing, he did. I let myself out of the cab. We'd only gone ten feet.

"Whatsa matter, lady, you crazy?" he called after me.

As I stepped up on the curb I thought about it. *Whatsa matter, lady, you crazy?* Such a throwaway phrase. So simple to say. No, I wasn't crazy. I knew what the word really meant. I had seen crazy people. I had seen people go crazy. My mother. My patients. In June, I'd seen a man go crazy and murder a series of prostitutes because he thought he could save them. Five women had died.

And there was someone else out there who was crazy. Kidnapping men, killing them and taking their photographs.

I always wondered how the courts could declare that anyone who had taken someone else's life was legally sane. It had to be an insane act to take a life that was not yours.

Thirty-Five

I walked the twenty blocks to the police station, hoping that I could convince myself to turn around and go home before I reached the front door. In my head, I ran through every one of Nina's arguments and some she hadn't thought of, but none was convincing. By the time I reached the precinct house I had worked out exactly what I could say and what I couldn't say in order to stick to the rules of my profession.

Noah was smart and he wouldn't need much. I would not have to betray anything the members of the Scarlet Society had told me. I'd just show Noah what I'd seen and he'd follow it through.

If, of course, he hadn't figured it out already. And if he had, so much the better. I'd pick up my bags, take myself home, get into bed and be able to sleep, because although I'd done the wrong thing according to Nina, I would have done it for the right reason. To save someone's life.

And no one but Noah would ever have to know.

My heart was beating loudly in my chest and my skin felt clammy as I walked up to the front desk, gave my name and asked for Detective Jordain. "I'd appreciate it if you'd tell him that it's important and that it will only take a few minutes."

The young officer dialed the phone, spoke into it, listened and then hung up.

"He asked if you would please wait for him in his office. He'll be with you shortly. I'll have someone take you there."

The corridor was busy—it was always busy here—and no one paid any attention to my escort or me. We turned the corner. Up ahead, coming from the opposite direction, were Detectives Jordain and Perez, and a woman who looked familiar.

You aren't aware of how quickly the synapses work: your eyes send the message to the brain, which supplies you with conscious information before you even have time to realize you are working on figuring it out.

Of course, the combination of pressed blue jeans, soft brown suede blazer and the ever-present worn leather briefcase were familiar. It had been the dark brown hair that had thrown me.

In my office, as Liz, a long-time member of the Scarlet Society, she was a blonde. But her eyes were the same and they were staring at me, as shocked as I was, asking me exactly the same silent question I was asking her.

What are you doing here?

What trust are you breaking?

I didn't wait to talk to Jordain. I had been completely wrong to go there. My escort was gone but I knew where to go. Turning, I rushed back the same way I'd come, as fast as I could without running, the shopping bags hitting my legs.

Out in the street it was raining again. I cursed myself that I'd forgotten to buy the umbrella at Barney's, pulled up my collar, tucked my head down and just kept walking, figuring I'd find a cab soon enough. After three blocks, I did.

I gave the driver my address, sat back, opened my bag, pulled out a roll of peppermints, popped two in my mouth and bit down, knowing that the instant intense scent of mint would obliterate the stale body odor that permeated the air in the enclosed space.

Inhaling the sharp, clean scent, I concentrated on the sensation of speeding through the nighttime streets and the sound of rain hitting the car's roof.

Thirty-Six

❧

It was just eight-thirty but it had been a long day and I was exhausted. I'd only been home fifteen minutes. The shopping bags were still in the front hall where I'd dropped them when I got in. I'd taken off my work clothes and had changed into leggings, a cashmere cardigan, and a pair of black suede ballet slippers. I'd even had time to stick some frozen thing in the oven and pour myself a glass of vodka with a splash of Rose's lime juice when the buzzer rang.

It wasn't really a surprise. I had gotten to know Jordain better than I'd thought in the short time we'd known each other. That he wanted to know why I had turned and left the police station when I'd obviously come to tell him something was not unexpected. But the reality of him filling the door frame shocked me.

I stared at the drops of rain on the broad shoulders of his leather jacket and in his silver-streaked hair. How long was he going to want to stay? How could I get him to leave?

"Can I come in?" he asked.

His eyes were too blue. "What will happen if I say no?"

"I'll come in, anyway."

"I guessed as much." I opened the door wider and he walked into my apartment.

"Is Dulcie here?"

I shook my head. "She's with her father."

He nodded and looked around. He'd been here before and he seemed to be remembering it, reacquainting himself with the space and my things in it.

"Did you eat yet?" he asked.

"No, I was just having a drink."

"That sounds great. I'll have whatever you're having."

Wasn't he going to ask me what I had come to tell him? Why couldn't he just get it over with? As I moved toward the bar, my mind tried to deal with a half-dozen different emotions at once. Had Nina been right? Should I stay out of the police investigation and let them find out who these men were and why they were being killed on their own? Or was I just thinking that because Noah was here?

I took a glass off the shelf above the bar. My hand was shaking. Did he see it? I poured the vodka, splashed in the Rose's. There was no ice. I left him, walked into the kitchen, put three ice cubes into the glass and went back to him. He was looking out the window and turned as he heard my footsteps. He walked toward me, took the drink, sipped at it, smiled, and then without putting it down or saying a word, pulled me toward him with his free hand and kissed me.

His lips were cold from the drink. He tasted of lime. He smelled of rosemary and mint. He pressed his whole body against mine and reminded me how it felt to be alive with every cell of your body, not just with your brain. The room fell away. The reason I'd gone to see him and the rain and the impropriety and the rules I was bending were all gone.

That the coming together of bodies could be such a delight, such a powerful force, that it could be so pleasurable was both a gift from the gods and a mercurial force of science. That I was still wary of it shamed me. That I was thinking of giving this gift back made me feel ungrateful.

Noah did not stop kissing me.

I lost my balance.

His arm held me up.

He knew even that.

I pressed into him.

He responded, reciprocated.

He did not stop kissing me.

I could not remember ever being kissed like that. I did not remember when a kiss was as good as fucking. When a kiss was as intimate as having a man inside me. No. More. More intimate. Noah breathed into me. I inhaled his breath. The rest of our bodies disappeared. The point of contact between us burned. I knew my lips would be bruised when we stopped. I only hoped his would be bruised just as badly. Months of long nights were in my mouth, spewing from me into him. My teeth gnashed into his, letting him know that he had waited too long to come back. I bit down on his lips, trying to punish him for taking me at my word. He had known better. I had counted on it. He had tricked me.

He bit back. He pushed back. He used his tongue like some kind of weapon, berating me for what I had prevented, castigating me for having kept us from being together before this. He inflicted the kiss on me. I accepted it as my sentence. I argued with my mouth. It had not been all my fault. He had not fought back. But he was fighting back now.

And then the pressure lifted. The lips became soft. The tongue teasing. The attack a caress. No, an apology. It waited for my apology back. I gave with my mouth opening wider for him, with my tongue stroking the inside of his cheeks. The kiss went on. Metamorphosing again into his invitation to me. A wordless inquiry to let him be in me. In this way and in other ways.

He put down his drink without breaking the kiss and led me to the couch, pulling me down with him. Still kissing me. Seconds went by. Minutes. How many? I don't know.

This is the problem with romance or love or whatever word you want to use. It distorts reality. The rush of hormones tricks you into thinking you are feeling emotions. And if there are emotions mixed in with the hormones, the distortion is even more profound. The way it was with Noah.

I pulled away. Got up. I paced. He stayed on the couch. I felt a pinprick of disappointment but pushed it away. It was better that we had stopped the kiss. I sat down in the chair opposite him.

"I like this room. Those chairs are in great shape. Original Grange?"

Noah was also a connoisseur of antique furniture. The one time I'd gone to his place in Greenwich Village, I'd been amazed at the quality of his mission furnishings.

"Yes," I said, nodding. My whole body was shivering, but I took a sip of my cold drink anyway, sucking on the ice, hoping it would numb my lips and extinguish the heat still burning inside my mouth.

"I liked seeing you at dinner the other night," he said.

Damn. He wasn't going to let me off the hook.

"So, this is a personal visit?"

"So you've put your armor back on."

I shrugged. "I'm tired. I'm worried."

"I know," he said, with so much warmth that I felt it surround me and settle on my shoulders like a soft blanket. "Talk to me, Morgan."

It was a more sexual and frankly erotic invitation than the long glissade of kisses had been. His words shot up inside me, making me clench my legs together to try to stop the instant and intense throb deep in my womb.

I, who knew exactly what to tell a patient, who could help people navigate the most complicated interpersonal relationships, had no idea what to say or how to think about this man and what he could arouse in me. I didn't even know where to look. Into his eyes? Not if I wanted to get out of this encounter alive. He could swallow me up. He could water down my logic, reduce me to feelings.

"You are a bad man," I said with a halfhearted laugh.

"Because I care about you even though you don't want me to—or don't think you want me to?"

"Don't be clever. And don't try to shrink me."

"I wouldn't dare." He was teasing and for a minute I didn't mind. For those sixty seconds, I wished that he wasn't a detective and I wasn't a therapist and I didn't have any information about the case that I knew was keeping him up at night.

"Noah, what do you want? Why did you come here?"

"To have a drink. To sit here with you. To listen to you."

It was a nice offer but I had to be on guard now—he was the line I could not cross. He was the temptation that Nina had so correctly warned me against.

I was a therapist. He was the police. He wanted to know what I could not tell him.

Except, I remembered, for one small thing. I'd gone there to help him. It wasn't fair of me to be angry with him now because he'd shown up to find out what I was offering. Be it myself or help with his case.

He got up. Came to me. Bent over and kissed me again. My head was raised to his. His hands went into my hair and his fingertips moved against my scalp. He raised me up so that we were standing body to body, the whole length of each of us against the other. His lips did not stop moving, nor did mine. His hands left my hair, moved to my shoulders. Then he unbuttoned my sweater, and everywhere he touched my skin I became aware of nerve endings that I didn't know existed. The tremors that overtook me shook him. He pulled back and gave me a smile that was as grateful as it was seductive. "Just from my fingers?" he whispered.

I nodded, thinking I could not have said anything even if I wanted to.

"Tell me," he said.

I shook my head.

"Tell me," he repeated.

I put my mouth up to his ear; he put the flat of his hand against my back. It burned. I was sure that in the morning I would be branded by his five fingers, that the red mark would never leave, that my skin would be scarred so badly I would be able to feel the ridges of the scarring.

"Tell me," he said once more.

And my whispering began. Words I couldn't hold back any more than I could have stopped him from touching me.

"I told you before. I don't trust any of it. I've heard every awful thing I can imagine that two people can do to each other. The way that passion poisons. The way that this kind of feeling becomes so big that other things are crowded out. It makes women weak, Noah. I talk to them. I help them. I try to figure out ways for them to find themselves again after they have been swallowed whole by this kind of touching. By the exact same sensations that you are making me feel…"

He worked the clasp of my bra, pulled it off me, lowered his head to my chest and circled my nipple with his tongue.

"Don't stop," he said. Exactly what I was thinking. But he'd said it first. He wanted my words the way I wanted his touch.

"It's not real. It's too tempting. It's fleeting. Don't you see? It's temporary. It won't last like this. We will suck each other dry and all that will be left will be the memory of passion. And then we'll try to live on that, to make that enough, and it won't be, but neither of us will want to admit it."

He had put my whole nipple in his mouth and was sucking on it. Acting out on my body exactly what my words suggested. The next second the warmth of his mouth was gone and the air was puckering my skin. One fingertip, slick with wetness from his mouth, made circles around and around my breast, teasing out more words.

"I will not do this, Noah. I can't. I know better than this. I feel what you are doing and I keep hearing all the people who've been in my office, betrayed by this. Who have fallen for the exultation of this only to find out that it is a mirage."

He didn't ask me to stop talking. In fact, as he undressed he asked me questions. Wanting more.

"What do you tell the women? The ones who fall for this? The ones who want more of it? Who won't let go of the hope that they'll get it back?"

He was naked now. Erect. His whole body strong and supple. I looked at him, not even hearing the words as they came out of my mouth. "I help them find themselves again. To separate the feelings from the fears. To see where their own issues interfered with the intimacy of the relationship.

To deal with their conflicts about wanting to be controlled and yet rebelling against it."

He undressed me until, like him, I was naked, and he gave me that smile again. I've never met a man whose smile pulled at me like Noah's did. It made promises; it reassured; it invited. It was a secret. A very different expression than the grin that he showed in public. This was a private face that was more naked than his body. He expressed joy—but a joy that was mingled with an acknowledgment of how tenuous any single moment was.

"Do you want me to control you?" he asked.

I shook my head.

"Do you want to control me?"

I shook my head again.

He lay down next to me. We were connected at a hundred different points. Slowly, his hands ran up and down my sides, warming my skin, electrifying it. I started to feel myself losing even more consciousness. I was trying to say words to him, to keep talking about the voices I heard in my head whenever I tried to get back to myself. About how difficult it was to get rid of my patients whenever I had tried to have sex. Before. Before the one time that Noah and I had been together. But I couldn't. Not anymore. Every place on my body that he touched had become aroused. My skin was going to orgasm. Not inside of me, not up high where it was dark and oceanic and the waves of blood were pounding—but on the surface of my body. My shoulders, my neck, the small of my back, behind my knees, the tops of my thighs, the soles of my feet: all of these places were humming with sensation. Setting my body reverberating. The words were gone in the feeling. The voices had been drowned out by the simple sound of Noah's breath, more hurried as the time went by.

Matched by my breath in my own ears. Even more rushed than his.

"Morgan," he said, so low that I wasn't sure I'd heard it until he said it again. "Morgan." As if he had found something he had known once but had lost.

Thirty-Seven

—⊷⟳⟐⟳⊶—

We lay on the couch afterward, wrapped in each other, stuck together from our sweat and the heat we were still generating. He kept kissing me. And I didn't stop him. For a long time, I floated on his lips until the sensations calmed and I remembered who I was. And who I was with.

"If you will stay out of my head," I said, pulling back, ending the kiss, not even realizing I had answered a question he had not asked out loud.

He nodded. Not in assent. Just in acknowledgment that he had heard me.

"That's wrong, Morgan. You need me in your head. You need to be able to talk to me. You need me to be able to listen to you."

"You can't not push, can you?"

"You didn't mind my pushing ten minutes ago."

"Don't," I said. Despite his levity, I was scared. And, of course, he knew it. So he moved away, reached for the long-abandoned drink, took a long pull, then asked, "What is this, by the way?"

"Vodka, ice, lime juice."

He nodded and took another long sip. "Not bad. See, you *can* cook."

I smiled despite myself.

"Speaking of food…" Noah stood, pulled on his pants and went into my kitchen. I found him there after getting my robe. He had just opened the stove and, laughing, was pulling out the pathetic, once-frozen, now dried-out chicken entrée. He threw it into the garbage and said, "Real food, Morgan. You need to eat real food."

He returned to the hallway and retrieved a plastic shopping bag that I hadn't even seen him walk in with.

Back in the kitchen he withdrew packages and lined them up on the counter. Then he opened the cabinets and took out bowls and mixing spoons, a frying pan and a pot.

He put water on to boil. Cut two of the three lemons he'd brought and squeezed them into a measuring cup.

"Strainer?" he asked without turning around.

"Cabinet under the silverware drawer."

I wanted to fight him. To get him out of there. And, just as strongly, I was so happy to sit down at the kitchen table and watch this impossibly sweet man cook for me that I didn't know how to stop smiling. Just for tonight, I thought to myself, I will forget about what Nina warned me about; I will not worry about what is going to happen between Noah and me, not worry about the murders and the newspapers and the women in the Scarlet Society.

He opened a container of cream and poured it into a saucepan. After turning on the flame, he stirred it slowly. Watched it. Stirred it some more. After another minute, he poured in the lemon juice, stirred the liquids together, swirling them with a wire whisk, and then turned the flame down.

Listing the ingredients he assumed I had, he watched me as I pulled them out of the cabinets. Then, moving over to the sink, he unwrapped a package of fresh scallops and washed them in the sink, gently, careful not to bruise the white flesh. Just as tenderly, he patted them down with a paper towel. His long fingers picked up one glistening scallop at a time and slowly dredged it, giving it a fine coat of flour, salt and pepper. With a knife, he sliced off a knob of butter and set it in the pan to melt.

While he waited, he opened a bottle of wine and poured us each a glass. By then, the butter was sizzling and Noah added the scallops to the pan. His whole body was intent on cooking this meal. The same way it had been focused on every inch of our bodies that had been touching fifteen minutes before.

The dry, crisp white wine he'd brought was an excellent accompaniment to the delicately lemon-flavored pasta and sautéed scallops. The tastes worked off one another— the buttery and salty flesh of the seafood giving up their perfume, softened by pasta coated with the lush cream, spiked with the tart lemon juice. For a few minutes, I didn't say anything but just luxuriated in the food.

Mixed in with my admiration of the detective's skill was a little resentment. I didn't want to admire him. Or look at his too blue eyes and strong cheekbones, or watch his hands bringing forkfuls of food up to his mouth and remember—

"Why are you really here?" I asked, knowing, sadly, what I was doing. Sabotaging a lovely night. But I didn't have any choice, did I?

He frowned. "I was hoping we wouldn't have to talk about that until after I'd made coffee. Want to take back the question? You're allowed to do that, you know. It's part of the rules when I make dinner. People who ruin the mood are allowed to retract their words. You have thirty seconds." He looked at his wristwatch.

"Wish I could. Why, Noah?"

"I came here hoping to find out that your visit to me at the station was a personal one. That after seeing me at dinner last week, you'd decided that you'd been wrong last June. That you regretted having stood me up and wanted to make amends and start over."

I shook my head. "It wasn't personal. I'm sorry."

"Are you, really?" His voice was suddenly edged with sarcasm.

I hated hearing it and yet was relieved. I was back in control.

"Okay." He gave a small sigh as if starting down this path was saddening him. "Why did you run out of the precinct then? You obviously came all the way downtown to see me. What made you change your mind?"

I shook my head. "Sorry, Noah. I can't tell you that."

"Can't?"

Damn, I'd given too much away with one word. I'd forgotten how sharp he was, like a magnet that picked up the slightest sliver of iron from a bushel of wood.

"We've followed Betsy Young. We know she's been to your office. I should have realized she wasn't just there to interview you. So she's a patient."

"No. I don't know Betsy Young. I told you that last week." I was confused. Why had he brought up the reporter now?

"You told me she'd interviewed you."

"Right. Over the phone."

"You never saw her, never met her?"

"No, Noah. I already told you that."

"If that's true, why did your eyes widen a mile when you saw her in the hall?"

I didn't say anything. I was too surprised. Betsy Young? No. The woman Noah had been escorting out of his office was Liz-without-a-last-name, from the Monday night Scarlet Society group, albeit with different hair.

Finally, I got it.

So that was why Betsy Young had called *me* to get a quote for her article on the first killing. She hadn't thought of me because of my involvement in the Magdalene Murders at all.

Shelby Rush had told me that many of the women who belonged to the society slightly disguised themselves when they participated. I hadn't questioned that. Of course they would. If they had any kind of public persona, they would want their participation in the society to be anonymous. And they couldn't just show up in masks all the time. Hence wigs turning brown hair blond, sunglasses, hats. Certainly not all of them changed their appearances. But Betsy Young had.

"I thought she looked like someone I knew, Noah. Someone I didn't expect to see there. It shook me up. I ran out. That's it."

"Is the person you saw with me a patient of yours, Morgan?"

"You know better than to even ask me that. If she were, I couldn't tell you, anyway."

"You're right. And I don't have to ask you. Because I already know. When I asked you why you ran out of the precinct, the first thing you said was *I can't tell you*. Not I won't tell you. Only one reason for that."

He stood and picked up our plates. His shirt was unbuttoned and I looked away from his bare chest. Not wanting to think about his flesh now.

"Don't do that, Noah. I'll clean up after you go."

"So, I've been dismissed?"

"I don't know what you expect of me. You come over

here to seduce me and once that's done you switch gears and start digging to get information that might help your case. How am I supposed to deal with all of that?" It was all I could manage not to scream. This had happened to us before. We'd gotten our roles mixed up. We'd crossed the line, and now I'd let it happen again. What was wrong with me?

I grabbed the plates—my plates—out of his hands. "This is my house. You can't come in here and take over. Uninvited. You can't."

The dishes sounded as if they had shattered as I dropped them into the sink. I didn't look to see if they had.

"You're right," he said in a low voice that curled around me like his arms had before.

Damn him for that, too. The easiest way to defuse someone's anger is to apologize. And I couldn't afford to have my anger defused. It was the only way I could get him a safe distance away.

I went back to the table to get the glasses and utensils. When I came back, Noah was standing at the sink filling my teakettle with water. In four steps I was by his side, pulling the kettle out of his hands and managing to splash myself and him with a wide arc of water.

"Glad that was still cold," he said.

"This isn't your kitchen!" I shouted. "I told you that."

"What are you so mad about? You love my cooking. I remember that you loved my coffee, too. I even bought chicory."

There was a whole subtext to what he was saying that I didn't want to hear, because after he left, when I was alone again, I didn't want to think about what else he'd implied.

He retrieved the kettle out of my hands before I realized what he was doing and finished filling it up.

"Noah, I'm asking you to get out of here. To leave me alone. And to give me back my goddamn kettle."

Ignoring me, he put it on the stove, turned on the burner and proceeded to fill the French press with some freshly ground espresso beans that he'd also brought with him.

"You might as well just sit down and relax, because I haven't had any coffee yet and I'm not leaving until I do. You know that about me."

His arrogance infuriated me. He laughed. The New Orleans accent even affected his laugh. The peals were long and drawn out, like his words, like his legs, like his fingers. I turned away. I did not want to look at him anymore. I did not want to feel my insides bubbling up again.

I didn't succeed.

Meanwhile, Noah took a pastry box out of the bag he'd brought with him, opened it and put the contents on a plate.

The raspberries glistened in their flaky tart crust.

"You can't throw me out. I brought your favorite dessert."

"You can't know that. How do you know that?"

"You told me. Did you forget?"

I didn't answer him.

The kettle started to sing and Noah returned to the stove to finish making the coffee.

"Take these," he said, handing me the plate and two forks. He brought the French press and two mugs.

As he arranged everything on the table, he said, "You don't have to tell me anything, Morgan. But you have to listen to me. There's nothing stopping me from giving you information about this case."

"Why would you want to do that?" The glistening raspberries were impossible to resist.

"Humor me."

My fork slipped in between two berries, through the custard, and crunched into the crust.

"No. Explain."

"Because I think you're involved. I believe that Betsy Young is your patient and I am afraid that, by treating her, you could put yourself in danger. And that if or when that happens, you won't come to me for help because of your professional integrity. Which, by the way, I think is very sexy no matter how infuriating it is. If I keep you informed, you will at least be able to protect yourself. And if, at some point, this case reaches a stage that's dangerous enough that you won't have to keep your information confidential, you might come to me."

I lifted the fork to my mouth. The smooth and crunchy textures battled for prominence. The combined but distinct flavors of buttery crust, tart berries and sweet cream were a perfect excuse for me not to say anything.

Regardless of the words, no matter the conversation, Noah and I were spinning. We fluttered around each other like butterflies preparing to mate. They dance, they flirt, they advance and retreat. Some species, when they finally do perform coitus, stay locked together for as many as a dozen hours.

"One day," Noah said in a voice so low I had to lean forward to hear him, "you'll stop fighting me."

"You're so sure." I had tried for a tone of voice that would suggest irritation.

"And you're happy that I am."

Obviously, I'd failed. I didn't answer. I wasn't ready to. And this time, Noah didn't push.

Once we were finished, we left the table and moved into the living area. Noah took the chair near the window, making clear his intention to continue the serious part of the conversation.

"We don't have anything. Perez and I are flying blind. Shit, we can't even find the damn bodies, Morgan. It's a crisis situation the likes of which neither of us has ever dealt with. I need something. A connection between the men. A suggestion in one of the shots to indicate where the hell those bodies are. Just one reason that the killer wants the stories to break in the paper first."

"I noticed something odd in the photos in your office."

He nodded.

I continued, speaking slowly, thinking out exactly how to phrase my sentences. I didn't question why I had finally decided to speak. Did not allow myself to doubt my decision. I was not betraying any confidence. I had not been told what I was going to tell him by any of my patients.

"The bottom of the men's feet are dirty."

He nodded.

"There are dozens of particles, scratches, rough spots, and there are the red numbers. But there was also a...mole...or a piece of dirt on Philip Maur's right foot, just where the number started. And there was something similar on Timothy Wheaton's right foot. Almost in the exact same place. At first, I just thought it was more dirt. But how could both men have a speck of dirt in precisely the same place?"

"That's something either Perez or I should have noticed."

"I could be wrong."

He got up. Urgent now.

I was barely able to breathe. Over and over in my mind I repeated what I'd just said, satisfying myself that I hadn't broken any confidence, just pointed out something I'd noticed. Besides, I didn't know what the mark was. I hadn't asked the women in my group. There would have been no way to explain that I'd seen the photographs that close up, for one thing. It was only my guess that a group like the Scarlet Society would engage in some kind of ritualistic behavior and brand their men.

He walked to the front door. I followed. "I've been living with those photographs. I've looked at them a hundred times." He sounded as if he had betrayed himself. He grabbed his raincoat off the hook in the hallway and shrugged into it. Once more, he hesitated before walking back to me.

"I didn't want to have to leave tonight," he said as he bent down and softly, as if he were a butterfly alighting on my lips, kissed me.

My center didn't hold. I felt weightless and lost for a moment. And then, just when the feelings would have become too intense, he pulled away, smiled at me with an expression that I would think about for days, and walked out.

Thirty-Eight

After Noah left, I retrieved the tape that Shelby Rush had given me and watched it once more. This time I was not curious about the rituals of the group; I was searching for Liz. Was she Betsy Young? Both names were nicknames for Elizabeth. It was possible that either the blond hair she sported in the therapy sessions or the brown hair I'd seen at the police station was a wig. Many of the women who belonged to the Scarlet Society disguised themselves, and that wasn't illegal. They had a right to their privacy and to keep their sexual predilections a secret.

That a woman in the group had gone to the police didn't bother me. In fact, I'd asked the group the day before to consider doing just that.

What I was having a hard time understanding was that a woman who'd taken an oath to keep the society a secret was also the reporter who had broken the news of the members' deaths. It was clearly a conflict of interest.

The only ethical way for a reporter to handle being in her position was to disclose it to her editor, take her chances, and hope her boss would let her cover the stories despite the collision of her professional and personal lives.

Had she done that?

If she had, wouldn't the editor have taken her off the story?

Certainly, she hadn't written about the men's involvement with the society in her stories. And from what Noah had told me, she had not disclosed it to the detectives working the case.

Why?

To hold something back from the authorities in case she needed ammunition? To protect the society? And if that was the reason, if she was keeping her promise to the society, then what was she doing writing the stories?

On the tape, the auction continued. Even if she were in this crowd, I wasn't sure I'd recognize her. Most of the women were wearing masks. Timothy stepped forward on the makeshift stage. I'd seen this footage before. It made me more sad this time than it had the other day.

Was it simply a coincidence that the killer was confessing through a reporter who belonged to the society? But I didn't believe in coincidences. So Betsy Young aka Liz had to have been chosen to break the stories precisely because she was a member of the society.

But why?

On the screen, Tim left the stage with the woman who had won him.

At that moment the phone rang.

"Hello."

"Morgan, I'd like you to come down and see what we found," Noah said. "I'm sending a car for you."

Thirty-Nine

For the second time in five hours, a rookie cop escorted me to the office at the end of the hall. I wondered how one night could last so long.

"Detective Jordain said he'd be right with you, Dr. Snow."

I sat down in the chair opposite Noah's and stared at the wall I'd seen a week earlier. The collage was different: a new layer of photographs, of another man, had been added. I wanted to turn away but I couldn't help staring.

Chicory-spiked coffee perked in the pot and a few beignets, covered in powdered sugar, sat on a white china plate that was definitely not police department issue. It made me smile despite my surroundings. Then my attention was drawn back to the wall. Mixed in with the photographs of the three dead men were papers, notes, newspaper articles and maps. Knowing Jordain, there had to be some kind of logic to the way the ephemera had been arranged, but I couldn't figure it out.

The men were so pale. You'd think they were asleep, except living people's skin is never that color. Looking at death is disturbing. But with the added insult of the sexual focus, it was also distasteful. Humiliating.

"How did you see those marks?" Noah asked as he walked in, holding a thick stack of photos. I smelled something sharp, chemical. But couldn't place it.

"I don't know." I shrugged. "It must just be that I'm shorter than the two of you. When I'm sitting here, the shots of the feet are at my eye level. I focused on them. They're too low for the two of you."

"We had enlargements done of all of the backgrounds on every single shot—searching for something, anything, to tell us where the bodies are. And we enlarged all the full-body shots…but…" He was shaking his head in disbelief, still trying to understand his oversight. "Anyway. You were right."

He walked over to the coffee. "Do you want some?"

"No." It was going to be well after midnight by the time I got home. I had to be up at six. I couldn't afford to overdo the caffeine or else I'd just lie there obsessing about Liz or Betsy or whatever I should be calling her. And about Noah.

It was surreal to be sitting in his office just hours after we'd made love in my apartment. Nothing intimate between us now—just the disquieting photographs.

"Here, take a look." Noah laid out half a dozen blowups of the three men's feet. As he was doing that, Perez and Butler came in. I'd met them both before and we exchanged greetings.

From the looks of both of them, Noah had called them back to work after they'd gone home.

"Just in time," Noah said to them. "Get some coffee, pull up a seat." He waited until everyone was gathered around the desk.

"Look." He said it slow and drawn out, making it sound like two words, not one.

In the first set of photos the feet were life size. This alone made me shudder. When an image is diminutive, even if you know you are looking at someone who is dead, there is a disconnection because of the size. You can be horrified but it's more of an intellectual horror.

As I stared at the full-size feet with red numbers drawn on them like graffiti marring a marble wall, my eyes blurred. I wanted to turn away and protect myself from the images, knowing I wouldn't be able to forget them.

The next group of enlargements offered some relief. Each showed only four inches of a man's right foot. Just an abstract canvas with markings on it. These could have been hanging on the wall of a conceptual art gallery in Chelsea, waiting for some brave collector to snap them up. Now that we were looking at the feet out of context, everyone saw what I had noticed.

There was a brown, circular mole. In the same spot on each foot.

Noah slapped another set of shots down on the table. Now the mole, and half an inch around it, had been blown up to fifteen or twenty times its size.

Clearly, it was not a freckle. Not a mole. It wasn't even brown anymore, but deep bloodred.

Scarlet, with black mixed in.

"It's a tattoo," Butler said, shocked.

"Are those intertwined snakes?" Perez asked, speaking over her.

Noah didn't respond to either of them. He was looking at me, because I was looking at those same images and had not said a word, not asked a single question.

I didn't have to.

I was the only person in the room who knew exactly what I was seeing. What appeared to the others to be a circle of snakes was two *S*'s, one flopped and overlapping the other. Two *S*s for the Scarlet Society. And to someone as smart as Jordain, my not asking a question or making a guess was suspicious.

Forty

The photographer arranged the lights.

Harsh white lights.

Hard to see anything but the glare. Not the face. Not the person. Just the bright white lights. And the voice coming from behind the camera.

"You look more forlorn in this kind of light. No filters to soften or flatter. But I don't have any need to show you off or make you look good. That isn't the purpose of these photographs. Fear is. The kind that wakes you up at four-forty in the morning, when it is still dark, and prevents you from doing anything but lying in bed, tossing and turning, trying to find a cool spot on the pillow, but knowing even if you do, it won't matter. The worry and anxiety is too deep to let you fall asleep again."

Bruce Levin blinked. It was sinking in. He wasn't dead yet. But he didn't feel right. He tried to get his eyes to open wider, to make some sense of where he was, but he couldn't. Someone was touching his chest. His thighs. The fingers felt like ice streaking across his skin. God he was cold. It occurred to him that he must be naked. He couldn't understand that, either.

"Don't worry," the photographer said to him. Or at least he assumed it was the photographer because he could see a camera looking down at him.

Bruce couldn't answer. There was something in his mouth.

His mouth?

His mouth was full of—what? It was tasteless and had wicked every drop of saliva from the inside of his cheeks and his tongue.

"Nothing will hurt. As long as you don't try to fight me. I don't like fighting." A laugh.

What was so funny? he thought. What kind of lunatic had brought him here and tied him up? More important, why? If he knew why, maybe he could figure out how to get free. But he couldn't think—not think straight, anyway. He wasn't sure if it was morning or night or how long he'd been here or even where he'd been before he was here. What had happened? Had there been an accident? Had he been hurt? Were there bandages in his mouth?

Bruce tried to concentrate on that. He was someone who could always figure things out. Complicated things. But now it was as if part of his memory had been cut out. That had to be the drugs. But what drugs? He'd taken his share of drugs when he was in college, but nothing made him feel this sick.

It took a huge effort but he managed to open his eyes. And this time he could see just a little bit more. It would have been better if he hadn't, since what he saw were hospital gurneys with shapes on them. Silent shapes. Naked. Pale. Freezing. How could he know that? He couldn't. But the air around him was so icy, he was so cold, those shapes had to be equally frigid.

The light glaring off the steel edges of the scissors

blinded him. Christ, that hurt! But he fought against the pain. At least it was distinct. At least it wasn't hazy the way everything else was. The scissors were coming toward him, toward his face…closer…and closer…and he thought, *I should prepare myself for this, but how?*

The fear now was so deep that it was inside of his chest and forcing his heart to race. Christ, he could hear the beating, and then the scissors moved toward his forehead.

Involuntarily, even though he made a big effort not to, he closed his eyes.

That's when Bruce heard the sound. It made no sense given the rest of what was going on around him. Blades. Cutting. But cutting what? A swish and hiss and after that the sandpaper sound of hair being shorn. His hair.

Why would anyone want his hair?

He was dreaming about someone he'd had sex with once. Someone whose body he knew as well as his own, but only the body. It was better to fuck strangers and not know what they were upset about or what their bosses had said to them that morning, and not have to worry about when they would start to expect more: more words, more actions, more commitments.

He liked his partners to tell him what they wanted him to do with their bodies. It put them in charge. And he liked that because he didn't have to use his imagination on how to please them. They told him. And by doing so, they took away the one aspect of sex that was the most dangerous as far as he was concerned.

Women fell in love with you, not because of who you really were, but because of the fantasy you fit. They kept silent and selfish about what they wanted, so you made it up as you went along, and God forbid if you guessed right, you bypassed go and became some fucking sort of hero. And then the only place you could go was down.

But this way, they made the rules. The women made you move right or left or up or down or lick or suck or bite or come or wait, and there was never the next morning when they'd look at you with their sloppy lovesick eyes and tell you that they had been waiting for you for a long time.

Because this way, you were no more to them than a dildo come to life.

He was hard.

Christ, in this place?

Tied to this steel bed?

Freezing his nuts off and scared out of his mind, he had enough blood running through his veins for some drug-induced dream to give him a hard-on?

No.

It was the gloved hand that was stroking him. Shit. The photographer's hand sliding up and down the shaft of his penis, slower and faster and slower, and his body was responding as if none of this horror existed at all.

He knew that there wasn't much connection between his cock and his brain. Hadn't that been proved to him hundreds of times? But this was even more insane. This time it wasn't just that his brain wasn't engaged, it was that his brain should have been fighting this obscene seduction. His brain should be preventing the erection. And it couldn't.

The tongue flicked out and licked him. Like a very aggressive cat. One long lick. A short one. A long one.

How could he let this happen? The inertia was hard to fight. Despite wanting to stop what was happening, the feeling in his groin was pleasure. It was the feeling in his stomach that he couldn't stand. The anxiety that wasn't abating even with the expert combination blow job and hand job he was getting.

Abruptly, it stopped.

Right in the middle of the massage. It ended with a laugh. Low and deep and crude. No words needed to be spoken in order for him to translate that laugh. It mocked him and his penis. It reduced him to the most basic animal, denounced his brain and his talent.

"That's all you get."

He shivered.

So that was it. Cut my hair, suck my dick, photograph me, and after that, when you are good and ready, you'll kill me. He felt nausea rise in his throat and hoped he would throw up and choke on it. At least then he could cheat this monster out of the pleasure of killing him—because surely that was the ultimate high here. Sex games, mutilation and finally murder.

The nausea rose again, came up higher, and after that receded, leaving an acid burn down the back of his throat.

Please, he begged some God he didn't know. Wasted thoughts. Whoever the fuck God was, he wasn't in here listening.

Please, make it quick. Make it quick. And painless.

That was when he heard the popping noise—the last noise, he thought, he would ever hear again.

Forty-One

~~~~~~~~~~~

My visit to Nicky and Daphne that Thursday started off badly.

The two of them were sitting on opposite sides of the room, not looking at each other and not looking at me.

Sometimes you really can smell emotions. I've always thought that the body emits scent to warn other members of a group—the way that wild animals do.

In that pretty sunroom, filled with the benign still lifes of fruit and flowers Daphne had painted before she'd discovered her talent for the male nude, I smelled fear, anger and lust.

It was an effort to get them to tell me what had happened before I got there.

"Why don't you want to talk about it?" I asked Daphne first.

"Because no matter what I tell you, Nicky is going to twist it."

"How about you let me worry about that."

She got up and walked to a hanging basket that held an oversized fern. I watched her pinch off a dead, withered frond. "Daphne?"

She turned, playing with the feathery and brittle leaf.

"I think it would be a good idea if you stayed seated. I know this is your house and that it seems normal to you to get up and move around, but it would be beneficial if, during our sessions, you remained seated. Just as if you and Nicky were in my office in the city."

Without saying anything, she sat down in the same spot on the end of the settee. She didn't look at Nicky. He didn't look at her.

"Daphne, you were going to tell me what happened before I got here."

She sighed. "Nicky tried to get me to have sex with him."

"Tried?" Nicky blurted out. Then he looked at me. "She came to the door ready for me. She ordered me to go upstairs with her. She knows that I respond to that kind of talk."

"You see?" Daphne said. "He's twisting it."

"Daphne. What happened when Nicky came to the door? How did you feel?"

"I was happy to see him. I love him. I want him here." She was shredding the fern into small fragments, letting them drop onto the pristine floor.

"Okay. So he came inside. You felt good about him being here. What happened then? Did you kiss him hello?"

"Of course I did. He's still my husband."

"She opened her lips. It wasn't a simple kiss. She's not telling you that."

I shifted in my seat so that I was facing Nicky now. "It might be better if you let Daphne tell me what happened first. Without interrupting her. After she's finished, you can tell me what you think happened. Do you see there's a benefit to working that way?"

"Yes. I do want to work this out. But she's playing games with me and—"

"Nicky?"

He stopped talking, took a deep breath, blew the air out of his mouth and settled back on the couch, prepared finally to let Daphne tell her version of the story.

The two stories they told were, not surprisingly, very different. Daphne's version was that Nicky made it clear as soon as he got there that if she wanted him to make love to her, he would be happy to accommodate her. She'd agreed and taken him upstairs. They had embraced. Begun to undress. He'd taken off his shirt. That's when she saw the scratches on his back.

"I asked him if he'd been to the society in the past few weeks. He lied and said no. At least, at first he did. He just wanted to have sex. He didn't care about the rules. About the promises. About how I felt about it."

When it was Nicky's turn, he said that Daphne had not asked him if he'd been to the society outright. She'd tricked him into telling her a lie of omission. And that was not the same thing as outright lying.

"What do you mean, a lie of omission?"

"She didn't ask me if I'd been to the society. She asked me if I loved her. I told her I did. Then she asked me if I really deserved to be let back into her bed. She didn't tell me that she'd seen the scratches. She set me up."

"He is taking his life in his hands every day that he goes back there," Daphne interrupted. "I know it and he knows it. But he's got some crazy death wish."

By the time the session was over, I'd managed to get them to stop reacting to each other's accusations and to allow each other to express anger. If they didn't at least do that, I explained, they'd continue to respond with knee-jerk reactions and their resentments would just keep growing.

"Before I go, Daphne, instead of using the old language, tell Nicky how you feel."

"I'm scared for him," Daphne said.

Nicky looked at her, smiled, and told her that mattered to him a lot. "I'm careful. Nothing is going to happen to me," he said.

"Do you really think that Philip wasn't careful?" Tears were running down her cheeks. "Or Tim?"

Putting her head in her hands, Daphne wept.

Nicky got up, went to her and took her in his arms. He held her and let her cry and rubbed her back and smoothed her hair.

I wished that I could do more and do it faster. Not for the first time as a therapist, and not for the last, I wished that I had more to work with than words and insight. I wanted a magic wand that I could wave over this couple so that they could act on the positive feelings they had for each other instead of tormenting themselves with desires and needs that were only keeping them apart.

Forty-Two

Despite having promised Dulcie that I wouldn't go to Boston for the opening of *The Secret Garden*, I couldn't stay home. I'd rented a car and left the city Saturday morning.

The fall leaves were blazing as I drove up the Merritt Parkway through Connecticut. The sky was cloudless and a pure cerulean blue, and the sun filtering through the trees made the countryside shimmer. But it was hard to let go of everything I was thinking and just enjoy the foliage or the day.

I hadn't planned on going.

After she left with Mitch at six-thirty that morning, I went into the den, pulled out the wooden table that held a chunk of rose quartz that I had been chiseling for the past six months, put on my goggles and went to work chipping away at the stone.

It was only a hobby but usually it soothed me. Once, I'd hoped I had talent. That was before I found out what real talent was. I'd been introduced to sculpting when my father had remarried. Krista is a successful sculptor who shows once a year at a prestigious gallery on Fifty-seventh

Street. Her work mesmerized me when I first met her, and taking my interest as a way to bond with me, she'd offered to teach me. I was only twelve, but I loved everything about the stone and the process and the tools. I was fascinated with the idea that the job of the sculptor—as Krista had described it—was to find the shapes hidden inside the rocks, waiting to be unearthed.

When I'm faced with a situation that makes me seek out the comfort of a mother figure, I first think of the woman who passed away in a drunken stupor when I was eight, who I had tried to save every day until she finally gave in to her weakness, or I thought of Nina, who had stepped in that same day, wrapped me up in her strong arms and never let me go.

Yet the bond between my stepmother and me was real, too, born of the stone and sustained by my love of the hobby I'd never given up.

That morning, excavating the sleeping form of a young child from a block of rose quartz didn't keep my mind occupied. I put down the mallet and chisel, called for a rental car, packed a bag and started to figure out what to say to Dulcie when I got to Boston.

About an hour and a half out of Manhattan, I pulled off the highway in Westport, Connecticut, and drove into town to get something to eat. It was twelve-thirty. The show wasn't until eight that night. Boston was only another three hours away. I had plenty of time.

Sitting in the local Starbucks, with a latte and a piece of pumpkin-walnut bread, I went over my decision again. By going up to Boston I was breaking my word to my daughter. But how could I stay away? This was her first professional performance. She was so nervous. I was so concerned. Even if I stood in the back and never told her I was there, I had to go.

How upset would Dulcie be if she saw me there?

I was on a seesaw. Torn between turning back and going forward. Neither direction seemed the right one, and then my cell phone rang.

"Hello?"

"Dr. Snow? It's Pam."

Pam was the operator who worked the phone service for the institute on weekends and evenings and called when there was any kind of off-hour emergency with a patient. "Hi, Pam." My voice was already tight while I waited for her news.

"You just got a phone call. From a patient of yours. She only gave me her first name—Liz. She said it's an emergency and it's really critical that she talk to you."

Forty-Three

An emergency request for an appointment from a patient who was somehow connected to the deaths of three men was as good an excuse as I could think of to get into the car and head back to New York.

I could be a responsible doctor and keep my promise to my daughter. While I knew the wrenching pain I felt backing the car out of the lot and heading south instead of north would stay with me, at least I wouldn't have to see the look of disappointment in Dulcie's eyes when she saw me at the play that night.

Since she had her blond wig on, the woman who was waiting for me was Liz. I was glad. I preferred for us to stick with a member of the group I knew, as opposed to the reporter I had never met.

She sat down on the couch; I took my seat. "What's wrong?" There was no reason to waste any time.

It was midafternoon and the sunshine filtered through the leaves outside my windows and made a pattern on the rug that shifted and changed each time the wind blew. Liz sat staring at it. Not saying anything. With her was a manila envelope that she clutched to her chest, desperately, the way I had once clutched my daughter to my own chest when she was sick with fever and I waited, panicked, in our doctor's office to find out what was wrong with her.

"Now there is a fourth man…" she said.

"When did you find out?"

"Early this morning."

"Have you told the police?"

She nodded and then frowned. "Why were you at the police station the other night?"

"Why is that relevant?"

"Because I need to know I can trust you. That you aren't telling them about the group."

"I'm not."

"So why were you there?"

"Liz, why did you want to see me today? What is the emergency?"

"How do I know I can trust you?"

"I don't know how to convince you other than to tell you that I take privilege very seriously."

"You are implying that I don't."

I hadn't said anything that should have made her say that. "Is there a reason that I should question your ethics?"

Her laugh was not jovial or kind, but rather slightly hysterical and panicked. "Of course there is. You are the only person who knows that I am not only the reporter who is getting these monstrous packages, but that I belong to the same sex club as the men who are being murdered."

"That's something that is bothering you?"

She stood up. Now the knuckles that held the package to her chest were white.

"Please sit down," I said.

She didn't. "Is it something that is bothering me? Are

you crazy? Of course it is. I haven't slept for days. I am breaking rules at the paper. I am breaking my word to the Scarlet Society. And both you and the police think that I'm the one who is killing these men."

"Please sit down." I was using the softest voice that I could. She was in crisis. Her whole body was trembling and she was slightly out of breath. Before we could have any kind of conversation, I had to calm her down. "I can help you if you'll just sit down so we can talk through what's bothering you."

She continued to stand, staring at me for ten, twenty, then thirty seconds, the only change the quickness of her breath and the look in her eyes, which deepened and became more troubled.

If she was in any way responsible, she was dangerous. And as one of the only people who knew about her complicity, I might be in danger. Was this woman capable of killing three—no, she had just told me four—men?

This was not the first time that I worried about my own safety with my patients, but usually I wasn't alone at the institute on a Saturday afternoon. Usually, there were people in the hall and if I screamed someone would come running. But no one was outside and I had nothing at hand to subdue her with if she became violent.

I stood, took one step toward her, and another.

She didn't move.

I took another step. We were within a foot of each other. I was looking in her face, but I could see her hands in my field of vision and they were still clutching the envelope. If she moved either hand to reach for something, anything else—a weapon?—I'd know and I'd have a split second to disengage her. I'd studied self-defense. I'd taken my daughter to classes, too. It was just smart to learn what to do. I could take Liz without any trouble as long as I kept my composure. As long as I kept my eyes on her hands.

"Why don't you sit down, Liz?"

"Betsy!" She yelled.

It was so sudden I almost overreacted, but I am trained to deal with someone in the midst of a psychotic break. Was that what this was? Years of work had prepared me for it. What was surprising was how few times I had witnessed it, considering the number of patients I dealt with.

"My Fucking Name Is Betsy!"

"Betsy. Betsy, I want you to sit down." I took her arm firmly in my hand and gently forced her down. She allowed me to seat her, and, that done, I pried her fingers apart and took the envelope out of her hands.

The minute I had it in my grasp, her whole body relaxed and her face crumpled into despair. The fury was dispelled. At least for the moment.

"I killed those men," she said. And then buried her face in her hands.

Forty-Four

Detectives Jordain and Perez were sitting in an unmarked navy-blue sedan across the street from the Butterfield Institute. The morning had started with a call from their officer who was working the mail shift at the *New York Times*. Betsy Young had gotten a fourth correspondence from Delilah.

The man in the photographs had been reported missing five days earlier. Bruce Levin was a celebrity real estate developer whose name was almost as well known as the people he brokered luxury apartments for. It helped that he had been married to a top model, with whom he'd fathered a pair of twins. The divorce had been in all the tabloids because of the exorbitant demands his wife was making and the claims she made about how much she spent on her children.

Like the other three packages, this one included a lock of Levin's hair in a small plastic bag and three photographs, all taken from the same angles as the previous shots. There were the same ligature marks around his wrists and ankles.

And as they expected it would be, the number 4 was painted in red on the soles of both of his feet.

What was different was the reporter's demeanor when she arrived at the precinct house. She'd written up her article and had brought it with her to the station house.

Previously, she'd been very professional, slightly nervous, clearly disturbed, but in control. Even to the point of being angry at Jordain and Perez for holding the articles too long—according to her—for not letting her reveal everything that was in the packages, and for insisting the *Times* not print all the photographs.

Betsy Young's star at the paper had risen in the weeks since she broke the story about Philip Maur, and with it, her attitude had become more strident.

Except that morning she had been subdued and completely shaken. Once the meeting was over, Perez offered to have a car take her back to the *Times,* which she agreed to. She was clearly too upset to think through why he was offering: that it would be even easier to tail her if she were in a cop car.

She'd gone back to work, stayed for three hours, and then taken a cab to the Butterfield Institute, getting out of the taxi with a different color hair than she'd had getting in. The detectives had talked about the wig and tried to come up with a reason for it. Like everything else in this case, the reporter's hair change made no sense.

Perez sipped at his coffee. They'd been in the car so long it was lukewarm. Jordain had finished his already but wished he'd bought two cups. They might be there for a while.

"We are so cold on this one I need a winter coat," Jordain said.

"I'm not as sure about that as you are."

"I'm betting she is not our Delilah. All I'm hoping at this point is that she knows who is, and might lead us to him."

"Well, something's going on. She's the most important crime reporter in the city right now, and that is more motive than anyone else we can think of."

"Talk about willing to do anything to get ahead, that's—" He was interrupted by his cell phone.

"Jordain,"

"It's Butler. I've got the information you wanted."

Jordain mouthed the police officer's name to Perez. "Good, go ahead. I'm waiting with bated breath."

"Well, I'm sorry to disappoint you guys, but I came up with absolutely nothing on Young being linked romantically with the last victim."

"Let me guess," he said wearily. "It's the same as with the other three. You talked to business partners, friends, doormen, and did some quick phone-record searches. No calls from our new Samson to Young's home number, cell number or office."

Perez shook his head after Jordain had filled him in on Butler's investigation. "Maybe she didn't know them. Maybe she saw them somewhere and for some reason targeted these four men—stalked them. Maybe she tried to date them and they all rejected her."

"And then she drugged them and killed them to exact her revenge? She's a perfectly normal-looking woman—even if she's a little pugnacious and aggressive—no reason to assume she's that hard up for a social life that if a guy said no, she'd go to this extreme. No, if this is tied in any way to her, it's the career thing."

A woman walking an apricot-colored miniature poodle stopped alongside the car while her dog sniffed at the sidewalk. She glanced into the window, saw the two men talking to each other, but didn't focus on them. Jordain watched her without looking directly in her face.

"Have we found out if there's another exit to the building?"

Perez shook his head. "Most buildings in the city don't have one. If this one does, and if she used it, it would mean she knows we are on her tail. So, do we get out and check and risk bumping into her, or do we wait? And how long do we wait?"

"Most sessions last forty-five minutes. We've got a ways to go."

"Do they ever let a patient go more than a hour?"

"Morgan would if it was important. If the patient was in crisis. She'd break a rule like that."

"But not break a rule for us?"

"She's got integrity."

"Oh, is that what she's got?"

Jordain arched his eyebrows.

"Come on, partner, I've known you long enough to be able to tell when you are interested in someone. Christ, I've been waiting for that to happen."

"Well, give it up."

"I've seen the two of you in a room together and—"

"I'm hungry," Jordain interrupted. "Do you have one of those nutrition bars you're always eating instead of real food?"

Forty-Five

❧⟨⊙⟩❧

After Betsy blurted out that she was responsible for the deaths of all four men, she sat there, head in hands, while I opened the envelope and inspected the contents. I'd seen so many photos like these at the police station I should have been inured to them, but the new shots made me sick to my stomach, and when I saw the red number 4 on the new man's feet, my head started to pound. "Betsy?"

She looked up. "They wouldn't be dead if I'd told the police about the Scarlet Society."

"What would you have told the police?"

"How can you sound so calm? You don't sound as if you care."

"Why do you think that?"

"You can't care about them—you didn't know them."

"But you did, didn't you? You had sex with them and talked to them."

She nodded.

"Did you care about them?"

"I cared about Bruce Levin."

I nodded, not surprised that Betsy had known this last man better than the others. Something had brought her to me.

"But I killed him."

"How?"

"I didn't do anything to protect him."

"Actually, you did. You wrote articles that were picked up on every television station and in every newspaper in the country. All the men involved in the Scarlet Society heard or read that news and should have been careful. Extra careful."

"I thought that, too. But they weren't, were they?"

"Or if they were, it wasn't careful enough."

"I can't go to the police."

"I didn't ask you to," I said.

"But you think I should."

"Betsy, I didn't say that. Do you think you should?"

"I can't. I took an oath to the society."

"But surely if you can prevent someone's death by revealing that information—"

"It's more complicated than that," she said.

She didn't have to tell me. I was as conflicted as she was. "Tell me."

"It's not just about the society. I tell the police, I will most likely get fired from the *Times*."

"Why?"

"If it were revealed that I knew about the society—was involved in the society—and that I kept that information from both the authorities and the paper…" She didn't finish the sentence.

I waited, and when she clearly wasn't going to resume speaking, I asked her what she had stopped herself from saying.

"I'd have to recuse myself from writing the rest of the stories and I can't do that. Not yet. It would be professional suicide."

"You have a stellar career, don't you? You've won Pulitzer Prizes. Would this cancel all that out?"

"You don't understand. It's not about avoiding getting into trouble. I've waited twenty years to get this kind of front-page space day after day. I can't possibly walk away from it now."

"It sounds like you've made up your mind."

"I've never equivocated on my decision."

"So why are you here?"

I could tell from the expression on her face that she hadn't expected that question. But blunt questions work in my favor. Not because I always expect to get truthful answers—patients lie to themselves and to me all too often. No, it was that unless you are a trained actor you don't know what your face is showing. Only the most devious and accomplished liars are practiced enough to control all of their facial expressions.

I can see pupils dilate or shrink. Can see lips tremble or sweat pop out on the forehead. Can hear an involuntary intake of breath. Or notice the pulse quicken by focusing on a prominent vein on the neck. Swallowing, gulping, blinking, squinting—all proclaim the lie.

Betsy wasn't a trained actress and she was acting guilty. Depending on the question, she couldn't meet my glance. Despite the cool fall air blowing through the window, wisps of hair were stuck to her damp forehead. She picked at a hangnail, kept crossing and uncrossing her feet at the ankles. Her mouth was dry—I could hear that.

Was she letting me witness her guilt on purpose? Was her confession about the smaller crime offered to distract me from thinking she was capable of the larger one? Was I supposed to believe that anyone struggling with her conscience this way over the infraction of not admitting to knowing these men could not be the killer? If I were convinced she was distraught about the minor role she had played in this drama, then I might not wonder if she'd had an even bigger role.

But I did wonder.

I was all too aware that the woman sitting in my office on that Saturday afternoon might have been responsible for the carnage she was reporting.

She had motives.

One she had discussed in group: she was getting older and the men in the club were no longer excited when she chose them. She saw it in their faces and the way they avoided her eyes—the way she avoided mine that afternoon. Betsy was a strong woman and she was angry.

How angry?

I didn't know that yet.

The second motive was the attention and power she was enjoying being the only reporter on the story.

Going against her claim of innocence was that she purported to be devastated over the deaths of four men she'd known, and yet she wasn't willing to do anything to help prevent the next crime.

But neither was I.

And that didn't make me a suspect.

Was she dangerous? Did she have mood swings? Inappropriate responses? Lapses in concentration? Inability to focus? The answers would help me make an educated guess, but she'd have to be in therapy with me for a few more weeks before I could assess whether she was psychotic. Psychotic enough to be a serial killer?

And there was the issue of her being female. Male criminals raped and killed serially. They easily had sex without forming connections. (Even healthy men.) But women were much less likely to engage in sexual athletics. Despite themselves, they made connections. The women in the group had attested to that when they'd bemoaned the fact that they couldn't go to Philip Maur's memorial service.

Certainly women could kill. A wife could murder her husband in a crime of passion if he betrayed her, but for a woman to kill four men she cared about, one after the other, because they didn't pay her as much attention as she would have liked?

It wasn't impossible, but it was highly improbable. Especially a woman who didn't exhibit signs of serious psychosis.

Certainly Betsy was involved on some level, but how? And what could I do about it? She had not exhibited any behavior to lead me to suspect that she was going to harm herself. She had not named any man other than the men who were already dead. I could only go to the police if I feared for her or had information suggesting she was going to harm someone else.

The law was clear on this.

That I had a group of patients who knew men who were being targeted was just on the wrong side of the line. I had already encouraged them to go to the police.

Now I would have to try even harder to convince Betsy to tell the truth.

Forty-Six

My ex-husband had called me early on Sunday morning and told me what had happened to Dulcie over the weekend in Boston so that I'd be prepared.

I waited for her to come home that night. Sitting in the den without the TV or stereo on, I listened for the click of her key, holding my breath. Aching for what my thirteen-year-old little girl had gone through.

I had to hold myself back from rushing over to her and wrapping her up in my arms when she opened the door. I waited as her footsteps echoed in the foyer and stopped sounding as she walked down the carpeted hall to her room.

Only then did I get up and go to her.

She was sitting on her bed, the suitcase at her feet. Eyes red-rimmed, her hair lank.

"Hi, honey," I said. Walking over to the bed, I sat down next to her, put my arm around her back and kissed her cheek. She buried her face in the hug. I didn't know that she was crying until I felt the reverberation of the sobs on my fingertips.

"I want to quit the play," she whispered through her tears.

"I know, sweetheart."

Her small head was nestled under my chin. I wanted to kill my ex-husband for persuading me to let Dulcie do this. *Life would offer enough pain,* I had told him. *Can't our child have her whole childhood before she confronts the vagaries of the professional world?*

Dulcie was crying so hard it hurt my chest.

I had held my mother like this, but then I was the little girl and she the adult. It hadn't mattered; her heart had still been broken by the audience. By the love she needed so badly but could never have gotten from strangers watching her act on a stage.

"Dulcie, I love you."

She nodded and hiccuped. "I want to quit," she said again.

"I know."

And I wanted her to quit. I wanted to call the director of the show and tell him that I was sorry but Dulcie had decided that she didn't want to continue with the play. I knew exactly the tone of voice I'd use so that he would understand it wasn't a conversation we were having. I was just giving him information and he would have to accept it. There were two understudies, and both girls were prepared to go on. And there was no reason that either of them wouldn't do just as good a job as Dulcie. And her school would take her back. They'd agreed to that. She'd been tutored the entire time. She'd get up to speed quickly. The director would try to convince me that Dulcie needed to stay. Or maybe he'd be relieved that she wanted to pull out. How dare he think that? Dulcie was perfect for the part of Mary Lennox.

I wanted to laugh. My pride and my need to protect her were mixed up with each other.

I hugged her tighter, knowing that I wasn't going to do anything that I wanted to do.

"It's dinnertime. I made your favorite."

"Made it?" Dulcie looked at me askance from under swollen eyelids. She was depressed but she was still her irreverent self. I had never been quite so happy to hear her sarcasm.

"Yes. First I purchased it at EAT, then I brought it home, put it on the stove and turned on the heat."

"That's not making it, Mom, that's heating it."

I laughed. She laughed and then fresh tears spilled out of her eyes, wetting her cheeks all over again.

We sat at the table in the kitchen and Dulcie proved that, no matter how upset she was, it didn't affect her appetite.

"I thought I was fine."

I nodded at her, listening to what happened in Boston on Saturday night.

"I wasn't even nervous. I mean, we'd had so many rehearsals. I really knew my lines. And all the songs. And I wasn't scared."

I nodded again.

"But when I stood up there. I don't know. It just stopped working. I couldn't find anything. Everything was wrong. It was the most awful thing. And they wrote about it. How nervous I was. Even unprofessional."

She started to cry again and I had to hold back from crying with her, in sympathy. She pushed the plate away from her, laid her head on the table, and started to sob as if it had just happened all over again.

I stroked my daughter's head but didn't say anything. I wanted to give her the space to feel the full brunt of the pain. Professionally, I knew that talking to her, trying to dilute the embarrassment and disappointment, would only dam it up.

When she picked her head up a few minutes later, the tracks of tears on her face made my stomach seize up. Of course I would let her quit the play. There was no reason that my child had to go through anything this terrifying. The world would offer up enough pain for her later that I couldn't fix.

This was something I could stop.

"I want to quit."

"Okay, let's talk about it."

"I don't want to talk about it. I just want to quit."

That wasn't okay, as much as I wished it were.

"Dulcie, we have to talk about it. It's much too big a decision not to talk out."

"Dad said I could."

"And I'm not saying you can't. We don't have to have the conversation now, but we do have to have it eventually." I cursed my ex-husband for giving her the okay without talking to me. Of course she could quit, but it wasn't good for her to make a decision like that without understanding why she wanted to and what it would mean.

I stood up and filled the kettle. "I'll make some hot chocolate. We can watch a movie."

"I hate that powdered hot chocolate. Instant!" She spat the word out as if she could taste the stuff and wanted it out of her mouth.

Inwardly, I sighed. She was acting her age. I couldn't blame her and I didn't want her to act any other age. But that didn't mean I could cope with it. Of every aspect of motherhood, the one that I had the hardest time with was the idea that I had to adore every facet of my daughter's personality. My daughter was stubborn and willful and sarcastic, and when she exhibited all those parts of her personality at once, it was as if a demon child had moved into her body and taken over.

I shut off the kettle and opened the refrigerator. "Do you want some cider? It's fresh; I bought it over the weekend. I can heat that and put some cinnamon sticks in it."

Usually she loved this fall beverage, but of course she shook her head. "No. I just want you to call Raul and tell him I'm out of the show."

"It'll be okay with you when the play opens in New York in eight weeks and you aren't in it? You won't regret this?"

She shook her head.

"I think instead of calling him, we should go down to the studio together tomorrow morning and tell him in person."

"No," she shrieked. "I can't. I don't want to see him."

On some mental checklist I noted her reaction to my suggestion, not sure yet what it meant. Why was that such an abhorrent idea? I sat back down at the kitchen table, next to her. "We don't have to do it when everyone else is there, Dulcie, but you have to see Raul and tell him yourself."

"I said I won't. There isn't some stupid rule that I have to."

"No, not a rule. But it's common courtesy. He chose you out of three hundred and fifty other girls. He's been working with you for months. You can't just disappear without explaining why."

"You tell him why. Mom—" She strung the word out so it hung on the air. If she had been younger, I would have acquiesced. Instead, I wondered what was really going on and why she wanted me to take over. Was it just a regression to wanting her mother to take care of her so she could feel like a little girl, all safe and protected after her foray into the unfeeling, the critical?

I didn't think so. Even when she was younger, Dulcie had never been the kind of child who wanted me to fight her battles for her. She'd never relied on me to handle her confrontations, nor had she been afraid of them. If anything, like my ex-husband, she seemed to get stronger when faced with adversity.

"Raul thinks I'm an idiot. An idiotic baby who had the worst stage fright than anyone ever had in the whole world."

I felt like a warrior who wanted to slay this dragon that had threatened my loved one. "He called you an idiotic baby?"

She shook her head.

"What did he say to you?"

"He told me…" She didn't finish.

"Dulcie, it's okay. I won't embarrass you with him. Just tell me what he said to you. I need to know."

Still, she hesitated.

"He told me…" she whispered.

I took her hand and held it between mine. Our fingers were almost the same length. I remembered a diminutive hand that used to grab onto mine with fierce strength. "What did he say, sweetie?"

"Nothing."

"Come on, tell me."

She burst into tears. I didn't think she could have that many tears in her. I scooted my chair closer to hers, gathered her into my arms and stroked her back.

"I…let…him…down… Oh, Mom… He won't want me to work with him anymore.…"

Finally, I saw the first glimmer of what was really going on. How could I have been so dense?

"Dulcie, all these weeks you've been asking me to pick you up from the studio ten or fifteen minutes late. Was it really because you didn't want me walking in on a rehearsal or was it something else?"

She looked up at me from under her thick lashes that sparkled with tears. "I just didn't want you to see me making mistakes."

"I believe that was one reason. What I am asking, and you know it, is, was that the only reason?"

She didn't have to say a word. I could see the answer in the way she looked away from me.

So many times during the last two months, I'd arrived at the studio to find Dulcie working with Raul on her part. They weren't alone—there were always other cast and crew around getting ready to leave and talking to one another—but she clearly was spending more time with him than the other kids were. I knew that was because she had the lead. But did she realize that was the only reason? Was she seeking him out because she needed help or because she wanted the attention he gave her?

"He never minded that I hung around after rehearsals to talk about my part." She was still in my arms and spoke her words into my neck. I could feel her breath, hot and moist, on my skin.

"I'm sure he didn't mind," I told her.

Dulcie didn't say anything else.

She wasn't eight or nine years old. She was thirteen. And now I knew she had a crush on Raul Seeger. Which was why my daughter was devastated that she hadn't lived up to her director's expectations.

"You have to call him for me, Mom, and tell him I'm quitting." Her words were still muffled.

"Dulcie, Dad told me that the review also said you

showed incredible range in your singing and you had serious star potential."

"They were just saying that."

"If they were just saying that about the good part, then why weren't they just saying that about the bad part?"

"I…don't…know."

All I had wanted from the beginning was for Dulcie to stay in school and put off having an acting career until after college. Now I was about to convince her not to give up the play, because this wasn't about her stage fright anymore. It wasn't about the play being too much pressure for her.

It was a conflict of heart. Her first. And I was not going to let my thirteen-year-old daughter give up her dream because she was embarrassed in front of the man she had a crush on—her director.

She was sitting up again. The tears had stopped but her face was stained.

"Can't Raul work with you on the stage fright? I'm sure he's had lots of experience with other kids."

"He said he could. All I had to do was ask."

"But?"

"If I asked him to help me Mom, he'd know how weak I was. He'd know I wasn't good at it and that I couldn't do it without him."

She was looking at me when she said it. And the way the light was shining on her face, I could see myself at the table reflected in her eyes.

"Well, that's okay, sweetie. It's okay to ask him for help. For him to know that you need him. He won't think any less of you."

I was hearing my own words. Knowing that I wouldn't think about them now, but that they had their own resonance for me, too.

"I don't know," she said hesitantly.

"Did you like being in the play—once you got past that first scene?"

She nodded, now almost ashamed to tell me, some part of her realizing that she had not been quite honest with me about the crisis.

"The problem was in the show on Saturday night, right?"

She nodded.

"What happened during the matinee on Sunday? Was it as scary?"

"Well, part of the time I worried about screwing up."

"What about the other part of the time?"

She got up and went to the fridge and pulled out a soda. "I guess it was okay," she said with her back to me.

"Okay? That doesn't tell me much. What was it like?"

She popped the top and turned around. "I wasn't really there. Mary Lennox was. I was sort of seeing what she was seeing. It was like the play was real, and what was real disappeared." She'd forgotten the embarrassment and was reliving the exhilaration of having slipped into another being's soul and inhabiting it for a while.

"Your grandmother used to tell me that," I said. A pang of loss, like a minor chord, reverberated inside me. You don't ever stop missing someone you have loved, you simply learn how to make the longing for them a piece of you. You learn that missing them is the part of loving them that never leaves, but that doesn't mean that every once in a while it doesn't catch you unawares and shock you with its potency. "So I guess you are going to have to stay in the play," I said.

"Why's that?"

"Because actresses have to act, honey. That's what makes

them feel alive and fulfills them. And Raul can help you. I bet he'll even like helping you."

"Will I have to ask him for help?" She frowned.

"Here's the thing, Dulcie. Even though you aren't going to like admitting that you need help, the person whom you are asking to help you—if he cares about you—will be very pleased. It will mean so much to him that you need him that he will never even notice that you feel uncomfortable about it."

Forty-Seven

❦

The long living room wall was covered with newspaper clippings. There must have been a good twenty-five stories cut out and taped up. Each one telling the story in a slightly different way.

Once in Italy, he had gone into a church. Was it in Siena? The whole back wall had been covered with slips of paper, different sizes and colors, each covered with handwriting. Every note had been a prayer. Some old and yellowed. Others with the ink still black and fresh. He had taken a picture of the wall of prayers.

This then was his wall of answered prayers. The men who had taunted him were getting what they deserved. One by one by one. The only thing he was sorry about was that, although they described the other photographs of the dead bodies, they weren't showing them. The silly small shots of their bare feet, with the numbers, were disturbing and gruesome, for sure. Graphic, too. In fact, if he were doing a cover for a book about these serial murders, he'd use this image of the insignificant filthy feet, so vulnerable with the bold bright red numbers printed on them.

His glance traveled from the number 1 on Philip Maur's

feet to the number 2 on Timothy Wheaton's feet to the number 3 on Grant Firth's feet. And now the number 4 on the bottom of Bruce Levin's feet.

Number 5 would be up on the wall next. But he could be patient. Today was for luxuriating in Bruce Levin's demise. He had been one of the worst of them. Laughing at his cock, flaunting his own erection. Stud. Fucking stupid stud.

He smiled.

Not anymore, he wasn't.

Paul Lessor wished there were someone he could tell. Because it was so satisfying that he needed to share it.

They had laughed at him and now they were dying.

And no one had any idea why.

On the news and in the papers, reporters kept asking: What connects these men? Why these four? What is their bond to each other? And the longer they searched and the more they looked and the more bodies that showed up, the more baffled they became.

Paul knew. The thing that bound them together was the deepest darkest secret each of these men carried. Secrets they each had gone to great lengths to hide so that no one could find out about their nocturnal wanderings, their willingness to subjugate themselves to the powerful women who had them lie down or stand up and kiss them or lick them or fuck them or massage them or bathe them, or the one who had even been so bold as to ask him to wipe her pussy after she had gone to the bathroom.

No. None of these powerful men—who ran companies and made money and ordered other people around—wanted anyone to know that they belonged to a secret society where they were as powerless as ants under a gardener's shoe. And so they had hidden their secret so well that neither their families nor the police or the reporters could find the connection between them.

It was late. After two on Sunday night. He should go to sleep. He would pay the price for this tomorrow when he went to work. But he wasn't tired yet.

He picked up the red magic marker on his desk and walked over to the wall of answered prayers and began to underline his favorite parts in the articles that had appeared in the weekend papers. And he wondered how much longer it would take until the secret leaked out. Until everyone who had laughed at him was being laughed at. That would be rich.

Forty-Eight

꧁⁓◦⁓꧂

"It's too bright in here. Can't you shut off some of the lights?" Anne asked.

"I'd like that, too," Ellen said.

The lights were not that bright. My desk lamp was on. The recessed lighting was at the same level it always was. I thought about the request, got up, and turned the rheostat down just enough to make a difference. Then I sat back down.

The group had assembled. Everyone was present except for Betsy, and I wasn't surprised that she hadn't shown up.

"Let's get started. If—" I had to remind myself not to call her Betsy. "If Liz comes we'll be able to fill her in."

"I think we should wait for her. She's the only one who isn't here," Davina said. "And this is the first time we've all been together since the last two articles appeared. This is the only place we can be together and talk about this."

"I understand that you'd like everyone to be here. But she may not be coming. And there is a lot for us to talk about. Is it all right with everyone if we proceed?"

I got a few lukewarm nods. Only Shelby spoke. "I think you're right, Dr. Snow. We really need to get started so we can talk about what's happened."

Over the last three weeks, the stress these women were feeling had become more profound. They were in shock. Disturbed. Confused. And flat-out frightened.

The conversation quickly turned to the four men who had been chosen and conjecture about why, out of the many dozens who were participants in the society, they were being targeted. No one could come up with a reasonable suggestion. It seemed random.

The group was also sincerely worried about several men who hadn't been seen at the society in the past two weeks. Were any of them missing?

"Maybe they just aren't coming to your evenings. Perhaps the news has scared them away. Have you tried to contact them?"

"Yes. But we can't do any more than leave coded messages. And we haven't heard back from them," Shelby said.

"I'm surprised anyone is still coming," Ginny said. "Why isn't everyone staying away? Why aren't I?"

"How do you feel about being there?" I asked.

"As if it's more important than ever to show up…" She seemed embarrassed for a moment. "It makes me feel even more alive. Like we are saying 'fuck you' to whoever this madman is every time we get together."

A few other women agreed.

"I think that is a very reasonable reaction. You want everything to go back to normal. It's a way of defusing the reality of what's happened."

"When I'm at the society, I can pretend that nothing has changed," Anne said.

"I don't feel that way," Davina said. "I don't think I can do this anymore. It's wrong. Like we are playing some kind of ghoulish sex game."

Shelby shook her head. "This isn't our fault, though. It's not something that we did. We're not responsible." She spoke too loudly.

Anne started to cry. "I'm tired of being sad. I don't think I'll ever stop being sad. It was bad enough when it was just Philip. And, after him, Tim. But now…four men…this is horrible. I think we should do something."

Shelby turned quickly to look at her. "I thought you and I already resolved that."

"Maybe it would be helpful to tell the group what you resolved," I suggested.

Anne turned directly to me. "I told Shelby I thought we should talk to the police."

I was glad that someone had brought it up again. If no one had, I was going to try and figure out how to suggest it myself.

There was only one connection between these men. It was the society that these women belonged to and participated in. Yes, now the police knew that each victim had a mark on his right foot that connected him to the others, but that wasn't much of a lead without knowing what the mark was.

"No." Shelby spoke sharply. "It's just impossible. What could we say? No one knows about us. The very last thing we can do is expose our membership. That would be disastrous. We'd never recover!" She was almost shrieking.

It was the first time since we'd started the group that she exhibited this level of emotion. And I was glad.

"It doesn't matter if it destroys the society," Anne said. She was angry now, too. "If it means that even one man's life will be saved, I don't see how we have any choice. I don't even understand how it can be a conversation."

"You can't be serious," Ginny said. "Are you willing to

have your husband find out? Your boss? Your kids? Your in-laws? Your friends? I'm not. I absolutely am not. Besides, what good will telling the police do? Aid them in warning all the men that they are targets? For God's sake, there isn't one man from the society who doesn't know that by now."

"Except it hasn't helped," Anne argued.

"This is not a discussion," Shelby said. "We all took an oath. So did every man who joined us. We cannot tell anyone anything."

"I think this is a discussion," I said. "And an important one."

Shelby turned on me. "You would. You talked to that reporter. Why did you do that? You told us that you would keep our secret with us. But you talked to the press."

The attack was easier for everyone to focus on than the discussion of whether or not they should talk to the police. Ten sets of eyes—angry, hurt and accusatory—turned on me.

"No, Shelby. I didn't go to the reporter. She came to me. And I didn't discuss anything about the society with her. You can be sure of that. My comments were about what we can expect from a sexualized serial killer. Not about the men who have been killed or what might tie them together."

"But you may still be talking to her. How can we know you aren't?"

I wound up explaining privilege to them once again. I needed them to understand that it was up to one of them to go to the police and help them in figuring out who was behind these crimes. At the same time, they needed to trust me if I was going to help them work through their anger, shame and guilt over what had happened.

"The U.S. Supreme Court established the psychother-apist-patient privilege in the federal courts in its *Jaffee v. Redmond* decision in 1996. The psychiatric community had always operated on this premise but finally it went to the courts. For almost fifty years, lawyers and doctors had been trying to clearly establish that communication be-tween patients and their psychotherapists was in need of a very high level of protection."

They were listening. Intently. Only Shelby seemed to be ignoring what I was saying. She was looking out the win-dow, staring into the tangled tree branches, lit by the street-lamp.

"There is another precedent—the Tarasoff case," I con-tinued, "which established just how far that privilege ex-tended. In that court case, it was decided that psychiatrists do have an obligation to warn a third party when a patient has threatened that third party. But none of you has told me the name of the next person or persons at risk. And as far as I know, none of you knows. So I have no right to go to the police myself."

"You are saying that as if you think we have the right to go," Cara said.

"An obligation to go," Anne said.

"No. No. That is just not going to happen," Shelby yelled, her head swinging around to face the group again. "What are you going to tell them? What names are you even going to give them? We don't know one another's real names, for Christ's sake. This is insane. We have a trust to uphold."

"At what price?" Anne asked.

No one said anything.

"We don't want you to talk to the press anymore," Shelby said to me, obviously trying to change the subject.

"That's not something that has anything to do with you, I'm sorry," I said as kindly as I could.

"It does. Don't you understand? If we hadn't hired you, if we hadn't paid you, you wouldn't know anything about this case. You wouldn't be getting your name in the paper. You wouldn't be getting patients because of us."

I am not made of ice. Pushed, I can get just as annoyed as anyone else. And yet, in this setting, understanding what I did about the stress these women were under—and Shelby in particular—I made an extra effort to control my own emotions so I could help them with theirs.

"Shelby, I didn't talk to the press to get more patients. Why would you think that?"

"We're giving you power," she said.

In her world, this was a transaction and power was her currency. Several of the women in the room nodded their heads, agreeing, understanding what she said. The very reason the society had been created was to allow them to act out their desires to metaphorically—and perhaps literally, from what I had seen on the videotape—be on top.

"You see it as power, but I don't. You hired me to help you cope with a disturbing situation. That doesn't put me in a position of weakness any more than it puts you in a position of strength. This isn't a battle between us."

"And it won't be as long as you don't talk to the press."

Davina had been listening intently, but saying very little. "Shelby, back off, will you? Can we just talk about what we might be able to do? How we feel about this? How to handle all this shit? I go to the office. I snap at people. I'm angry. Then I get sad. I want to cry but I'm afraid that, if I let myself cry, my friends or my family will ask me what's wrong. What the fuck am I supposed to tell them? How do I short-circuit the grieving process so I can get back to my life?"

"You can't. You—" I looked around and focused, one after the other, on each of the women. "None of you can short-circuit this process. That's why it's important to talk it out here. To feel free to let out whatever you want to." My glance stopped at Ginny.

"I have something I want to let out," she said. "I think I know who might be behind this."

Forty-Nine

Nina must have been waiting for the group to leave because she came to my office within five minutes of the last woman going. "Can we talk?" she asked.

I nodded. "But not now. I have to get home for Dulcie."

"Do the two of you have plans for dinner?"

"No."

"Why don't I go home with you? We can walk. Talk on the way. Then the three of us can get a bite."

She didn't wait until we reached the street but started in as we descended the staircase from the second floor to the lobby. "We have to work this out," she said. "It's not good for you or me. And it's not good for the institute."

It had been several days since our argument, and that was a first for us. In all the years since my mother had died, Nina and I hadn't ever had an argument that had lasted longer than a few hours.

"It's even worse for the four men who are dead," I said.

She opened the heavy door that led to the street. It was evening already, but like so many other days that fall, the weather was relatively warm. I was wearing a blazer with a sweater thrown over my shoulders and knotted around my neck. Nina had on a camel-colored shawl, theatrically draped around her.

The stores were well lit, and as we passed boutique after boutique I saw the two of us mirrored in the glass. I was so used to seeing our reflections, side by side.

"Are you going to change your mind about how I've been handling the Scarlet Society?"

"It's the police I have the problem with," Nina said. "That and why, knowing how I felt, you brought the issue up in our weekly meeting."

"I didn't know I was being censored."

"Can you stop acting like a chastised teenager and lay off the sarcastic tone?"

"Will that help? I'm still not going to agree with you about this. Things are only getting worse," I said, and told her what had happened in the group.

That took us to Seventy-fourth Street, where we stopped and waited for the light to turn so we could cross. "We've fought before, but we've never been on such opposite sides of the argument. I want advice from someone who's willing to help me explore my options, and you are rigidly holding to your own position."

Her eyebrows came together and her eyes narrowed. "You are still doubting my judgment?"

"You taught me to look at every side of an argument when dealing with patients. To assume nothing. But you're being stubborn about this."

"Morgan, do you know the name of any person who is going to be targeted?"

"You know I don't."

"Do you know the name of anyone who is targeting members of this society?"

"I don't. One of the women in the group thinks she might. But that isn't the point."

The light changed and we crossed together, still in step.

"It is. What you should be doing is working with these women to help them deal with their grief and counseling them about how they feel about their activities. And while you are doing that, you should be working on your paper about the changing level of sexually aggressive behavior among women who have assumed high levels of power."

"Do you care that four men have been killed by some madman?"

"You're insulting me, Morgan."

"I can't believe you are being so stubborn."

"Why?"

"Because it's not as black and white as you are making it out to be. These men are being killed. The only thing they have in common is the Scarlet Society. One of the members of that society is a reporter who is breaking the stories, who shows manic tendencies and exhibits signs of stress and guilt. And who has hidden her profession from the other group members and hidden her knowledge of what ties the men together from the police and the *New York Times*. Add to that another member who told me tonight about some guy who was paranoid and possibly bipolar, who had left the group before the killings started, and who seemed to have a lot of anger toward several of the other male members. So that's two possible suspects. And the police don't know about either of them."

"The police know the reporter. You told me they do. And I'm sure they think she's a suspect."

"Based on the fact that she's breaking the stories. Yes, possibly. But they'd take that much more seriously if they also knew she'd had sex, for God's sake, with every one of those men, is feeling completely unattractive and is jealous of the younger women in the group."

We'd stopped for another light. The wind blew and a crimson leaf fell off a tree and across Nina's face. She brushed it away and it drifted to the pavement.

"We have a job to do, Morgan. That job does not include doing the work of the New York Police Department."

"We are doctors. Our job includes saving people's lives."

"That's very naive. We just do the best we can. We're not superheroes."

"I agree with you. That's why we can't make decisions like the one you are making. In other words, we have to remain silent at any cost?"

But the light had changed and Nina had started crossing the street. She hadn't heard my question. Or she hadn't known how to answer it.

Fifty

He had only slept for four hours, and fitfully at that, because he was anxious. The *New York Times* was always delivered to his apartment door at five-thirty. Would there be another article this morning? Another mention of the last murdered man? Another criticism of how long the police were taking to make any headway with the cases?

He padded into his kitchen in his Frette terry-cloth robe and turned on the kettle. While the water boiled, he took out a Limoges cup and saucer, a silver teaspoon and a box of loose black tea. He filled a bamboo basket with the tea leaves, pinched a sprig of mint off the plant on his windowsill, rinsed it and dropped it in the cup just as the kettle started to sing.

As he poured the water, he heard the thud of the paper on his doormat and left the tea to steep while he retrieved the *Times*.

Sitting on the couch, the cup on his coffee table, he scanned the front page. Nothing. It took about five minutes to search through the National section and the Metro section, looking for any press about the Scarlet Society murders.

Nothing.

This was going to ruin his day. Was going to make the low-level depression he never escaped escalate to mid-level.

No. He couldn't give in.

Abandoning the paper, he returned to the kitchen, heated up the water again, toasted an English muffin, slathered it with raspberry jam from Fauchon in Paris, and took his breakfast back into the living room. He knew what to do. He'd done it before and it had helped.

Half of the muffin in hand, he stood in front of the wall of articles and, beginning with the very first, reread them. He didn't skip a word, and paid even more attention to the sentences he'd underlined with the red marker. Some particularly pleased him; others annoyed him.

He had read each of these articles dozens of times by now, but it still never got boring. He loved seeing the black type on the newsprint, the way the serifs bled into the paper, the way the lines marched like soldiers up and down the page, in perfect formation. More than once, he lost the meaning of the words, forgetting that each connected to the next to make a phrase, which added to the next made a sentence, which added to the next made a paragraph. Instead, he saw the straight lines and curved forms, the dots and dashes and negative spaces between them. He ran his finger over the designs, seeing the patterns in the way the margins broke and how the indents made holes. And there was the abstract design of his marker—the only color amid the monochromatic type. An artist, he appreciated the way he'd slashed through the colorless information with red, marking all mentions of when the loved ones had last seen the victims alive and what the mood and manner of the men had been. He'd also highlighted direct quotes from the

police—specifically Detective Noah Jordain. No matter
how well he couched what he said, it was all too clear to
Paul that Jordain really had not made any inroads in identifying a suspect or discovering the whereabouts of any of
the bodies.

Paul had starred—again in red marker—every instance
in which the reporter had hinted at what the connection between the men was. It was very subtle. He wondered how
many people had picked up on it. Had the police?

"The scarlet numbers on the bottom of his feet were…"

In each article, Betsy Young had referred to the color
of the markings that way. It was always scarlet. Not red,
which would have been a much more obvious choice. Or
vermilion, which probably would have been the choice of
anyone educated in the study of color. Not bloodred, which
would have been slightly flowery for the *New York Times*,
but a possibility considering the crime.

No. She had used *scarlet* as her adjective of choice.

Who was she, and what did she know?

He thought of going down to the *Times* offices and
meeting her. Trying to trick her into revealing her knowledge of the Scarlet Society.

But how?

He resumed rereading.

There was one section he'd accentuated for entirely different reasons. He looked at these two paragraphs now, focusing on them, wondering yet again about this sexpert and
how smart she really was.

Dr. Morgan Snow, a sex therapist who works at the
Butterfield Institute and who was instrumental in
solving the recent Magdalene Murders, said that
there are signals in photographs the paper has

chosen not to run that these might be crimes of a sexual nature. In one, an unseen photographer shot directly between the victim's legs. There is black-and-blue bruising on the victims' wrists, ankles and testicles. This, said Dr. Snow, strongly suggests a sexual component to the crimes.

"Black-and-blue discoloration often indicates S & M. Restraints can heighten both the sense of control and submission in sex play," said Snow.

He liked Dr. Snow's observations. He'd heard about the Butterfield Institute but he hadn't been there yet. In his search for the right doctor to help him, the institute had been next on his list. Maybe it was time to go there. He had reason enough with his personal problems. He could make a convincing case that the purpose of his visit was other than to discover just what Young had shown Dr. Snow, and what she really believed about the motivation of the killer. He was desperate to hear someone describe the photographs to him in person. To listen to the soft and hard sounds of the words that would detail the malevolent restraints and the defiled bodies. To actually have someone talk to him about the black-and-blue marks and what they suggested about how painful and humiliating the abuse was that these men had suffered before they had been killed.

Walking back into the kitchen, Paul heated the water once more. The next cup of tea was even weaker than the last. Too much caffeine too early wasn't a good idea. He hadn't taken his medication yet. He had another fifteen minutes before he would open the amber pill bottle and spill the poison into his palm. The calm would be welcome, the dullness would not. Every day he teetered on the edge of not taking the pills. Occasionally he didn't. Those days he was not himself. Or he was more himself than on the other days. His dick could get hard again if he didn't take the pills. It would swell and rise up and remind him of what it felt like to be in control of his own body. But his mind would rebel. His head would explode. He would want to lie on the pavement on the sidewalk and have women walk all over him with their high heels. He would want to wipe out every other man who got in the way of him and those women. He would be on fire with wanting and hurting. And then he would crash. The depression would overwhelm him. Rob him of any desire to eat or sleep or stand or walk or go to the bathroom or make an effort to dress himself.

It was all too much. It was all enough.

Abandoning the inadequate tea, he opened a cabinet and pulled out the thick New York City phone book. Flipping through the thin pages, he found what he was looking for, and using the bright red marker that he took from his bathrobe pocket, he copied down the address and phone number of the Butterfield Institute.

Fifty-One

Despite the soft, late afternoon sunlight Paul Lessor had not taken off his black wraparound sunglasses.

"I have been to quite a few therapists," he answered as he crossed his right leg over his left knee. The perfect crease in his pants broke.

I wanted to see his eyes. "Is the light too bright, Paul? Do you want me to lower the blinds?"

"Yes. That would be better."

I got up and walked to the window. In its reflection I could see that his head did not turn to follow me, but rather he looked over at the door as if checking to see that it was closed. His movements were slightly slower than normal. I recognized the lethargy and guessed that he was on an antipsychotic drug.

We'd get to that.

After returning to my seat, I expected he'd take off his glasses and was disappointed when he didn't. "I closed the drapes. You can take off your sunglasses," I suggested.

He made a move to do what I asked but his arm stopped midair and hung there momentarily before he lowered it again. "I need to leave my current therapist," he said. "Leave him. Sooner than later."

"Tell me about him and why you don't want to stay. You don't have to give me his name if you don't want to, but I'd appreciate knowing it."

"Why do we need to talk about him?"

"I'd like to understand why you are looking for someone new before I refer you to someone in the institute. I want to choose the right doctor."

"You're going to give me a referral?"

"Yes. This is a consultation."

"I know that. But I thought it was a consultation with you. So you could be my therapist."

"I might be, but that's not how we work here. First we have to do an evaluation. I might not be the right doctor for you."

He shook his head, and the well-styled sandy hair fell into his eyes. "I really came here to see you. To be with you."

The sexual undertone was barely there, but I heard it. The way his voice had lowered to another register on the last few words. The sly way his lips formed the words and then ended in a half smile.

"I'm flattered. But may I ask why?"

"I've read about you in the paper. I did my homework. I think we belong together."

He was connecting to me too quickly. We had not yet formed any kind of bond. Paul Lessor had projected a relationship prematurely.

"Are you currently on any medication?"

He hesitated before he said, "No."

I assumed he was lying. He'd waited too long to answer me. I'd know for sure if I could see his eyes, but the dark lenses prevented me from reading him.

"Have you ever been on medication?"

"Dr. Snow, I have to ask you something. It's very important."

I nodded.

"Do you know the reporter who is writing about those murders? The ones where the victims have those red numbers drawn on the bottoms of their feet?"

"Can you tell me why that matters?"

"I'm concerned about the situation."

"Yes, it's very serious."

"Do you know anything about those killings? Has the reporter shown you the photographs? Do you know something that isn't in the papers? It's why I picked you, because the reporter interviewed you specifically."

I hoped that my face remained placid, I didn't give anything away, but a tiny flicker of fear shot through me. I leaned forward, trying to lock eyes with the man who sat across from me, but only guessing where I was looking.

"Can you tell me why?"

"Because I am very concerned. I told you that."

Instinct warned me that he was connected in some way to the killings.

"But why are you concerned? Did you know any of those men?"

"No."

"Why are you concerned?"

"Do you really think it's a good idea to help that reporter?" he asked, ignoring my question.

"Why wouldn't it be?"

"You might get hurt. It really could be dangerous for you to get involved."

"It's kind of you to be concerned for me, but why do you think that I might get hurt when all I did was talk to a reporter over the phone?"

I studied him while he thought about how to answer. Was he wearing a hairpiece? His sunglasses were too big, too wide. Was it to hide from me? Was he here in disguise?

He rubbed his hands together almost obsessively.

"Maybe we could talk about you and how you are feeling right now," I said, changing the subject on purpose, stalling, trying to assess the situation and figure out what to do.

"I'm much happier than I've been in a while," he said.

"That's good. How long have you been happy?"

"For the past two weeks."

"Can you tell me what it was like before you were happy?"

He didn't answer. In fact, he seemed to forget where he was as his hand went up to his chest and slipped inside the blazer he was wearing. He frowned. Felt his chest for another minute.

"Maybe I should go," he said suddenly. "I think I need to go."

"Why?"

He shook his head back and forth several times. "I just wanted to warn you about getting any more involved with that reporter."

"I thought you were here to find a new therapist."

"No."

"You just came here to warn me?"

He nodded. He was still holding his hand on his chest in a pose reminiscent of Napoléon. "You could get yourself in a lot of trouble, Dr. Snow."

"How?"

"By trying to interfere. That's what therapists do. You interfere. But none of you really knows what you're doing. You just guess. I know that. I've been part of your guessing game. I keep trying one of you after another and all you do is suck my strength."

"How do we do that?"

He continued talking as if he hadn't even heard my question. "Do you know how powerful it is to be weak? When someone wants you to obey them and you do, you become the feeder, the nurturer. You have the authority then, even though it seems exactly the opposite. But the therapist I'm going to has taken away all that and the other men don't understand. I tried to explain it to them. They just laughed at me."

I was having a hard time following him. "What men?"

"Don't you understand? I thought you would."

"I don't. I would be happy to help you find a therapist who can work with you."

His hand was still inside his jacket, pressed to his chest. "That is not the point. I told you, didn't I? I came here to warn you that you are in danger. Don't you see that?"

"How?"

"You're meddling. This has to be done. And it has to be done in a certain way. It's not over. There are more men who have to be punished, and you can't interfere."

He stood up, and as he did, something fell out of his hand, flashing as it hit the floor. Quickly, he bent over to pick it up. When he stood up, his jacket didn't fall back correctly and his shirt was exposed. On the right-hand side, where he'd been keeping his hand, was a round wet spot.

When women are breastfeeding, their breasts can leak. I knew that; I'd breastfed Dulcie. Men rarely lactate but they can under certain conditions. Suddenly, the dots were appearing faster than I could connect them. I needed to keep him in my office for a few more minutes and call the police. Clearly, he was involved in the killings.

Nina's admonitions didn't apply here. Paul Lessor wasn't yet my patient. This had been a consultation. And he had threatened me. That gave me the right to tell the police.

And he was lactating. He was probably suffering from other side effects of the drug. I took a chance that he was.

"Your mouth is probably really dry, isn't it? We still have a half hour left. Why don't you just sit down, let me get you some water. Then we can relax and you can tell me what you mean about my being in danger."

He was still agitated, but something I'd said had reached him and he sat down as I'd suggested.

As I moved, I explained exactly what I was doing. "I am going to get up now and go ask my assistant to bring in a carafe of ice water. With two glasses." I continued talking as I walked to my office door, opened it and took two steps in the direction of Allison's desk.

"Can you bring us some ice water?" I said, loudly enough to be sure Paul could hear me. Leaning forward, I whispered in a voice I prayed he wouldn't be able to hear, "Call 911. Then call Jordain."

Raising my voice again, I added, "Yes, two glasses."

I walked back into my office, leaving the door ajar. He couldn't see that; his back was to the entrance.

As I came back around toward my desk, I saw what had fallen out of his pocket: a straight-edge razor blade. He held it in his hands, playing with it as if it were no more harmful than a feather.

"Could I see that?" I asked, hoping that he couldn't hear any fear in my voice. My stomach cramped. I forced myself to think clearly. I did not have to be afraid. Even if he jumped up and came at me with the small blade, I was prepared, I knew how to protect myself.

He was playing with it so that it caught the lamplight and gleamed. Then he rotated it and a flicker of light moved from my wall to the floor, then flew to my face and into my right eye. I blinked. He shifted it again and the shimmer jumped to the window.

"Why do you have that?"

"I make collages—just one of the tools of the trade," he said, as if I were a child and he were explaining to me.

"Oh? Do you work at a magazine?"

"No."

"What kind of work do you do? Are you a photographer?" I was almost afraid to hear his answer. I held my breath. If he said yes—

"I thought you wanted to know about the danger you are in."

"I do."

Allison appeared at the door and knocked.

"Oh, good. The ice water," I said. "Thank you, Allison."

He jerked around, moving as quickly as he could, but still circling a fraction more slowly than someone who wasn't medicated. He hid the razor blade in his hand so that she couldn't see it. I hoped his reflexes were off just enough so that he would cut himself with it, distract himself.

"I don't want anyone in here with us," he said, nodding his head in her direction.

"She won't stay. Allison is just bringing us some water. Your mouth is dry, isn't it? You need the water. Allison, you can put the pitcher and the glasses on my desk. Thank you."

"You're welcome," she said to me. Her hands shook as she put down the tray.

"That's good," I said.

She didn't move, just stood in front of me, staring at me.

"Thanks, Allison," I said again. "We can handle it from here."

She left without looking back at the man on the couch.

After her footsteps retreated, Paul said, "She didn't shut the door."

"No, she didn't."

"I'd like it better if the door was closed. I don't want anyone to come in." He had taken the blade out and was examining it again. His beloved talisman. His shining toy. His power. His strength.

I got up. How much time had passed since I had asked Allison to call the police? How long would it take for Jordain to get here? What if he wasn't at the number Allison had for him? What if she hadn't gotten in touch with him? No. She would have said something. The number she had for him was his cell phone, wasn't it? Wasn't that the number I'd put in the book last summer? Yes, it had to be his cell phone. Because he'd always answer his cell phone, no matter where he was; he'd told me that when he gave me the card with the numbers written on it. Besides, I wasn't in immediate danger—not as long as I could keep Paul Lessor talking. And I could do that, I told myself. No matter how nervous I was, that was my job, that was what I did every single day. I helped people open up. Cut through their barriers. Bled out their emotions.

I could do it with him.

And the surgery, so to speak, would keep him occupied. I hoped.

Fifty-Two

Jordain, Perez and Butler were all hunched over the last set of shots Young had received. They were still waiting for all but a few enlargements they'd requested. But there were more than enough to work with. Or to be frustrated by. Everyone on the Delilah team was overworked, over-tired and feeling the pressure of an investigation that had never gotten past go.

"Delilah is nothing if not consistent," Perez said. "Look at this. Every one of these four guys has marks around their wrists and ankles at the same points. It's almost as if he uses his own previous photos as a template to make sure that the restraints are exact."

When Jordain went to sleep at night, he saw multiple images of these men, all four of them, as if his brain was a hall of mirrors. They went on into infinity, their ghostly figures screaming at him for not stopping this carnage.

He stood up and paced from one side of the room to the next, letting his eyes relax and scan the hundreds of photos that now entombed him. If he stopped focusing, perhaps he could pick up a pattern that they might have overlooked.

Just one more clue.

The two detectives plus Butler, as well as dozens of other cops, continuously mined the photos for something that might lead them to the discovery of the bodies or the apprehension of the killer.

All they had was the tattoo, but they still didn't know what it meant. Perez had sent out copies of the small interlocking shapes to police departments across the country, as well as the FBI. If they could figure out what the mark signified, they would at least know what tied the men together.

"We need one fucking break," Perez said as he popped the top on a can of soda. His back was killing him. They'd all been working sixteen- and eighteen-hour shifts for days, and he was overtired.

"We have to make the break ourselves. We can't wait anymore," Jordain said.

"What can we do that we haven't done?"

"Find the fucking connection." It was not like Jordain to raise his voice, but neither was it like him to be involved in a case as cold as this one. In his fifteen-year career with the police, he had never had a murder investigation with less to go on. "For Christ's sake, we don't even have the bodies. Why? What possible reason is there for the killer to be hiding these bodies from us and yet giving us the proof of his crimes?"

Perez had nothing to say.

"That's a really good question, Noah," Butler said.

"It's only a good question if it gives up a good answer. Right now it's just more bullshit." He slammed his fist down on his desk.

Butler jumped.

"Listen, this is not doing any of us any good," Perez said.

"What isn't?" Jordain asked.

"Losing our tempers. Not sleeping. Looking at these damn pictures hour after hour when there is just nothing here."

"Do we have anything new on Young?" Jordain asked as he broke stride in order to pour himself yet another cup of coffee.

"No. Nothing. We've had this tail on Young 24/7 since day one. And the only thing the woman has done is go to work, go to the gym, go visit some friend over on East End Avenue a few times, and go to Dr. Snow's office with a wig on. Three Monday nights in a row. And one Saturday afternoon. If anyone knows anything, it's your friend."

Jordain glared at his partner. "We can't get the reporter to reveal her sources. We can't get the doctor to violate privilege. There's nothing illegal about her going undercover to get a story or wearing a wig to protect her privacy at the clinic."

"Then we aren't going to get a break. It's that simple. Something has got to give. One of these women has got to decide that she wants to help us more than she wants her own professional—"

Jordain held up his hand. "You're right. We're tired. Let's not push it. Neither of these women is breaking any law. We have to assume that neither of them knows who the killer is, because if she did, and she is any kind of human being, she'd tell us. Even a seasoned reporter jonesing for a big story can't just sit back and let more and more and more men be murdered. And that goes for Morgan, too. Privilege be damned."

Noah was holding back a dozen emotions. He was furious with his partner for even suggesting Morgan might be withholding information, and he was guilty for wanting to protect her if she was involved. He was frustrated that he didn't know how to reach her emotionally and that he still cared about her. He was angry that the case was getting in the way of him having any kind of time with her, if she would even agree to see him again.

He was forty-one years old. He'd been trying to give up on the idea of finding his ideal for too long. He'd pretty much assumed the best he could hope for was that one day he'd get tired of looking. Then he knew he'd finally have a shot at a decent relationship. He'd almost gotten to that point when he'd met Morgan.

Morgan.

He knew better than to think he could ever fix what was wrong with anyone, but he was certain that he was what she needed. And he was even more certain that if Morgan had what she needed in a man, she could finally heal herself.

His cell phone rang. He pulled it off his belt, opened it, barked a hello and listened.

"Let's get out of here," he said as he shut the phone and headed to the door. "We might finally fucking have something. Fast."

Perez wasn't sure, but he thought his partner sounded frightened. He'd only heard his voice like that once before. The night that Morgan Snow got herself trapped in a madman's apartment.

Fifty-Three

Had minutes passed? Or hours? My glance never left Paul Lessor's face. I didn't shift my head or avert my eyes from him, but in my peripheral vision I glimpsed shadows pass by in the hallway outside my door. I would know when Jordain came. If he came.

Now there was only silence out there and the distant ringing of a phone. Then more shadows.

And finally ten movements in one.

The door was thrown all the way open as a blur of figures rushed in, and before I could focus, the action stopped and everything stilled.

Jordain held Paul's arms behind his back. Perez had a gun pulled on him. Three other uniformed cops took position around the room.

In normal time, the scene came back to life as Butler slapped a pair of stainless-steel bracelets on Paul's wrists.

"Paul Lessor, you are under arrest," Perez said, and proceeded to read him his rights.

Paul stared at me as he spit out one word over and over. "Bitch. Bitch. Bitch."

Butler and a cop I didn't recognize took him away.

Jordain walked over to me.

"Are you all right?"

I nodded, not yet trusting myself to speak. Once it was over, the terror had overwhelmed me. I had not allowed myself to think that the killer had been sitting in my office for the past thirty minutes, idly playing with a razor blade.

"We need to know what he told you," Jordain said. "You think you can come down to the precinct?"

I tried to find the words. To calm myself. To let it sink in that there was no threat of danger anymore.

Jordain kneeled down next to me. He put his hands on my knees. The warmth of his flesh coming through my pants seared into my skin. It was the only thing I was aware of. The heat of his hands. I focused on my desk, on the silver-framed photograph of my daughter. Dulcie's face swam in front of my eyes. What would have happened if Paul Lessor had hurt me? Worse. Killed me. Dulcie without me? She'd be all right. She had her father. But she'd be one of the lost girls. Motherless daughters who never quite understand why they never feel whole.

"Morgan?" Jordain's voice pulled me back to the present.

"He is on Thorazine," I blurted out.

"How do you know? He told you?" He was excited. "It's important. It is one of the few pieces of information we had about the murdered men. At least one of them had been drugged with Thorazine."

"He started to lactate. It's one of the side effects of being on Thorazine for an extended period of time. He put his hand under his jacket and kept it there. When his jacket fell open and I saw the wet spot, I knew. I remembered. You'd said Thorazine was on that hair sample. And he kept talking about the men. The other men. That they de-

served this. And that I would be in danger if I interfered."
I was talking too fast. It didn't matter, Jordain was following. His eyes were keeping me centered. I felt safe.

Even there, in that chaotic moment, I hated that false
sense of security. It reminded me of his power over me.
How he could make me talk about things I didn't tell other
people. How he made it seem as if he could keep the harm
away.

"He's got a driver's license, address. Lives in the city."
Perez had come back into my office and was filling Jordain in. "I'm sending Reston and Douglas over there now."

"Morgan, can you come downtown with us?" Jordain
asked.

"I made a tape," I suddenly remembered.

"You did? Why?"

I couldn't remember for a second. Then my head
cleared. "We always tape consultations. The potential patients are informed. It's not unusual."

When I stood up my legs were wobbly. The betrayal surprised me. Jordain put his arm out and it amazed me how
easy it was to lean on him. I got my equilibrium back, let
go of him and, straightening, walked across the room
steadily on my own steam. The tape recorder was small but
in full view on the lower shelf of the coffee table by the
couch.

I shut off the machine, popped the tape out and handed
it to Jordain. "I need it back. You can make a copy, can't
you?"

"Yes." He practically snatched it out of my hand. I
stared at his fingers. I remembered them playing piano.
And playing me a few nights ago. I couldn't make the connection between that man and this detective.

"What is going on in here?" Her voice was strident and

furious at the same time. Nina had never sounded so outraged. Perez and Jordain turned but she ignored them. Her anger was not directed at them. She glared at me. Whatever our attempt at reconciliation had accomplished the other night, it had been undone by having a contingent of policemen inside the Butterfield Institute taking a patient, even a potential patient, away in handcuffs.

Fifty-Four

Perez and Jordain stared at the living room wall. In its way, it was eerily like their own wall at the precinct house. Lessor had papered it from one end to the other with every newspaper article about the Delilah murders. There was a design to the black-and-white clippings, graphically annotated with red markings: a map of a madman's mind.

Jordain started at the right, Perez at the left. They walked from one end to the other, reading mostly to themselves until they found a section that Paul Lessor had underlined. Those they read out loud.

The two policemen who'd gotten there earlier showed the detectives what they had found in their search of the apartment.

"Did you find anything at all that could suggest where the bodies are?" Perez asked.

Both Reston and Douglas said they hadn't, but they showed the detectives the medicine cabinet full of pill bottles, including Thorazine and half a dozen other antipsychotic drugs. Most of them were half full.

"He's been on everything," Perez said. "It's a freaking drugstore in here."

An hour later, the wall had been photographed and, piece by piece, the art director's lair had been dismantled. Nothing had been found to lead them to their next destination in this search.

Often serial killers take souvenirs of their victims, but nothing in the apartment suggested that Paul had done this. There were no weapons. No restraints. There was no evidence of any blood on any of the man's clothes, but they bagged all of his dirty laundry from the hamper in the bathroom so that the lab could go over it.

"This place is so small there's nowhere he could hide anything, but just in case he brought those men here, let's get the place printed."

One of the backups went to work on that.

"I don't like this guy as much as I thought I would," Jordain said after two and a half hours.

"Why's that?"

"Other than his obsession with the stories, there's just nothing here."

"I'm betting he's got some other place somewhere. Out of the city. He's a successful art director at a big publishing company. Probably makes more than enough for a weekender upstate or even in the Hamptons."

"We'll know that as soon as we get a court order for Lessor's bank statements, mortgage papers, phone records. It sure would solve a lot of problems if I am wrong and you are right."

"And this time I bet you wouldn't even mind," Perez said.

"Not one little bit."

Jordain was sitting at Lessor's desk. Everything was neatly put away. One thing that had struck him about the whole apartment was how uncluttered and organized it was. Even the newspapers on the walls were carefully cut out. The underlining was all done in the same red ink.

He opened the maroon leather address book that sat in the right-hand corner of the maroon leather desk pad. Inside, page after page was filled in a studied and artful handwriting.

Nothing was out of order.

"Let's get this cross-referenced," he said to Douglas.

Butler had spent the past few days entering the information from each of the victims' address books and PDAs into a computer. Cross-references might lead them to the killer. Or to someone who knew all four men. Or who might at least know what their connection was.

So far there were only a few matches in the books. A movie theater. The New York Department of Motor Vehicles. Bloomingdale's. And a few restaurants, but that wasn't all that unusual. They all lived in Manhattan, were all well off, were all professionals.

Maybe Lessor's book would offer up something else.

Jordain had picked up the book and was about to bag it when he shook his head. "Jeezus…"

"What is it?" Perez spun around.

"We are so fucking stupid sometimes." He pulled out his cell phone and dialed Butler. She answered on the first ring.

"Take off his goddamn shoes and socks and tell me if he's got the mark on his foot."

Fifty-Five

Nina listened to my explanation of what had happened in the consultation with Paul Lessor. She'd frowned when I described the razor blade and how he had held it up in the light. She'd leaned forward when I explained how he had started to lactate and how I'd put that together with a long-term Thorazine patient and what I knew from Jordain about the victims possibly being drugged with Thorazine before they had died.

Nina's loyalty to those she loved was legendary. And so was the depth of her anger.

Over the years, everyone who worked with her had seen her go into battle for a patient, oppose interference from outside authorities, fight off family members who were detrimental to the patient's regaining his or her mental health.

In the past four months, I had seen her angry more often than in the past thirty years. First over my involvement with the police in the Magdalene Murders, and now with the Scarlet Society case.

But that had been nothing compared to this.

What she said after I finished came hurtling out with a

suppressed force that surprised me. She didn't yell; in fact, her voice was like a whisper. But harsh. Her mouth was pursed and the vertical lines above her upper lip—usually almost invisible—were white with rage.

"You do not call the police to come into this institute and take a patient away in cuffs."

"I explained to you he was not a patient. He was here for a consultation. But that was a ruse. He was here to threaten me, Nina. He had a razor blade. He knew things about the men who have been killed. He *was* threatening me."

"How do you know that he was dangerous? How do you know he wasn't simply delusional? How do you know that razor blade wasn't only a prop?"

"I don't, but I couldn't take a chance. The man had a weapon."

"You have worked with hardened prisoners. You know karate and self-defense. We all do. You know exactly what to do when someone comes at you. If he had a gun, if you were here alone at night, that might have been different. You weren't. He didn't. You were out of line here, Morgan. You were looking for an excuse to call the police. You've been looking for an excuse for days."

"That isn't true."

Her well-shaped eyebrows arched high in disbelief. "Isn't it?"

"Are you insinuating that I'm lying?"

"No. I'm assuming that you are not facing the truth."

"Have I ever done that before?"

"That doesn't mean you are not doing it now," Nina said. "You're not dealing with how you feel about this detective."

"I am dealing with what I know about this spate of killings."

"We've been over this before, haven't we? What you know about the Scarlet Society can't help the police. But that's not the issue here. We're talking about you calling them here."

"I'm telling you that he was threatening me. That I thought there was a real possibility he is the killer and that he had come to make sure I didn't help the police figure out who he was. Why he thought I could, I don't know. Something about what I'd been quoted as saying in the paper. But how much of this matters anymore? They have him in custody. No matter what he did or didn't do, the man brought what I perceived as a weapon into my office. Nina, what if he had jumped on me and cut me? What if he'd lucked out and slit an artery?"

Something softened in her face. A motherly concern, the reality of what I was saying? "You know, don't you, that I'm on your side?"

"You have a funny way of showing it. You aren't looking out for me, Nina, but for the institute."

She frowned. I could see hurt mixed with returning anger.

I stood up. "I have another patient. And this isn't going to get us anywhere. You have to trust me on this."

She stood, too, so we were facing. Neither of us moved to embrace the other. One of us should have.

And then the moment was interrupted by a knock on the door.

"Dr. Snow, Detective Jordain is on the phone."

Fifty-Six

Dulcie was standing in the middle of the living room. I was on the couch, more relaxed than I had been in days. Jordain had Paul Lessor in custody. The danger was over. Dulcie was telling me about her rehearsal.

"Once we were all there, Raul sat us down in a circle and we went over everything that had happened in Boston."

She wasn't just telling me what had happened but performing for me, as if it were a scene from the play. "He asked each one of us what we thought, both positive and negative. No one mentioned me freezing up. No one."

"Well, Dad said it wasn't something he thought many people even noticed. I'm sure it felt to you like it lasted for hours, but he told me it was only a minute or two."

"It did feel like hours, sort of like time had just stopped. And it was so quiet and everyone was looking at me and I couldn't figure out what to do next."

"It sounds really awful," I said. "My mom told me about it when it happened to her."

"Did she ever throw up because she was so nervous?" Dulcie asked. "Raul said some really big actors and actresses throw up even after years of performing. Can you imagine that? If I kept throwing up, I'd quit. Don't you think you would?" But she didn't really give me a chance to answer. There was more to tell about the healing that happened this day. "So then Raul told us there were more reviews and he read them to us."

"Were they good?"

"All three of them said that I was going to be a star. That I had everything it takes."

"Did they mention your stage fright?"

She shook her head. "No. Pretty amazing. I really thought they would." Dulcie was more serene than I'd seen her in the past few weeks. The opening was still eight weeks away. The writers were reworking two of the songs and some of the dialogue. The cast and director were reblocking some of the numbers that had tripped them up in Boston.

I'd talked to Raul for a few minutes while Dulcie was gathering up her stuff that evening, and he assured me that her stage fright was much less severe than he'd seen in far more experienced performers.

"I wouldn't worry about her," he'd said.

"If you can find me a mother who doesn't worry about her daughter, then she's not much of a parent."

I looked around, making sure Dulcie wasn't nearby and couldn't overhear me, and broached the subject of the suspected crush. "It seems perfectly natural to me but I wanted to mention it. To let you know."

"Goes with the territory," he said matter-of-factly. "First time it happened I was floored. Had no bloody idea what was going on. But that was a while ago. I've gotten awfully good at spotting it. And if I do say so, I've figured out how to strike a good balance of staying involved without appearing interested."

After Dulcie finished recounting her day, we'd gone into the kitchen to make real hot chocolate, with melted bittersweet chocolate and milk. Actually, Dulcie was preparing it to ensure its success. I was sitting at the table and keeping her company.

That was when Noah called and asked if it would be okay if he came up.

"Is this business...?"

"Or pleasure?" He finished the part of the sentence I hadn't asked, partly because Dulcie was in the room and partly because it was easier for me to assume it was business.

"I think you have to tell me," I said.

"Tonight, it's business. But it's always a pleasure to do business with you, Dr. Snow."

There was a playfulness back in his tone that seemed appropriate. I could only imagine how relieved he must be to have detained the man who had eluded and confounded him and the rest of the department for almost a month.

I didn't ask him if it could wait until the next day. If it could have, I knew he wouldn't have called.

"Do you like hot chocolate?"

"Are you making it?"

"No, Dulcie is." They'd never met, but he knew about her, had seen photos of her, and had been interested in her drama career.

"Then the answer is yes."

Fifty-Seven

"So, you're the actress," Jordain said as he took Dulcie's hand to shake it. "Tough gig. How are you holding up?"

"Okay," she said.

I could tell that she was curious about him. I'd explained that he was coming over to talk about a current case, but she wasn't quite sure. She had some sixth sense about him. The same sense, I supposed, that I always had about her. So she hadn't just inherited my mother's love of acting, she'd inherited my intuition.

"I think openings are just the worst," he said.

Dulcie looked at me with a crease between her brows, silently throwing accusations across the room like darts. I shook my head at her.

"I didn't tell you that, Detective, did I?" Dulcie asked.

"No. I play piano, Dulcie. Jazz. I've done some big gigs. I know the drill. I know the shakes."

"How long did it take you to get over it?" she asked in a fascinated voice.

"Never got over it, but learned to live with it. Lots of deep breathing. And focusing. Waiting to go on, I ask myself why I'm doing this to myself. And I always have the same answer. Because I want to make the music. Damn the audience."

He was so good at being charming that it was almost suspect. I was glad I wasn't going to have to see him anymore now that the case was solved. He was probably very good at lying, too. The other night with him had been an aberration. One I was not going to put myself in a position to repeat. He'd taken advantage of how stressed I was. How worried I was.

"Hey, it's getting late," I said, seeing that Dulcie had finished her hot chocolate. "Why don't you get ready for bed?"

She gave me the pouty-mouth look that was the precursor to an argument, and I intercepted whatever it was that she was about to say.

"This is nonnegotiable."

"Yes, Dr. Sin," she retorted with just a shade too much sarcasm. I let it ride and repeated the suggestion that she take herself off to bed. She stopped at the door and turned to Noah. "It was really cool that you told me that stuff. Thanks."

"It was nice meeting you. And I'm really looking forward to seeing you in that play," Jordain said.

"Are you coming?" She seemed pleased, which really surprised me. Her response was immediate and heartfelt.

"If your mom invites me."

"If she doesn't, I will."

I'd never seen my daughter flirt, and it shocked me. Not pleasantly, either. I had a jolt of foresight: in one split second I jumped from this one comment to her dating and me being home at night waiting to hear her key in the door.

Jordain and I went into the den.

"Is it him for sure?" I asked.

"Not sure. We think it's him. One very interesting development is that he's got that tattoo on his right foot, like the victims."

"He does?"

Jordain nodded. His gaze focused on me. Unwavering. Intense. I wanted to look away but knew that would be suspect. I wanted to tell him, too. Just two words. But he didn't need to hear them. He'd get them out of Paul Lessor now.

"What are your next steps?" I asked.

"We're running the prints we found in the apartment. We're checking his address book against the four address books we have of the victims. We're looking for anything that ties these men together. We're interviewing people he worked with. Trying to pinpoint where he's been for the past few weeks. Looking for anything out of the ordinary. And about a million other things." He stifled a yawn.

"How long has it been since you've slept more than four hours at a stretch?"

He smiled. Damn. That long, slow, slippery slide of his lips that affected me somewhere deep inside.

"Morgan, is there anything you can tell me about that tattoo?"

He knew that I knew. But how? Damn him again. I shook my head. They had him in custody. They'd figure it out now on their own. I wouldn't have to betray any confidences or break privilege. I was almost light-headed with relief.

"But you know something we don't."

"Noah, don't, please."

"Shit."

"If you're going to start badgering me then I'm going to ask you to leave."

"What do I have to do for you to ask me to stay?"

I didn't say anything. A wave of cold spread over me. I gave an involuntary shiver.

"Why do I frighten you?"

I shook my head.

He didn't relent.

"Do you even know?" he asked.

I shook my head again.

"I have a few ideas."

"That's good," I said sarcastically.

"You want me to keep them to myself?"

"Yes, but I have an awful feeling you aren't going to."

"Have you been out on a date with anyone since your divorce?"

I could have told him that it wasn't any of his business. Or just refused to answer. But I knew he wasn't going to give up and I didn't feel like fighting. Or at least that was my excuse. "No."

"Do you think that's giving your daughter the right message?"

"What?"

We were sitting together on the couch, far enough apart that we weren't touching at all, but close enough so that I could smell his minty cologne. Close enough for him to reach out and brush my hair off my face.

"You know your hair is the color of the molasses that my mama used to cook with," Noah said. "And your voice sounds like the water that whooshed by in the river outside our windows late at night."

"You are shameless."

"I'm smitten. I have been since I first met you. And even more than that since the other night. I didn't think you'd be so hard to get over."

"You make me sound like a flu."

"Nope. The opposite. Being with you makes me wide awake, more aware of everything—of colors, tastes, even the smell of the air. After we're together, when I'm alone again, there's this sad riff that settles on me."

I looked down, not wanting him to see the flush in my cheeks.

Smart man, he went back to what he'd been saying about Dulcie. "So do you think it's a good idea for your daughter to see her mama give up on men? For her to see you throw yourself into your work and her? It's too much pressure on a kid. It's inhibiting to a teenager to have to worry if Mama is lonely and sad."

"When did you get a degree in child psychology?"

He ignored the attitude in my voice. "Is her father dating?" he asked.

I nodded.

"Not good for another reason. Makes it look like men are stronger than women."

This was like needles under my nails. Paper cuts on my fingerpads. Insects biting at my cheeks and neck. A dozen tiny unpleasant feelings erupted in me at once.

"How dare you," I accused.

"What? Too close for comfort?"

"I am as strong as any woman she will ever meet. She sees that every day. I didn't fall apart when my marriage did. I didn't go running after a dozen men just so that I wouldn't be alone. I didn't start drinking or taking tranquilizers or doing anything unhealthy. I slept through every night. I never even intimated how lonely I was."

He let my last few words linger in the air. It embarrassed me when I realized what I'd inadvertently said.

"Like who? Who told you how lonely she was and put all that pressure on you?"

My head jerked of its own accord. The sudden rush of tears that came to my eyes shamed me. He'd fooled me again. Once more getting me to tell him things and express feelings that I'd never admitted to before.

With one hand under my chin, he turned my face toward his. Reaching out with the forefinger of his other hand, he stopped a tear that was sliding down my cheek.

"You don't have to tell me, Morgan. I can guess. But I want you to know you can tell me. It's this crazy thing between us. I know things about you without knowing how. Will it help if I tell you it scares me as much as it scares you?"

"If it scares you, why don't you go?"

"Because feeling scared like this is a big part of being alive." And then without giving me a chance to object or move, he leaned forward and kissed me.

It was generous. Sustaining. He took nothing. Gave all.

Through my lips he transferred his want. His willingness to wait. His utter helplessness in the face of his desire. I accepted it all. Gave nothing back. He didn't fight for it. Or try to pull it out of me. It was enough for him to offer it up to me.

"One day you'll want to give it back," he said in a deep, low voice that was like darkness falling. "I know you will. I don't think I'm wrong. About other things, yes. But not you. Don't ask me why. There is no reason on earth except I just know. It's like when I have an idea for the piano. Sometimes it can take months for me to search out the whole composition. But that's okay. The idea of it keeps me going. Because I know in my fingers, in my inner ear, in my soul, that the rest will come if I can just give it time."

He kissed me again, this time putting a hand on each of

my shoulders and pulling me very close to him and enfolding me in his arms.

For thirty seconds...forty-five...I just forgot. I wasn't there. Not a woman sitting on a couch in her den with her daughter sleeping in another room. Not a therapist who had information that this policeman would do anything to get.

The sound of his blood beating in my ears and the feeling of his arms sheltering me blocked out any world that I knew or was used to.

Finally, before I could pull away, because that was what I knew I had to do, he did. Standing, he smiled down at me, a little wistfully. "You make me ache," he said, and, without giving me a chance to say anything, left me there, sitting on my couch, looking around my den as if I'd never seen it before.

Fifty-Eight

The bad news came at noon the next day, like it always does with a phone call.

"Shit," Perez said with such vehemence and anger that Jordain had no doubt what had happened. "Shit, shit, shit. Damn."

"Another one?" Jordain asked.

Perez nodded at his partner as he continued on the phone. "Don't go anywhere, we'll come there." He hung up. "That was Douglas. Young got another package this morning. We're gonna have to let Lessor go."

"He could have mailed them before we got him."

"Nope. The lock of hair isn't just in a bag. This time it's wrapped up in a nice little cut-out of today's *New York Times* article saying we have a suspect in custody."

Jordain felt sick to his stomach, but there was no time for that. Grabbing the bottle of Pepto from his top desk drawer, he unscrewed the cap and chugged the viscous pink liquid while Perez waited.

"Where was Young last night?"

"Home all night."

Jordain threw the empty bottle into the garbage pail and they left.

Fifty-Nine

The detectives spent the afternoon examining the photographs that Betsy Young had received that morning. Every detail of these new shots matched up to all the previous ones. Five portfolios of brutally graphic images of five men who had been defiled and killed.

How?

That remained a mystery.

Why?

They didn't have a single clue. In fact, the list of the unknowns was one hundred times longer than the list of things they knew.

Louis Fenester was, like the others, laid out on a hospital gurney. The light source hit him evenly so that there were few harsh shadows, but that did nothing to soften the hard edges of the man's angular physique.

He had been thin enough to start with—his girlfriend had delivered photographs of him eight days ago when he hadn't come home after going to the gym. Now his ribs were protruding, his cheekbones arched over deep hollows in his face. He looked as if an overeager sculptor had gouged out too much of the marble with his chisel. Fen-

ester no longer looked human; he could have been a stone
effigy on top of a sarcophagus. His skin was like white
marble, without the luminosity.

Around the man's wrists and ankles were the same rings
of green-and-blue-and-purple bruises that all the men had
exhibited.

Like the four others before him, plus Paul Lessor, Fenester had the identifying tattoo on his right foot. But what
did that mean? Lessor had steadfastly refused to tell them
anything about the mark.

Fenester lay in what seemed to be the same room with
the same dull gray backdrop behind him that had been in
all the other shots. Nothing revealed the nature of the
chamber of horrors beyond that sweep of even, toneless
color.

The pallor of death had overtaken Fenester's body so
that although it was a color photograph, there was none in
the man's skin. The only vividness in the shot were the
number 5s on the man's feet. Bright red. The same hue as
the leaves that were decorating the park and the city streets
that time of year. What did Young call the color in all her
articles?

Jordain tried to remember.

She never just said red, she was more specific.

Yes, scarlet.

When Officer Butler came in, both detectives looked up.
She had a satisfied smile on her face. After the deep disappointment of the day's events—of having to release Lessor, of knowing that Young wasn't looking like a suspect,
either, of having to inform Fenester's girlfriend and family of his grisly murder, of dealing with the fury of their
boss that they were back to square one—Butler's expression buoyed them.

"You have something?" Jordain asked. "What is it?"

She nodded as she approached the table, littered with photographs of the dead man, and put down a computer printout that had squiggles of blue ink all over it.

"We got Fenester's phone book keyed into our ever-growing database and we have one number that is showing up in all six."

"The restaurant?"

She nodded. "It's called S's in one. Shel's in one. It's in Lessor's phone book but he had it listed in the *P*'s and identified as 'Pete's friend's place.' Now, in Fenester's PDA, it's listed under S. No notation. Just the number."

"So you checked it out?" Jordain asked, leaning forward, fingers frozen on the desk, body rigid, waiting.

"It's a cell phone. Listed to Pine Realty. We're working on getting the billing information."

"Give me the number."

Jordain punched the speaker button on his phone and dialed.

The three of them listened to the hollow sound of the phone ringing twice and then they heard a click. Butler's sharp intake of breath was audible in the split second between the phone being picked up and the announcement starting.

"There's no one here right now, but please leave your name and number and someone will get right back to you. Appointments and schedules of events can also be found online."

Jordain hit the button to end the call.

"Appointments I can understand from a realty company. But events? What kind of events?" Perez asked.

"Open houses for other real estate agents?" Butler offered.

"Neither of you actually think that is a real estate office, do you?" Jordain asked.

"How long will it take to get the name and address of whoever pays the bills?" Perez asked Butler.

"About an hour. If we are lucky."

"Well, let's not bet on that. We haven't been lucky so far. Not with one damn thing," Jordain complained. "We have had five corpses, no idea of where they are hidden, a man with a mental disorder whose glee at the killings makes my blood run cold and who refuses to help us with one piece of information. Oh, I almost forgot, we have a red tattoo that links everybody up to one another." Jordain got up, walked to the window and opened it. He leaned out, pressing the palms of his hands into the rough surface of the brick sill.

Horns honked, people shouted, cars roared by. The afternoon traffic was at its peak. Even though the air was tainted with the city smells, it was fresher than what was inside the office. He breathed in. Deeply. The end of October was usually colder than this. Or was it just that the air wasn't even close to being cold as compared to the case?

Ice.

He was not used to coming up short. But he couldn't think of a single case he'd ever worked on without a body or a crime scene. That was where leads came from. The body and the place the body was found.

Once you dealt with the concept that the victim was a man or woman who had a job, a family, a spouse, sibling or child who would be bereft, whose life would from this day forward never be the same, once you swallowed hard a few times—even though you'd been through this so many times you should be inured to it—you dealt with the clues. The hair and fibers. The skin trapped under the fingernails. The weapon. The blood on the floor. Or the sheets. The bullet casings. The contents of the victim's stomach. The note in his pocket. The torn picture in her purse.

You could get somewhere with just one find. And you had a hundred places to make it.

But this insanity? Photographs and hair in sanitized plastic bags that mothers slipped sandwiches in, that were sold in every damn supermarket in the whole United States? Manila envelopes that couldn't be traced because every office supply store in the damn country sold them?

"Hey, look at this," Butler said, interrupting Jordain's thoughts. She was leaning over and examining one of the shots of Fenester's midsection that had been enlarged.

"What is it?"

"He's got some kind of shadow on the underside of his left thigh. Or is it a shadow? Whatever it is—this is something I haven't seen before."

Jordain went back to the table, bent over her shoulder and looked down at what she was pointing to.

It didn't look like anything in any of the other shots. One deviation from the exactness, but, just to make sure, he picked it up and carried it the length of the photo-papered room, holding it up and comparing it to the other shots taken from the same angle.

To him, the collage of death-scene shots didn't look macabre—he was used to it. But to anyone who might have walked in who wasn't with the department, the wall would be something they would never forget. There were hundreds of photos of male body parts. The same section in a dozen different magnifications. Some recognizable, others enlarged to the point of abstraction.

"No, nothing like this on any of the other men's legs."

Returning to Butler, he put the photograph down and pointed at the oblong irregular pattern she'd noticed.

"I don't think it looks like a bruise. But it sure does look strange. What's wrong with it? What is that splotch?"

Jordain picked up two other shots at random, turned them over, and used the blank white paper to create a frame around the area so that there was nothing distracting them from it.

All three of them stared down.

"What the hell is it?" Perez asked.

Jordain squinted. He put his hand down and moved the white frame in just a little closer so he could focus even more clearly.

"Holy shit," Jordain muttered.

Butler looked up.

Sixty

The dosage of Thorazine had been easy to administer. Pills crushed in water. Water taken greedily. Zombies willing to lie down and sleep. Everything about them subdued. The walking dead. The sleeping dead. The dead. Nothing woke them. That was right. Nothing could wake the dead. But the dead would strike fear in the hearts of those who knew about them. The dead would warn the living to stay away. To be better than these men had been. To behave.

Behave.

Such an easy word. Such a luscious concept.

Easy, the photographer thought, everything had been easy. Blessed. The whole plan had been blessed. The men did not see a stranger waiting for them. You do not fear someone whom you know. They came willingly. Too willingly, in fact. They were actually accommodating.

There was nothing to worry about. The monitor was on. If anything went wrong, the photographer would hear it.

But what could go wrong with the sleeping dead?

Each man had been a study in color, shape and form. To light each of them, to capture the image, to get the angles right, to develop the film carefully had taken talent.

The result had been professional, even though the photographer was only an amateur.

Arrrrg.

A sound?

Arrrg.

A moan?

Arrrrrrrg.

What was wrong?

Work tools, dropped without thought. A splatter of red spilled on the floor. It didn't matter. Not now.

Arrrg.

Run, faster. It was so many steps from the studio, through the hall, down the steps, through the cool brick-lined room, past the thick steel door built to withstand invasions and hold a family of six for days or weeks.

Arrrrrrrrrrg.

Getting closer. Closer. Closer.

The man writhed on the stretcher. Beat against the restraints. His face was pale, sweat dripped from his forehead into his eyes. He was screaming into the gag.

It had been important to memorize the side effects of Thorazine in case of emergency. Few were serious. Only one was deadly: a heart attack. And the photographer knew what a man having a heart attack looked like. He looked like the man strapped to the gurney.

Fingers fumbled to unbuckle the restraints.

It had been hours since their last cocktails. His drugs would just be wearing off. Why would the attack come now? It didn't matter.

"Can you get up? Let me help you up."

Arrg.

He was moving, sitting up. In pain and slow, but thank God he was standing.

"I'm going to take you to the hospital. You'll be fine. Hold on to my arm. Let me help you."

Prayers? Yes, prayers said silently that the man would be able to traverse the distance from here to the car. He was walking. Doubled over in pain. Slow. But putting one foot in front of the other. Lifting his legs. Step. Up. Step. Up. Prayers said silently that the man would be okay during the ride to the hospital. Because the man couldn't die. That would be murder.

Sixty-One

My appointment with Nicky and Daphne was a welcome interruption to my week. Since the resurrection of my argument with Nina the day before, I was uncomfortable at the institute. We'd had two—no, three—fights in as many weeks, and each pushed us further apart. I found myself staying in my office. Avoiding walking in the halls. I knew sooner or later we were going to have to figure out how to work out our differences and that my avoidance of her was cowardly and childish, but that didn't make it any easier for me to confront her. To do that, I would have to confront how I felt about Noah Jordain. And I wasn't prepared to do that. Not yet.

At least in the car, I'd have forty-five minutes to clear my head on the way up to Connecticut.

I took the North Street exit off Merritt Parkway, drove for ten minutes, took one turn, then another, drove five minutes, and finally pulled up in front of Daphne's house. I was fifteen minutes early, but I didn't care.

I parked in the driveway.

There were orchards to the right of the house and I didn't think that anyone would mind if I took a walk.

Everywhere I looked, a tapestry of leaves obliterated the grass and changed the distant landscape into a fauvist painting.

As we get close to death, we lose our color, we lose our beauty. I had seen my mother, sickly and thin, her hair stringy, her once peach-colored skin gray and ashen when she had become unconscious.

As leaves die, they alone become more beautiful. As they perish, they offer up a palette of screaming colors.

The wind blew and hundreds of lemon-yellow aspen leaves took wing, dipping and soaring on the breeze, flying around me, as colorful and as graceful as butterflies.

It had been slightly overcast when I got out of the car, but the cloud cover had blown away and the sun shone now and illuminated the landscape around me and the house beyond.

I walked toward it, getting closer and closer until, with the sun shining like that, I could see right into Daphne's studio. There were several large canvases on display. About three feet away, I stopped. No, that's not accurate. About three feet away, the painting I saw through the glass stopped me.

The portrait on the easel was of a man. Naked. Sitting in a chair. His head lolled to one side. His expression was slack and lifeless. His flesh fell in folds.

The painting was darker around the edges and lightened as it came closer to the center, so that there was a brightness on the man's midsection. At the very center of that spotlight, displayed the way a diamond is exhibited in one of Tiffany's windows, was the prize—the most detailed and lovingly painted part of the canvas: the man's flaccid and very small penis.

Something was familiar about the composition. What?

Where had I seen it before? I looked at the next easel. Another portrait of a naked man. He was standing, leaning really, against a wall. His shoulders slumped. He looked out, imploring, begging for help.

Daphne was more than accomplished. She was masterful. She captured emotions and intentions as well as any artist whose work hung in a gallery.

Like the other painting, this one employed a halo effect so that, after being assaulted by the man's expression, I was drawn to the dead center of his body. His penis was wrinkled, red, shrunken. Impotent.

Overall, Daphne's style was luminous and detailed, but nowhere on the canvases did she lavish more detail and time and create as much grotesque beauty as with the genitalia.

That was when I saw the third painting.

The nausea rose quickly. I didn't expect it, so I didn't have time to prepare myself for the violent way the image struck me. I put my hand out, reaching for a tree branch, and held on while I vomited on the newly fallen leaves.

And then I ran toward the house.

Sixty-Two

❦

Ronny White watched the silver Mercedes SUV pull into the parking lot of the emergency wing of the Greenwich Hospital and noted the license plate.

The hospital was well staffed, well appointed, and catered to the inhabitants of the town's population of 60,000, who were among the most wealthy in the United States. He liked his job. The hospital never got crazy busy like a big-city hospital. Great doctors worked there, imported from large cities to cater to the needs of the well heeled. Most of all, Ronny liked the visitors and patients who tipped him lavishly for watching their six-figure cars.

The driver who had just turned in to the lot was handling the car erratically, a sure signal to Ronny of an emergency. He called the front desk and told Lucie to send out some staff. "There's a problem coming in."

This was one of the things he could do: watch who was coming and going in a way that you never could in one of those giant hospitals in a metropolitan area.

"He's having a heart attack!" the driver shouted at Ronny as the car came to a stop in front of him.

Ronny nodded. "Don't move him. They are on their way

out and—" He didn't have time to finish when two order-lies and two nurses arrived with a stretcher.

As soon they got the man out of the car and onto the stretcher, the driver threw the car into Reverse and screeched out of the parking lot.

Ronny stared at the retreating Benz, trying to memorize the plates. He thought he had it, but he wasn't sure. The car had been moving too fast. Who leaves someone in that condition at the hospital and then drives off? A criminal, Ronny thought. Or a drunk. Either way, he should call the police.

The man was on the stretcher now. They were rushing him into the E.R.

Jeeze.

He'd seen a lot in the four years he had been working in Greenwich. Rich folk cried no different than poor ones. They sat down in the parking lot in the middle of the afternoon and curled up in a little ball and just wept. He'd seen kids, no older than his sister's kids, riding up in fancy cars, stubbing out their cigarettes, running in to pay a visit to Mom or Dad and coming back out jabbering on their cell phones. He'd seen mothers bring in babies turning blue and ambulances delivering patients with every ailment and injury there was.

But he had never seen a man, stark naked, with re-straints on his ankles and wrists, wheeled into the emergency room at four o'clock in the afternoon. Hell, at any time.

And he hoped that he never would again.

Sixty-Three

The front door was shut, but not locked. Opening it, I called out Daphne's name. No response. Running, I went from the foyer, to the living room, through to the kitchen, into the den, the whole time calling her name. Over and over.

"Daphne? Daphne? Daphne?"

Silence.

This was not the kind of house to leave unlocked. Besides, where was Daphne? She was an agoraphobic who had not left the house in six months, and yet she wasn't home now, when our session was scheduled? And where was Nicky?

Alone, any of those things would have concerned me, but together with seeing those horrific paintings, I was seriously alarmed.

Had Daphne read the articles about the men who had been killed, men who she, too, had known from her more active days as a participant at the Scarlet Society, and used her talent with brushes and paint to give voice to her nightmares?

Yes, that had to be it. It was the only possible explanation.

I walked into the studio. Maybe Daphne was there, in a corner I hadn't seen. Maybe she was wearing headphones and hadn't heard me calling out.

The light splashed through the windows onto the gruesome canvases.

They were portraits of powerlessness.

"Daphne? Daphne?"

No answer.

There were three doors in the studio besides the main one. The first led to a bathroom. Daphne wasn't there. The second opened on a supply closet and she wasn't in there, either. As I closed the door, I thought I heard something and turned, scanning the room. Static was coming from the monitor on the marble fireplace mantel. I moved closer to it. A monitor picking up noises from where? I carried it with me as I moved toward the third door.

The first thing I saw was the red light that washed over the cabinets and tabletops. The smell was stringent and sharp. I hadn't known what it was the first time I'd been to the house and I'd mistaken it for something else in Jordain's office, but I understood now.

Daphne had told me that she took photos of her subjects and worked from them, as well as working from life. Of course she would have a darkroom of her own.

The ruby glow illuminated the bottles of chemicals and the plastic baths. The trays were empty, but there were at least a dozen photographs hanging from clips on a line running from one end of the narrow room to the other.

Dozens of shots of a face. Devoid of everything but desperation.

It was the face I recognized from the painting.

Where was Daphne?

I still had the monitor in my hand, and when it came to

life I almost dropped it. The noise sounded like an animal in trouble. Or was it a human being moaning?

My fear suddenly surged into panic. I tried to figure out what to do.

The groans continued.

I ran from the studio, back out to the foyer, looking, searching for some clue that would tell me where Daphne was—because by now I was sure she was at the other end of the monitor.

Nothing in the living room. Nothing in the den. Nothing in the kitchen. But in the pantry off the kitchen there was a door flung open. Had it not been open, I never would have seen it—it was disguised to look like shelves.

Down a flight of steps.

In my hand, the moans continued.

Into a dark wine cellar where I was greeted with dank earth smells.

Wine and vinegar, sour smells.

And something else.

Putrid human smells. Urine. Feces. Filthy flesh.

In a house? In this house?

"Daphne?"

The moaning was no longer coming just from the monitor. Now I could hear it in the distance. It was down here with me. Not far.

Gagging on the odors I was following, I continued calling out Daphne's name and listening for the returning squawks. Could Daphne be making those sounds? There was more than one person moaning. Who was she with? Where were they?

I went through another opened door, this one disguised as a shelf of wine bottles. Down three more steps. How low into the earth was I descending?

The scent of human waste was overpowering me. For one second, I wondered if I was going to be able to go on. *Breathe through your mouth,* I thought. *Don't even allow yourself to smell this.* I pulled out my cell. No signal. Damn.

I took the last step and found myself in a large, windowless chamber. The center of the earth. The basement's basement. And facing me, as my eyes adjusted to this deeper darkness, lurid proof that there is no limit to the depravity of the human mind.

Sixty-Four

Four men were lying tethered to hospital gurneys. I didn't want the carnage to be real, but it was.

Who brought these men here? And where was Daphne?

Sweat rolled down my back. My legs shook so badly I had trouble standing.

My mind was not functioning.

Arrrg.

I heard the sound and screamed. What was happening?

The dead do not talk.

They do not moan.

But these men were moaning.

In the gloom, I saw the bright red marks on the soles of their feet. Numbers painted—of course, painted—painted in red.

2
3
4
5

There was no number 1.
Why was that gurney empty?
Where was number 1?

The chorus of grunts entreated me. When I was an intern on the psychiatric ward at the hospital, I had seen faces like these. They were drugged, sedated.

Thorazine.

Damn it.

None of us had thought of it—the men were not dead.

Damn it.

All of us—Jordain, Perez and I—had been looking for a serial killer. I'd studied everyone I met connected with the Scarlet Society for just one woman who exhibited any of the personality traits of a mass murderer: a psychopath with no regard for human life. A monster who killed for thrill and sexual satisfaction.

We all knew the stats.

Eighty-eight percent of serial killers are Caucasian men aged twenty to forty. More than seventy percent of them operate in a specific location or area. In a chart of serial killers' childhood development characteristics created in 1990, the three most dominant behaviors included daydreaming, compulsive masturbation and isolation.

They are dominant, powerful and controlling men. Who often have trouble perceiving the difference between themselves and God. Many believe that God is, in fact, telling them what to do.

By keeping these men prisoner here, by drugging them and holding them against their will, someone had committed a grievous crime. But it was not the work of a serial killer. Not the work of any kind of killer at all. Every one of these men was blessedly alive.

We had all been looking for the wrong kind of criminal. Of course we hadn't found him.

I moved among the men and, one by one, felt for their pulses and undid their gags, rushing, my fingers fumbling. There was too much to do at once. Triage was all about quick decisions. First, make sure everyone is alive. Check to see if anyone is in a life-threatening crisis. Then worry about their comfort.

None of the men appeared to be in acute danger.

Yes, sedated, but clearly not dehydrated or starved.

And not dead.

Not at all dead. I needed help now.

I pulled out my cell phone again—there was still no signal. We were too deep in the bowels of the earth.

I had to get to Jordain. As soon as possible.

"I am going to go and get you help," I said to the men, and then turned to go back up the dark, steep steps.

Sixty-Five

~~~~~⊙~~~~~

Nicky stood in the doorway, blocking my way, but he wasn't looking at me. His mouth was open and he was as pale as the men lying before him. Except some of their paleness—that dead look we'd all seen in the photographs—was paint. I'd seen the palette and the brushes upstairs. Daphne was an artist. She had used her talents to create the impression of death, disguising their flesh tones with a light gray paint before she took their photos.

As Nicky took in the scene, I knew, because I had just been through the process, that his brain was trying to understand and accept what he was seeing. It was clear from his reaction that he was not involved in this abomination.

"We have to call the police," I said. "Now. Quickly. Can you get me to a phone?"

He didn't move. A vein on his temple throbbed to the beat of some atonal tune.

"Did Daphne do this?" His voice wavered with the question.

"I don't know."

"How..." His voice broke.

He was still in my way. "Nicky, we need to call the police. Please, let me go upstairs, let me call an ambulance. The police."

He was not listening. "My wife. Did she do this?"

"I don't know, Nicky."

"Are they dead?"

"No, but every one of them is in danger. We are in danger. You and I. Daphne is, too. Please, we need to go upstairs and call the police."

"Do you know where she is?"

"No."

"You know she did this, don't you?"

I nodded my head.

"And you know why she did this, don't you?"

I hadn't been able to imagine why anyone would have done it when I'd first arrived in the dungeon. As I was bending over those living cadavers and listening to their hearts, it was impossible to guess. But now, seeing Nicky's sad, sick eyes, I did.

"Yes," I said as I tried to get past him.

"It was to scare me away from the society, once and for all. To make me think that if I kept going I would be next."

"Nicky!" I yelled at him. "Stop. Not now. We can talk about all of this once I call the police." But we didn't get anywhere. Daphne had found us.

"Nicky?" Her voice was strong and certain and commanding. "What do you think you are doing down here?"

Sixty-Six

~~~

Officer Butler carried the enlargements of the fifth victim's right thigh, and as she walked she flipped through them, watching as the area in question got larger and larger and larger until it filled the whole sheet.

Her mouth opened in astonishment just as she crossed the threshold into the room where Jordain and Perez were waiting.

"You are not going to believe this. It's like he's got a splotch of living flesh here. Is it possible the rest of him could be painted?" She looked up. Neither detective had even heard her.

Jordain and Perez were on the speakerphone, listening and struggling into their jackets as the conversation hurried on.

"Yes, yes, he has the number 1 written on both feet" came the disembodied male voice.

"Okay. We're on our way," Jordain started for the door.

"Greenwich Hospital, that's what exit?" Perez shouted.

"Exit three on I-95."

Butler hurried along with them, getting the story as they rushed through the halls, out of the station house and into Jordain's car.

"A man was brought to the emergency room at Greenwich Hospital about thirty minutes ago. Heart attack. Naked. And, like you heard, with red numbers on the bottoms of his feet."

"Have they confirmed it's Philip Maur?"

"He's conscious. Says that's who he is. Wife is on her way up there, too."

Jordain pulled the car out of the parking spot.

"There's one odd thing," Perez told Butler. "The doctors found streaks of grayish white paint on his legs."

"I know," Butler said, handing him the photographs.

Sixty-Seven

Philip Maur's wife was sitting by his bedside. The heart attack had been Thorazine-induced and had done only minor damage. She held her husband's hand and wept silently, muttering the same five words over and over.

"I thought you were dead. I thought you were dead."

Jordain and Perez stood in the doorway, finishing up their conversation with the doctor.

"We won't stay any longer than we have to."

"I'm going in with you, just as a precaution."

"That's fine," Perez said.

"Do you know where you were?" Jordain asked after he and Perez had identified themselves and told Mr. Maur how happy they were that he was alive.

Phil nodded. "At her house," he said in a hoarse voice. He licked his lips. Once, and then again. His wife handed him a glass of water. He drank from it slowly. All the way down.

Jordain was impatient but didn't show it.

"You were at her house?"

"We were all at her house."

"All?"

"Five of us. Tied up like…" His voice cracked and he started to cry. Damn. But he could no more stop the tears than he could let go of his wife's hand.

"You and four other men. Are all of them dead?"

He shook his head. His shoulders heaved.

The doctor moved in, ready to stop the interview if the monitor showed any change in the man's heartbeat, but the pattern stayed consistent.

"I know this is terrible, Mr. Maur, and we are very sorry to have to ask you to talk about what happened, but we need to find the house. We need to find the people who did this to you."

Phil was shaking his head vehemently.

"Everyone is alive. Drugged. But alive…" A sob escaped. "I'm sorry…never meant to…" The tears flowed. His wife was staring at him.

Jordain figured that Phil was not going to say anything with his wife sitting there. He sought out Butler's eyes and motioned to Mrs. Maur with a slight incline of his head. She walked over, gently took the woman by her arm and said, "Mrs. Maur, could you just come outside with me for a few minutes? I have some questions I need you to help me with."

Once she was out of the room, Jordain took her place by Phil's bedside.

"All that matters right now is finding out where you were. Where the other men are. So we can get to them in time. Do you know whose house it was?"

He nodded.

"What is her name?"

"I didn't mean to…"

"There is time for that later, Mr. Maur. Right now, we need to know where you were and where those other men are being held."

"I only know her first name. The name she used."

"What do you mean?"

"I don't know if it was her real name. A lot of them didn't use their real names."

Jordain felt as if he were deep under water, struggling to get to the surface where it was light.

He wrote down the name that Phil gave him. Only a first name. Not much help. "Where was the house? Do you know that?"

"Somewhere in the country. Sorry, I was already groggy by the time I got in the car."

"Do you remember how long it took her to drive you to the hospital?"

"No. It felt like five years."

Sixty-Eight

The detectives and the local police stood in the parking lot of the Greenwich Hospital discussing how to go about finding the house.

"Big town, small population. We've only got 60,000 people living here, but the township covers more than forty-eight square miles, much of it backcountry. Big houses on lots of acres. Canvassing would take days."

"And all we have is a first name, and we're not even sure it's a real first name."

Butler approached. With her was a uniformed cop from Greenwich along with a man wearing black pants, a white shirt and a black jacket with a hospital insignia on it. She introduced the man to Jordain and Perez.

"We've got something," she said. "Mr. White here saw the woman who dropped off Phil Maur. He noticed the car because of the way it came careening into the lot. And like he does with all the cars that park in Emergency, he took down the license plate."

"You are a good man," Jordain said as he took the piece

of paper with three numbers and three letters written in black ink. He looked at it and handed it to the local detective.

"Shouldn't take me more than five minutes."

"Make it three," Jordain said.

Sixty-Nine

Daphne stood in the shadows of the staircase. Her hair was wild, her blouse was pulled out of her slacks. There were sweat stains under her arms. Her mouth was twisted into an angry grimace. "What are you doing here?" she screamed at me.

I didn't have much time—only a few seconds while she was still in shock at seeing me—to push past Nicky and then get past Daphne in an attempt to get upstairs and out of there. To get to a phone. To get away.

But before I knew what was happening, Nicky fell on me and the force of his body pushed me to the floor. My shoulder started to throb. Nausea came in waves. I knew from experience that my bone might be broken.

Nicky sat up. "You pushed me," he was saying to Daphne in a dazed voice.

The pain in my arm was making me dizzy, but I managed to sit up, too.

"Why did you push me?" Nicky asked his wife. He was on overload, trying to work out the meaning of what was happening, not understanding anything.

Behind me, the men were screaming and shouting.

Daphne was standing over her husband and me, staring down at us; in her hand was a gleaming pair of scissors. Her back was to the staircase, blocking it. To get to it, I'd have to push past her.

"Get up," she said to him.

Nicky did what she asked.

Slowly, despite the pain, I got up, too, keeping my eyes on the scissors. She was three or four feet away from me. I wondered if I could lunge at her and throw her off balance. The scissors weren't much of a weapon against two of us. Nicky could take them out of her hand in one movement. But he was just standing there, rubbing his chin, staring at his wife.

"Nicky?" I said. No response. "Daphne, please put down the scissors. You need to call the police. I'll help you. You won't even go to jail. You just need help. Everyone is still alive. You will be fine. But you have to put down the scissors and let me get to the phone."

She laughed at me and looked at her husband. "Do you see, Nicky? You have to see. I did all of this for you, not to hurt anyone. I had it all planned out. I even picked Liz to send the photos to because I knew that she hated you all so much she'd enjoy making you cower. I guessed who she was. Saw her at a party. Lucky me. Screw conflict of interest. I knew she wouldn't be able to resist the temptation of keeping the story for herself. That she'd do everything she could to feed the police the bare minimum while milking the news. She didn't want the crimes solved—she wanted power over all of you, and I was giving it to her. I wanted you to live with the fear. Day after day. And have it grow in you. Until the fear was so big it overpowered the lust."

He was just nodding.

"You have to give it up—you understand that, don't you? No more going to the Scarlet Society."

Daphne was talking to him in a more strident tone of voice than she had used before in my presence, and her face was arranged in a mask of power that was the opposite of the sensitive, loving wife I'd met the two previous times. Which woman was real? The wife who only wanted her husband to be faithful to her? Or this aggressive, powerful woman crazed with jealousy?

"Daphne, we have to call the police now." I was using a calm voice, hoping I could reach her and break through her rage, but she was ignoring me.

"Nicky, do you understand?" she asked.

He nodded his head.

"You have to do what I say from now on, Nicky. All right?"

He nodded.

"Come here."

He moved closer to her.

She reached out with her free hand and stroked her husband's groin with her fingertips.

It seemed that we had all disappeared—me and the four naked men strapped to their gurneys. They were talking and shouting, but she was not hearing them. She continued to rub her husband until a smile curved her lips. She'd made him hard. Despite the plight of these men, the stink of the torture chamber, the imminent danger and the shining weapon, he was under her spell.

Her fingers curled around the bulge in his pants, squeezed it, and then unzipped his fly and pulled his penis out.

"See, when you listen to me, when you accept me for who I am to you, when you don't fight me, it's fine. You're hard, aren't you? You're nice and hard. And that's for me. Because I know how to treat you."

Nicky had slipped into a sexual fugue state. His eyes were shut. His lips parted. His face muscles went slack. Daphne leaned down and sucked on his penis. Up and down, licking him as she swallowed him.

This was my only chance. How concentrated was she on proving her erotic domination of her husband? How much did she want to show him, or herself, or the other men in the room, that she had the power and could command them all?

Enough so that I might be able to inch away?

Seventy

I took one small step forward. Daphne didn't miss a beat. She raised her head away from her husband's crotch and pointed the scissors at me.

"You aren't really serious, are you?"

Nicky was somnambulistic, focused only on his wife's wet lips. He didn't seem to know—or, if he knew, didn't seem to care—that his erection was exposed.

"Nicky, I need you to help me," I pleaded, surprised at how pathetic my voice sounded.

Daphne's other hand moved to her husband's penis and grabbed ahold of him hard enough for her knuckles to turn white. He was not at all aware of me.

I didn't know how to reach him. Daphne held the scissors in her right hand, continued stroking him with her left and leered at me. "Don't move," she said.

I looked right at Nicky, took a breath and in a clear, loud voice said, "Nicky. She's been lying to you. She's not agoraphobic. But she is dangerous. She needs serious help. Psychiatric help. And you are the only one who can make sure she gets it. I know you want to help her. You came to me to get help for her."

His head had fallen back, he was more lost than ever in his sexual stupor. My voice was probably a hiss in the background compared to the sensations he was feeling.

Daphne did not stop her ministrations.

I inched forward again.

Daphne stopped moving her hand.

Nicky's head jerked back. "No—" he cried. "Please don't stop."

"I'll finish after we deal with her. We have to tie her up. We have to protect ourselves."

"Please…don't stop." He was still reeling from her interrupting his impending orgasm. "Please…" he repeated.

"As soon as we figure out what to do with this little mess." She was torn between keeping Nicky sexually engaged—knowing that was the key to keeping him on her side instead of the side of reality—and at the same time she needed to figure out how to stop me. The scissors in her right hand shook from her trembling. "Nicky, we have to strap her down on the gurney. You have to get up. You have to help me."

Nicky turned. His eyes were glazed with lust and need but some of it dissipated as he looked at me.

I knew that the only shot I had was to convince him that his wife needed help and he was the only one who could ensure that she would get it. If he really loved her, whether it was a healthy love or not, I was going to have to bet on the fact that he would want to save her more than he wanted to hurt me. But would he? Or more to the point, could he? I didn't know enough about their relationship yet to know if he was subservient to her only sexually or in other ways.

"Nicky, we can help Daphne."

"Shhh…" She leaned closer to him and kissed him behind his ear. "Nicky…" She took his hand, put it up to her mouth and sucked in his thumb, going down on it and then pulling up slowly.

"We have secrets to keep now, Nicky. Your secrets with the society. My secrets here. We have to bury them. Both sets of secrets." She went down on his thumb again.

What was she planning to do to keep her secrets? What could I do to stop her? There was no way to protect myself. All I had—all I ever had—was my voice. But how could I compete with her? He was a man addicted to giving up power, who found it sexually arousing. His wife knew that.

"I'm sorry," she said to me. "I don't know what else to do. You're just too big a part of the secret now. You have to get up on that table."

I didn't argue. At least I could act as if I were going to obey. The longer I could stall her, the greater chance I had to talk Nicky into helping me.

"I can help you figure out what to do, Daphne. I can help with the police so you don't have to go to jail."

"I don't think so." She laughed and I cringed. It was a deranged laugh. A power-sick cackle that went through my body like a shot of pain. "I know how to help myself. I'm going to bury the secrets. I've known that I could do that all along. This bunker is twenty feet under the house. No one knows it's here. My grandfather had it built as a bomb shelter. It's not in any of the plans. Once Nicky and I walk out of here and shut the door behind us, no one will ever be able to find any of you. It wasn't my plan, but I always knew it was a backup."

Nicky seemed surprised by what she was saying. I could see that in the narrowing of his eyes, in the way he put his lips together in a tight line.

"Nicky." I made my voice as authoritative as I could. I

had learned from my session with Paul Lessor what I had done wrong. I was not going to waste the one shot I had left.

He didn't turn.

"Nicky!" I shouted at him with as much venom as I could put into the two syllables.

He reacted and turned to me.

"You must listen to me, Nicky." I kept my voice dictatorial. "Daphne loves you. She loves you enough to kill five people if she has to. You have to take away the power of her love. If you don't, you'll allow her to destroy both of you. You'll wind up keeping her secret for her. You understand what I'm saying, don't you? Yes. Of course you do. I know you do. You've had a secret for years. The Scarlet Society has been your dirty secret. And you know how that secret controlled you. You know that, Nicky, don't you?"

He was listening. Her fingers on his crotch were not distracting him from the tyrannical tone of my voice, or from the meaning of my words. I was ordering him to listen with every single syllable I uttered.

For one moment, Daphne had forgotten the most important thing.

Her husband was not addicted to sex.

Nicky was addicted to a woman overpowering him. To a woman demanding something from him. She was being too soft. Her need for his help was blinding her. She was seeing him as her savior and that was not the role he craved. He wanted to be a slave. If only she had stopped asking him to help her for just one minute and made him obey her, she would have won. But she didn't do it.

"Listen to me, Nicky," I commanded. "You bastard. You have to listen to me. Daphne needs you so much. She wants you. That's all she wants. She doesn't control you. I do. She is weak. Like you. I am the one with the power."

He was completely focused on what I was saying now. "You don't want to be the big brave man and give Daphne what she needs, what she *needs*, Nicky. You want to give me what I demand."

Daphne's hand was urgently racing up and down his erection. "Nicky...help me."

"No!" I screamed at him, hoping that Daphne was too far gone to understand what I was doing, that she wouldn't try to figure out why he was responding to me.

He was completely focused on me now, what she was doing to him might have merged with my voice, but it was my voice more than her actions that absorbed him.

"Nicky, I am ordering you to take the scissors out of Daphne's hand. NOW!"

He turned to his estranged wife. The fact that she still had her fingers wrapped around his penis didn't seem to be registering with him anymore. He slapped her hand away as if it were an annoying fly and reached for the scissors.

She was faster than he was. Pushing past him, she ran at me, her hand raised, the scissors pointed at my chest.

"Nicky, stop her!" I yelled. He went flying after her.

I ran in the other direction. Stopped seeing, just blindly moving, racing to find a corner of the room where she couldn't get at me. All I could think of was Dulcie. That I had to protect myself for Dulcie. I had to get home to my daughter.

Daphne followed me, enraged, ready to do battle with the *other* woman, with all the *other* women whom Nicky responded to when he no longer responded to her.

"Nicky, stop her!" I yelled.

She was a blur rushing me and then she was gone. Nicky had pulled her back. The two of them lay on the floor in a heap.

I heard weeping. Daphne's sobs. Nicky lay on top of her. He was finally flaccid. "Daphne, Dr. Snow is right. You know she is. We have to get you help. We can't make this worse than it already is."

She stared at him. There was an expression of disgust on her face: her lips were twisted into a grimace, her nostrils flared. With a huge burst of energy, she got her arm loose. She still had the damn scissors clutched in her fingers. She raised them over her head.

They came down. An arc of silver light gleamed in the gloomy basement.

The sound was that of a small animal caught in the night.

I cringed.

Daphne stopped moving. The blood leached out, turning her light pink shirt deep red.

Nicky shouted something I couldn't make out and knelt down to her.

"No. Don't touch her, Nicky. Go upstairs and call the police. Depending on how the scissors are lodged in her chest, you could hurt her more if you try to pull them out. Just go. Now!"

He stared at me. "I can't leave her," he whimpered.

"If you don't, she's going to die for sure. Go. Now."

Seventy-One

Nicky didn't have to leave Daphne's side after all.

The police—including Jordain and Perez—had found the house and were already inside and on their way down the stairs when they heard the scream.

Ambulances had followed them to the house, expecting to find the other men there—hoping to find them.

Within ten minutes, all four men plus Daphne, who was unconscious but still alive, had been taken to the local hospital in the waiting vehicles. Nicky pulled himself together, zipped up his pants and went with his wife. Holding her hand. Holding back tears. Glued to her side. Two local policemen had accompanied him.

One of the medics examined my shoulder. He didn't think it was broken—I had too much movement and not enough pain—but he suggested I get it X-rayed by the end of the day.

Jordain, Perez, Butler and two local detectives remained behind to lock down the crime scene. But first, Jordain was taking care of me.

We sat on the steps of the house amid a spattering of dried yellow and scarlet leaves, and I tried to remember how to breathe normally.

His hand on my back moved back and forth. "Square breathing, okay? In, one, two, three, four. Hold, one, two, three, four. Let the breath out, one, two, three, four. Hold, one, two, three, four," Jordain intoned. It was an exercise that most therapists use. Focus. Breathe. Relax. I'd taught it to him. Now he was using it to help me.

I did not know how I had gotten outside, how long I'd been sitting on the ground, how long Jordain had been sitting next to me, or when he had taken me in his arms. Nor did I know when my cheeks got so wet.

Finally, I stopped crying and my breathing had slowed down.

"I need to go back in there. Will you be okay for a few minutes?"

I nodded.

"I won't be long," he said.

I panicked as soon as he left me, though. Turning, I watched his back retreating into the house, repeating his last few words over and over. *I won't be long. I won't be long.*

Once he was back inside, I took a deep breath. I had to calm down. Everything was all right now. Five men were alive. Even Daphne's wound was not life threatening.

Reaching into my bag—how did I still have my bag? I couldn't remember, maybe Tana or Perez had given it to me—I pulled out my cell phone and called Dulcie. I didn't think about why I needed to do that or what time it was or interrupting either her classes or rehearsals.

She answered on the third ring.

"Mom?" She'd looked at the caller ID.

I put my knuckle into my mouth and bit down to force myself from sobbing.

"Hi, sweetie." I was surprised how shaky my voice

sounded and was suddenly sorry I'd called. The last thing I wanted to do was worry her.

"What's wrong?"

I shook my head, realized she couldn't see me. Using all my effort and what few acting skills I had, I forced a matter-of-fact voice. "No. Nothing. I just was thinking about you. Wanting to make sure you were fine. You are fine, aren't you?"

"That's soooo weird."

"Why?"

"For absolutely no reason my shoulder hurts. Not bad. But enough for me to have to take some Tylenol."

"When did it start?"

"About a half hour ago."

"You sure? You don't need to go to the doctor?"

"Yes, Mom, I'm sure," she said in that thirteen-year-old you-worry-too-much-Mom voice.

"Nothing happened? It just started hurting out of the blue?"

"I guess. Maybe I bumped into something. I don't know. But it's okay now."

I felt the pain throbbing in my own shoulder. I *did* have to go to the doctor. I didn't believe in coincidences, so how was it possible that we'd both hurt ourselves in the same place on the same day?

"Mom?"

"Yes, sweetie."

"I have to go. They're waiting for me."

After we said goodbye, I held the phone in my hand for a few seconds, just staring at it. It was so difficult to focus. There was another call I needed to make. There were other people who needed to know what I'd found out. Not the wives and girlfriends and families of the men who had been found, the police would tell them. But the other women, the secret sisters who cared in their own way. They deserved to find out, too, now, from me, not from some television report or newspaper article tomorrow.

Shelby Rush answered right away, and without going into too much detail—because I didn't think the police would want me to do that—I told her what had happened.

Once in group, Shelby had said she could not yet feel grief for the men who had died—worry, despair, confusion, anger, yes—but she couldn't cry for them.

Now, finding out that they were alive, she burst into tears. And I sat and listened to her sobs.

"How did she manage to keep them there?" Shelby finally asked.

"They were drugged. Enough, it looked like, to keep them in a zombie-like state. But probably not so much that they couldn't eat or drink."

"She tied them down, didn't she? She left them there. Under her control."

"Yes."

"It's like a game we played in the society." Shelby's voice quavered. "But we never hurt anyone. We never did anything to hurt anyone. You said they are all alive. You said that, didn't you?"

"Yes. It looks like she took care of them. In her own strange way," I added.

"It's so awful. Five men. Trapped. Like animals. For weeks."

"Shelby, I need to go. But I wanted to call. And to ask you to let everyone know."

"Yes. Of course."

"One more thing—can you do me a favor and call Liz first?"

"Yes, but why?"

I couldn't tell her—that would be breaking a confidence. It was going to be up to Liz to explain it all to Shelby, and I was certain she would. Liz was a talented woman who had work to do on her self-esteem but she'd get there.

I couldn't have known then that Jordain had already asked Tana Butler to call Liz, or Betsy, as the police knew her, and give her the promised exclusive and that she was driving up to Greenwich even now.

The final story in the series would be hers. The one story she could write without the police censoring her. That she would, in fact, write with their help.

My last call was to Nina.

"Are you sure you're all right?" she asked after I'd explained what had happened. There was no sign of anger in her tone anymore, only concern. Nina was the closest thing I had to a mother and this is how mothers react. They forget and forgive everything you've put them through when your safety and well-being is at risk. Something I knew better from being a mother than a daughter.

"Well, I'm in one piece. My shoulder's a little banged up, but it's nothing. I can wait till tomorrow to deal with it."

"You're not alone there, are you?"

"No, Noah is with me." I looked over. He was a few feet away, talking to Butler, glancing back at me every few minutes.

"I want to talk to him. You need to go to a hospital now and be checked out. I'll go to the theater for you and get Dulcie later. Did you call her?"

I told Nina about the coincidence. "How can that be?" I asked.

"Love does that. It connects us in ways that sometimes defy logic. Now," she said, "I want to talk to Noah about taking you to the hospital."

"Nina, please. I've been through hell and I know I've been banged up a little, but I don't need the hospital. A doctor tomorrow. I'll do that. I really am fine."

And I was.

Wasn't I?

"Yes, sweetie, you are. You're smart and brave. And I'm proud of you."

What had she heard in my voice? How nervous I was? How distraught? All the emotions I'd been hiding from Dulcie, from her?

Jordain returned just as I was getting off the phone.

"Are you ready to go?" he asked.

I nodded and he helped me up. Keeping hold of my arm, we began walking down the steps, away from the house.

The stench of the dungeon had not dissipated. I gulped at the air, taking in huge breaths, struggling to clear the scent; still the odor persisted. I inhaled again, more deeply, more desperately.

"What are you doing, Morgan?"

As I told him about the smell, the tears flowed again. He reached out and wiped them away but his gentleness only made me cry harder.

He opened my bag and found my roll of peppermints and put one in my mouth.

I was like a rag doll. He could move me and sit me and stand me up and feed me. It didn't matter. Who had I been fooling? I couldn't do it all without any help. When would I learn that sometimes I had to let the people close to me in a little bit closer.

Dulcie. Nina. Maybe…even Noah.

To learn that I might have to accept that one day I could wind up needing more than what I got back or wanting more than anyone could give. I might wind up being disappointed and let down. I might.

But if my thirteen-year-old daughter could learn that lesson, certainly I could make an effort to learn it too.

I just wasn't as optimistic about how good a student I was going to be.

We were on the path now, walking through the elaborate English garden I'd admired the first time I'd come to Greenwich three weeks earlier. Most of the flowers had long since stopped blooming, except for some daisies and one of the rosebushes. I leaned over the last of the season's full, old-fashioned, pink roses. I breathed in. The perfume was almost too heavy. Too sweet.

Taking a step back I crushed some of the daisies. The white and yellow flowers were bright and too cheerful. It made me sad that I had crushed them and the tears came again. From where?

How could there be so many?

Jordain's arm led me farther down the path. Crimson and scarlet, lemon and russet and rich brown leaves from the oak, maple, and birch trees sprinkled this part of the walkway. We passed wide hosta beds, the leaves still full but yellowed and withering.

Growing among these plants, towering over them, were butterfly bushes. The one plant that I knew the most about. The purple, lavender, and white flowers were mostly gone, except for three or four that had bloomed late. When the first frost came, they would freeze.

That was when I saw her. Fragile, strong, and so beautiful.

How long had she been there feeding? Was she even

real? I stopped moving and beside me, so did Jordain. The brilliant monarch couldn't be a hallucination because he was staring at her, too, watching her fold her orange, red, and black wings up behind her black body and continue feeding.

We stood side by side without saying anything.

The butterfly took her fill of the last of the season's nectar, spread her wings, lifted up and hovered in the air for ten or twenty seconds.

I held my breath.

She was hesitant at first, trembling on the wind, waiting for some mysterious clue from the breeze to tell her what direction would speed her onward to her destination. Still tentative, she circled the bush once more and then suddenly, somehow instinctively sure of where she was going, she took flight and soared.

And then Jordain took me home.

* * * * *

Acknowledgments

To the whole team at MIRA from Donna Hayes, Dianne Moggy, Margaret O'Neill Marbury to everyone in the sales force, art department, editorial department, marketing department, publicity department and mail room. What a wonderful home, I have. Thank you all for your hard work, creativity, and warmth.

To all my friends and associates but with special thanks to Lisa Tucker and Doug Clegg, two amazing authors, and the indefatigable Carol Fitzgerald—the trio who talk me through my books and hold my hand the whole time.

To Mara Nathan who is my key to Morgan Snow's world and my Nina. To Randi Kraft for her eye and her friendship.

To Chuck Clayman who tried to keep me from mistakes with legal issues. (My failures are not his.)

To Gigi, Jay, Jordan, Daddy, Ellie, Doug and Winka too, for all the love, with love.

Please turn the page for a preview of
THE VENUS FIX, *the next title by M. J. Rose*
featuring Dr. Morgan Snow and
the Butterfield Institute.

In THE VENUS FIX, *women who get paid*
performing on Webcams viewed by hundreds
of thousands of men are dying online as those men
watch on. Morgan gets involved in solving
the crime by working with a group of
high school teenagers—boys who are obsessed
with Internet porn—and girls who are
competing for their attention....

Don't miss this riveting story, on sale in July 2006!

Damn, it was freezing. He'd opened the window to chase away the smell of the beer and pot and sex, but then he'd fallen asleep, and now it was so cold he didn't even want to stick his head out from under the covers to see if she was still there. But Timothy wanted to come again more than he wanted anything else, so he did it, he pushed the blanket down just enough to peek out.

In his darkened bedroom she was the only thing that he could see. Still there. Still naked. Her lovely breasts with the pink-tipped nipples pointing up.

His erection stirred.

Timothy was awake now, the dreams replaced with a fresh fantasy of what the next minutes would bring. She was golden. That was the best way to describe her: the tawny color of her skin, the long blond curls, and the feeling inside of him that burned like a sun when he was in her glow. And all he had to do was lie back and let her magic work on him.

None of the girls at school were this experienced.

Or this gorgeous.

Or this willing.

Penny was sitting in the big red armchair where he'd left her—her legs spread, playing with a dildo, smiling at him. But it was one weird smile. He leaned forward. Nope, she didn't look right. She was shaking a little and her mouth was sort of contorted into a sick clown's grimace. Then her head fell forward, her back heaved, and she vomited.

Timothy had fooled around with a lot of different crap, but this was weird. What kind of pervert would think this was hot?

Usually Penny was coy and sweet and sexy. Sure, she was a little kinky sometimes with the crazy-shaped dildos she used, but she wasn't moving any of those magic wands in and out of her now.

"Penny," he whispered. "What are you doing?"

Her answer was an agonized groan. Low and feeble. Like the sound a wounded animal might make. Nothing like the exciting sounds she'd made when she was riding the lubricated pink plastic dildo and coming right along with him.

Maybe she wasn't acting. Maybe she really was sick. Food poisoning made you sick like that. He'd had food poisoning once. She looked sick, didn't she? Her skin was slicked with sweat, her hair was flattened to the sides of her face, and her eyes looked glassy and feverish.

She looked like she needed help. Now. Fast. But what could he do?

Grabbing the blanket off the bed, he wrapped it around his naked waist and started for his bedroom door. Then he stopped—there was no one home. His parents were out. Geez, what was he thinking? Thank God they were out because Penny, sick or not, was way off limits.

He looked back at her. Yes, she was still moving in that slow motion, sick way, her moan now a low constant sound that made him want to put his hands up to his ears and block it out.

He grabbed the phone.

He'd call for help. But who? The police? An ambulance? Amanda? Would she know what to do? No, she might tell her mother. He couldn't risk that. Besides, what if he was wrong? What if this was a game? What if Penny was acting out some perversion by request? He knew she did that sometimes.

He glanced back at her, at her small hands gripping the arms of the chair, at her feet, so fragile and inconsequential, at the worn carpet he'd never noticed before. Everything looked sort of pathetic now—the meager furniture, the really small television—except for the view out the window. He'd never noticed any of this before. He'd always been too busy, under her spell. But not now. Not anymore.

Pick your head up, Penny. Look at me. Tell me what's going on. What I should do?

She threw up again.

He dialed 911.

"State your emergency, please."

At the same time he heard the voice, the screen went black. He ran to the monitor and stared at it, seeing only his own ghostly image staring back.

Penny was gone.

What the hell?

He hit the back button to see if the problem was his computer or hers. The site he'd been to before hers popped up. He hit the forward key.

Her site was gone.

"Hello?" shouted the voice on the other end of the phone. "Hello?"

A dozen thoughts hit him all at once. They were going to ask him who he was, and he was going to have to tell them, and then his parents would find out he'd broken the rules again, and God only knew what they would do to him this time. He had been going to all those stupid therapy sessions at school and his parents were finally easing up on him, but if they found out about this…what would happen then? Besides, maybe he was wrong. Maybe Penny had only been acting out some sick game.

"Hello?"

"Hello." Timothy finally answered.

"Can you tell me what the emergency is?"

"It's not…I don't think. What if it's not an emergency?"

"We have a car on the way to your house. Are you hurt?"

"No. It was a mistake, it's not an emergency."

"Are you all right?"

"Yes. It's not me. I thought someone…I thought someone was breaking in…but it wasn't…I was asleep."

"The police are on their way. They should be there in less than thirty seconds." The operator's voice eased and softened.

Timothy heard the intercom buzz in the kitchen, hung up, ran out of his room and down the hall, the panic rising like bile in his stomach.

He pressed the button.

"Yes?"

"Timothy, the police are here," the doorman announced. "They said it was an emergency. I'm sending them up."

"No!" he shouted at the doorman. "No. Let me talk to them."

There was a pause. Then: "Timothy Marcus? This is Officer Keally. Is there something wrong up there?"

"No."

"Are you sure? You called 911."

"Yeah, but by mistake. I was asleep, dreaming, thought I saw…heard something, but it wasn't real."

"Are you sure you don't want us to come up and check things out?"

Timothy actually hesitated. Should he tell them and face the consequences? Deal with whatever his parents would do to him? He had seen something weird on the computer, hadn't he? She was sick, wasn't she?

Or did some sick fuck convince Penny to act out his perverted scenario?

"I'm sure," he said into the intercom.

M. J. ROSE

32197	THE HALO EFFECT	___ $6.99 U.S.	___ $8.50 CAN.

(limited quantities available)

TOTAL AMOUNT	$ _____
POSTAGE & HANDLING	$ _____
($1.00 FOR 1 BOOK, 50¢ for each additional)	
APPLICABLE TAXES*	$ _____
TOTAL PAYABLE	$ _____

(check or money order—please do not send cash)

To order, complete this form and send it, along with a check or money order for the total above, payable to MIRA Books, to: **In the U.S.:** 3010 Walden Avenue, P.O. Box 9077, Buffalo, NY 14269-9077; **In Canada:** P.O. Box 636, Fort Erie, Ontario, L2A 5X3.

Name: _____
Address: _____ City: _____
State/Prov.: _____ Zip/Postal Code: _____
Account Number (if applicable): _____

075 CSAS

*New York residents remit applicable sales taxes.
*Canadian residents remit applicable GST and provincial taxes.

MIRA®

www.MIRABooks.com

MMJR0106BL